KNOW THYSELF

As my eyes adjusted, I noticed the profile of a man in the front passenger's seat. He put a cigarette between his lips and lit it, then leaned forward so that I could see his face in the flame of his lighter. I wanted to move closer, but there was a wire mesh barrier between us.

His features were familiar—the unruly white hair, the mole on his upper lip, the green eyes.

It was me.

Other Avon Books by
Jeff Bredenberg

THE DREAM COMPASS
THE DREAM VESSEL

THE MAN IN THE MOON MUST DIE

JEFF BREDENBERG

AVONOVA

AVON BOOKS · NEW YORK

THE MAN IN THE MOON MUST DIE is an original publication of Avon Books. This work has never before appeared in book form. This work is a novel. Any similarity to actual persons or events is purely coincidental.

AVON BOOKS
A division of
The Hearst Corporation
1350 Avenue of the Americas
New York, New York 10019

Copyright © 1993 by Jeff Bredenberg
Cover illustration by Alan Craddock
Published by arrangement with the author
Library of Congress Catalog Card Number: 92-90433
ISBN: 0-380-76914-X

First AvoNova Printing: January 1993

AVONOVA TRADEMARK REG. U.S. PAT. OFF. AND IN OTHER COUNTRIES, MARCA REGISTRADA, HECHO EN U.S.A.

Printed in the U.S.A.

RA 10 9 8 7 6 5 4 3 2 1

I
Benito

Fried squirrel.

Sounds like something the grubbers might have for Saturday dinner, doesn't it?

Ha—maybe they did. Maybe it was only feigned disgust that twisted the face of the old gardener, Albert, as he held the crispy critter up by its singed tail. Maybe, the moment I turned my back, his mouth gave way to a flood of pent-up salivation as he packed the little rodent off to his shanty at the edge of the grounds. There, I imagined, with a flurry of his ragged smock, he would present his Ma with the furry morsel. Her eyes would bulge with delight, and. . . .

Oh, stop it.

If I go on with that kind of reverie you might consider me a Separatist of the worst kind. Which perhaps I was, although I like to think a tad better of myself before . . . well, before that fried squirrel did a Cuisinart job on my life.

All of this began the morning Elvis, my Cyber wife, downloaded the twice-weekly medical diagnostics. It was just before breakfast up in the study dome. I was pressing one of those round BandAids over the punctured vein in the crook of my arm and staring through the rounded glass. Thirty stories below, the willows were barely visible through the rain clouds moving in. I remember the lingering thought exactly: *I can build an amusement park on the Moon, but still there's no better way to sample blood than to gouge a hole in my skin with a metal stick.*

There were many indignities, at the time, that I thought I should be exempt from.

So Elvis was sucking in the diagnostics with her usual frown of consternation. She tapped her finger in perfect seconds on the rim of the computer key pad—one of the earliest of the human mannerisms I had programmed into her. As the download progressed, the terminal screen flashed white and then black again in the same one-second intervals. I decided then to factor in syncopation the next time I popped the lid on her CyberGo.

To save a few minutes' reading time on the terminal, Elvis had hooked the computer's feed cable into the 103-prong port just above her left temple. When the download was done, she jerked the cable free and patted her short black locks into place again.

"The cancer's spreading pretty fast," she said to my back. "You gotta go to the Moon."

I turned from the rainy landscape. "Maybe I can fit it in late next week—after I finish up with the union geeks from Disney Division."

Then she gave me the pouty-lips expression, the heart-melting gesture I purloined from the genetics of a twentieth century entertainer.

"Bay-buh," she murmured, "yo blood readouts say you takin' 3.86 times the recommended dosage of Libricotum and 2.4 times the *legal* level of Zenithialate B. Honey chile, you die this time, what makes you think I'll pour you into the TeleComp again? Maybe I'll juss dump you into the composter with the potato peelin's."

She had a point. For the last few weeks I had been sloshing through a wash of sedation. I felt no pain. The puncture in my arm for the blood test had brought no discomfort—it was just that the sight of the stuff soured my belly.

I paused, with a touch of drama—just the way I would have it done in one of my company's holovids. Hmm. How is it that I, the owner of the largest entertainment conglomerate under the sun, could keep the same Cyber wife for forty-three years, save for a few component updates? I asked her, "Elvis? You love me?"

She pretended to think it over, swinging her head so that her silky hair flew back. "Yeah," she said, "guess I love ya."

The next day I called the home office in Philadelphia to leave word for one of the VP's, Del Wortham, to handle the union matters. I had out-of-town business, I explained. I didn't mention *how* out of town the business was. Habitually I avoided mention of the Langelaan Tele-Compositors—a point of jealousy. I'm the only one in the company approved by the Interplanetary Commerce Commission for TeleComp travel. One of only a few dozen people on the planet with regular access to one. All others in the company—VP's on down—have to cool their heels on the shuttle when they have business on the Moon.

The chief secretary in the Philadelphia offices hesitated on the line. "But Mr. Funcitti, Del Wortham is on that fishing trip in Maine. Perhaps Brian Dietz could handle the union meeting."

"Wortham took his satphone along on the trip?"

"I assume so," she replied.

"Then get him in. If he's not on the case by tomorrow afternoon, have building services clean his office out. Move Brian Dietz into it. *Then* have Dietz handle the union meeting."

There were a few seconds of silence on the phone as the secretary stared stonily out of the holo screen. Then came a curt "Yes sir."

I flicked the phone off and walked to the TeleComp at the back of the study. I punched the Start-Up button. The booth door popped open, the interior light blinked on and the lighted console buttons inside flashed to life.

"Elvis!" Where was she? I glanced at my watch and saw that I was two minutes early. Elvis was not human enough that she would arrive early, or late for that matter, for an assigned duty.

But the preliminaries were easy enough that I could handle them myself. I sat back in the padded booth and strapped my legs and left arm in. The armrest whirred, and a moist brush whisked across my palm, scouring away just enough skin to get a genetic reading. (Now, why can't a painless device like that do the blood test, dammit?)

A familiar message appeared on the interior terminal:

> Identification: Benito O. Funcitti...
> confirmed.
> ICC clearance...
> confirmed.
> Please enter Langelaan TeleCompositor receiver
> coordinates.

With my free hand I pecked in the twelve-digit number on the key pad. The screen responded:

> Destination 3451–7721–1032 is...
> the private TeleComp receiver registered to Fun City
> Corp.
> Lunar station, Sector 32.
> Does this destination coincide with your travel plans?

I typed in "Yes." Elvis leaned her head into the booth and glanced at the progress on the terminal. The next question appeared on the screen:

> Do you wish to employ medical or genetic code
> restructuring features?
> If so, please establish MediComp link.

I reached for the key pad, but Elvis clicked her tongue reprovingly. She pushed my wrist against the armrest and flipped the restraining strap over it so that my hand was immobilized.

"I'd better do this," she said, "or you'll turn yourself into a smoked ham or something." Then her fingers flew over the key pad, ordering up the restructuring that would strip away my cancer while I, or a digital version of me anyway, was being beamed through space.

This was the part that took several minutes—and numerous feeds from our mainframe. Once, Elvis rapped my knuckles, saying, "Quit squirming, chile. You'll blow the whole entry, and we'll have to start from scratch. Ya might even lose your travel window."

Finally, though, the photonic surgery was arranged. Elvis pecked me on the nose and whumped the door shut. In the darkness, the dull green of the terminal was flashing:

"T minus 198 seconds, T minus 197 seconds..."

Nitrous oxide was hissing into the booth, and I breathed deeply, counting along with the computer as my mind numbed. How nice it will be, I thought, to be done with the cancer—for a couple of years, anyway. How nice it will be to have enough lung capacity to smoke again. How nice it will be to not need the painkillers. How nice it will be: A short working vacation on the Moon.

"Elvis," I murmured with rubbery lips. I couldn't remember whether the intercom was on, but it was worth a try. "Call ahead for me, okay Hon? Tell 'em to have a martini ready. And a pack of Winstons."

I awoke in the dark, which was not right. There were no welcoming terminal messages. There was no martini. The air in the Lunar station receiver was warm and stale. That's what happens, I told myself, when you stay away for four months—the operation can get pretty ragged.

Movement was impossible—my limbs were leaden. I calculated the dose of nitrous oxide I must have consumed, then crosschecked that, as best I could recall, with my current levels of Libricotum and Zenithialate B. No. Nothing that would cause such paralysis, as far as I could remember.

And then the problem became clear. I could not move

my limbs because they were still strapped down. Which meant that I was still in the transmitter booth in my study in Longwood Gardens, and not on the Moon. Restraining straps were not necessary on the receiving end of a TeleComp—recomposing an inert life form posed no problem for the biolaser compositors. It was in the *transmitter booth* that movement caused complications.

"Elvis!" I shouted, and the name fell dead against the padded walls of the booth. Instinctively I knew—from the soundless apparatus, from the putrefying air—that the transmitter was dead.

"Elvis!" I called up in my mind a blueprint of the house power systems. In a locker on the ground floor of the building was a bank of six massive transformers—a veritable substation that converted raw power from the electric company. They provided enough juice to light a small city of grubbers. Five of the transformers, however, were just enough to meet the demand of the TeleComp.

If the five transformers had blown, and apparently they had, perhaps the sixth was buggered as well. That would mean that the house was electronically dead, too, or nearly so. Along with Elvis.

A droplet of sweat rolled down my nose.

I pushed wildly against the restraining straps, trying to use my forearms as levers to force them open. When I felt the crunch of cartilage, I stopped. *I* would break before the straps did, and the painkillers would let me.

I was smothering now. Breathing this air was like sucking in frothy cotton. Where once my vision was black, now there glimmered a hundred whirling stars. They would grow, I knew, and fill my head until I passed out.

A high-pitched whine needled at my ears—the final hallucination of a dying man, I supposed. Then a weak shaft of light slashed across the darkness. It grew bolder and brighter as the excruciating sound scraped my eardrums. I was dead now, being tortured in a surreal Hell. I was dead now, and sweating rivers into a sopping shirt. I was dead now, and screaming.

The light was pouring from a hole in the wall of the TeleComp housing. In that jagged hole I recognized a set of fingers and then understood the noise—the shriek of titanium being slowly ripped aside. By Elvis, somehow. Goddamn.

I was blubbering. "Elvis, the straps. Just get one strap, one hand loose. . . ."

When the hole was large enough, the metallic ripping stopped and Elvis' hand came through slowly, centimeters at a time. Her power reserves were almost nil now, squandered on ripping the TeleComp open. She would be bleeding every trace of residual energy out of the entire dead building now, sucking every VDT, every transistor for the merest spark just to keep moving.

It took three minutes, but finally her thumb and forefinger closed on the tab of the restraint. She pulled back, and the moist chemibond gave way.

I was free. Elvis was dead.

The trouble with space needle architecture is that during total power failure, of course, the lift does not work. Thirty stories of spiral staircase weigh heavily on a heart accustomed to leisure and lungs at one-quarter capacity.

As I said, the gardener Albert found the fried squirrel amid the tangle of damaged transformer wires. He tossed the offending critter into his pickup truck and found a flashlight for me. My trackers, and their emergency equipment, were entombed behind dead hangar doors.

Against his protests, I sent Albert home to telephone Philadelphia Electric and have a repair crew sent out. I rooted around the first-floor storerooms until I found one of the power packs that Elvis uses when she leaves the house. Then it was back up the thirty floors of spiral staircase. After forty-three years of marriage, a man's gotta have his wife.

By the time Elvis and I were back to ground floor, Albert had returned. He looked grim.

"Power company says it could be several hours," the

gardener said. "Maybe midnight."

Albert now wore a hooded slicker against the drizzle. He jabbed a thumb over his shoulder. "You'd best come out ta the house an' wait."

For a couple of decades I had not seen the inside of the little house that I rent to Albert, and a vague feeling of dread washed over me.

"Why thank you, Albert," Elvis replied sweetly. "We'll ride down with you." Already I was regretting that Elvis did not have the benefit of the defunct mainframe computer. Usually she had much better sense than this.

Among grubbers, it was a common enough shanty, I suppose. All of the living spaces were contained within two stories of structure—stone outside, wood and plaster within. It was an early twentieth century relic that had been a caretaker's home even back then, when Longwood Gardens had been owned by a family of industrialists—du Bois, du Peau, du Pont, something like that.

There were separate rugs laid all about the ramshack, woven out of sheep's wool or some such fiber. The furniture had been fashioned from dark, polished lumber. Light was supplied by free-standing lamps—an eerie, uneven illumination. The heating was equally spotty, emanating as it did from low wall vents.

Albert introduced his Ma, Grace-Lee—a chunky grayhead, maybe ninety years old, a no-nonsense woman. We passed an hour in polite conversation in the living room. Before I could fashion a suitable protest, we were at the dinner table having salad and stew and warm bread.

"Your time being so precious," Albert said over his wine glass, "I hope the outage did not interrupt business much."

I coughed politely and glanced at Grace-Lee, knowing her to be a devout Catholic and probably not approving of TeleComp travel. "Well, I was about to beam to the Moon, actually," I said, "that being the most expedient thing— yeah, busy as I am."

Down at her end of the table Grace-Lee snorted. Elvis

nibbled quietly at a spoonful of stew, her eyes rolling left and right. Her chemical innards actually could make some use of the nutrients. The rest she would expel in private, as we all do.

"Butcher machine," Grace-Lee said. " 'Scuse me, Mr. Funcitti, but you know I have ta say it—butcher machine."

The TeleComp had gained almost worldwide acceptance, except among Catholics and some fundamentalist sects. The problem lay in the method of transport: In a transmitter booth, biolaser scanners create a replica of the traveler in digital code, molecule for molecule, which is beamed across space. In the receiver booth, the compositors rebuild that traveler using the molecular reserves held in stock—sort of a cosmic fax machine. When the transport is complete, the confirmation signal is flashed back to the transport booth, where the original is destroyed. The traveler remains intact in every way at his new destination—every memory, every worry, every wart, every scar. Unless these characteristics are altered in the photonic surgery options.

I did not mention to Grace-Lee the obvious irony: that my own TeleComp had nearly smothered me. Butcher machine, indeed. "A harmless, painless process, I assure you," I said, although there would be no convincing her. "We'd not be much among the planets today without it."

"An' that would be fine with me," she huffed. "To kill a living being for the convenience of commerce is not my idea of progress. There's too much against nature that people such as you are taking in stride." Her jaw nudged almost imperceptibly in the direction of my robotic companion. Being married to my gardener, Grace-Lee would know that Elvis was not human.

Several moments of embarrassed silence followed—three of us were embarrassed anyway. Elvis toyed with the stew and had no sense of such discomfort. It was not part of her makeup.

"Well," I managed finally. "It's a fine stew, ma'am. . . . What sort of meat did you say this was?"

* * *

When Albert dropped us off at the darkened house, there were three white vans parked in front and a dozen men milling about with flashlights and yellow raincoats.

"They should have ya powered up again in no time," the gardener said. "But if not, come down again and we'll put ya up in the spare room." He drove off into the rain, toward his shanty and his disapproving Ma.

I put an arm around Elvis and we trotted for the protection of the door overhang. We were met there by a somber young man, thirty years old or so. His raincoat was unzipped, revealing a white business shirt, a conservative tie, and a shoulder holster.

"You power guys," I asked, "you always—um, pack fire like that?"

He tipped his flashlight into my eyes, a singularly rude gesture for which he did not apologize. "My name's Sachs, inspector for the ICC. Could I see some I.D., please?"

I opened my wallet and nodded toward Elvis. "My wife," I said.

"Mr. Funcitti, would you come with me, please?" The inspector strode back into the rain and opened the side door of one of the vans. He waved me into the rear compartment and closed the door, leaving me alone in the dark. I had assumed that he would walk around and take the driver's seat, but he did not. He returned to the door overhang and was saying something to Elvis.

As my eyes adjusted, I noticed the profile of a man in the front passenger's seat. He put a cigarette between his lips and lit it, then leaned forward so that I could see his face in the flame of his lighter. I wanted to move closer, but there was a wire mesh barrier between us.

His features were familiar—the unruly white hair, the mole on his upper lip, the green eyes. It was me.

My chest began to tighten. "The transmission. . . ."

"Botched terribly, I'm afraid. Oh, *I* came through fine. Never felt better—ha, can smoke again. But on this end, hmph. When the system engineers figured out what had happened, I beamed back right away through the Philly offices of the ICC. Wouldn't do to have you setting up house here as if you owned the place."

"Doesn't the law say. . . ."

"I double-checked with the ICC, and you—*we*—remember correctly. They plan to dispose of you quickly and painlessly." He sighed sympathetically.

I fell back against the seat, and the words came slowly. "I don't suppose it surprises you to hear that I don't want this to happen."

"Legally, man, you don't exist. The only genetic code that the Government will recognize is mine—as restructured and registered this morning during TeleComp transmission." His voice carried that peculiar tone of someone quoting law.

I glanced about in a panic, and my fears were confirmed: There were no door handles on the inside of the van. The windows were reinforced with wire. "I don't . . . want . . . to die."

He tapped his head. "You're going to live a long time, up here. In my head, we are precisely the same man, the same blob of gray matter."

"Save for a few hours' memory."

He gave me a hard stare and pushed smoke out his nostrils. "Save for a few hours. Yeah." He paused then, and I knew that the words that were about to come would be well rehearsed. How odd to know another person this well, even better than I know Elvis, a being of my own creation.

"You know, the ICC fellows tell me this has never happened before, and it's quite uncomfortable for all of us. Not only because I *build* TeleComps, but because the ICC has been such a champion of the devices—"

"Because we bribed the right people," I noted.

"Hmp. You know, I actually considered the benefits of having a second self around—twice the productivity, no?" He sucked on his Winston, and the tip glowed in the darkness. "But the ICC would hear nothing of it anyway—the outcry that all of this would stir up. No. The, uh, problem has to be dealt with quickly and quietly. To do anything else could cause quite a lot of trouble, you understand.''

I managed a nervous laugh: ''Yeah, don't I know it.''

He rolled his window down a few inches and flicked the butt of his cigarette out. ''Look,'' he said, ''I know this doesn't help much, but you're a dying man anyway. The cancer's gone too far for you to go under the knife, and the ICC'd never let you ride a TeleComp again.''

The man on the other side of the barrier—my other, healthy self—coughed lightly. I smiled: He was already ruining a fresh set of lungs. At that moment I knew we were two distinct people. How could it be otherwise when you hated someone so much?

''Thanks,'' I said. ''It's been nice knowing ya.''

He turned away, opened his door and stepped out. As he did, the lights flickered on in the house.

2
Kodas

Doc comes back in the door sputtering and wiping her mouth like she does when she's been sucking gas—has an open jar of the tracker-piss in one hand and a plastic siphon in the other.

"Low-Diolomogen detergent fuel, from the taste of it," she tells me, shaking her head. "Bottom-of-the-line Exxon, I'd guess. Customers staying here sure go for the cheap stuff."

She sets the jar on the nightstand by her bed and clicks her tongue. "Mmmmm, *mmm*. Somebody been smoking in bed again at the Motel 99, and it's sure to cause a fire."

I flick a thumb toward her tuber and keyboard on the desk and go back to my work. "That's a perfectly good potato-head you've left out. Gonna let that tuber bake, huh?"

She shoves both palms under her belt and gives me that hunch-shouldered, exasperated look. I guess the whole world's pretty stupid when you're nineteen. Or has Doc turned twenty yet?

"*Kodas*, I'm going to check your nose first, remember?" she says. "I'm going to change the bandage—'less you want your nostrils to go to rot. Then I'll enter the progress in the tuber, and *then* I'll packer 'er up."

"Okay," I tell her—the kind of "okay" that tells her to calm down. Sometimes I think she's my goddamned daughter or something—not a physician at all. "But we gotta go. Rule Number thirty-eight: When the motel manager starts asking what line of work you're in, you've stayed too long."

"That's rule Number forty-two, I think."

"Hmm. Make it seventeen."

"Eighteen."

"Okay."

We go on like that—I don't know why. If we really had any rules, there wouldn't be enough that you'd have to number them. But I've noticed that Doc seems to prefer her rules even-numbered. Again, I don't know why.

I have one more juice-pack to fill. Seven of the briefcase-sized batteries are by the door, charged and ready to load into the tracker. The electrical socket intended for the television is pulled out of the wall. The detached wires are getting pretty hot and putrid. They're standard, low-rent construction, not intended for anything remotely like this kind of abuse—portable batteries that can suck up a thousand francs' worth of juice. But I twist the wires onto the terminals of the last juice-pack anyway (at worst we'll have us a slightly premature fire) and then I strip off my rubber gloves.

Doc leads me into the tiny bathroom, and there we are in the cracked mirror: skinny little Doc with her adolescent chest barely lifting the front of her T-shirt; me hunching down to get a look in the looking glass as she peels away the strip of gauze from the center of my face.

"Still looks pretty worm-eaten," I tell her. "You'll get a fire-rod in the mudcup if my nose is infected."

Doc shrugs and shakes up a bottle of thick, clear liquid. She pulls out the applicator brush and runs the goop down the rows of minute stitches on each side of my nose.

"The healing's progressing just fine," she says. "In a week, the swelling'll be gone. In three weeks, the scars'll be near-invisible. You're going to lose a few freckles, but otherwise you won't notice a thing—I studied up this time."

The liquid congeals, and Doc cuts out a new strip of gauze, smaller this time.

"Studied up," I reply. "You *always did* do a perfect job of white skin—those milky little lickers you take up with in that theater crowd. Give 'em cut-rate boob jobs. Umm. But dark skin—have I shown you the job you did on my left butt cheek lately? Looks like a worm-eaten chess board.''

"Hey, *you* always gotta have something new—the latest SentiaTerminal implanted, or some volume enhancer the Westies cooked up. Well, experimental is experimental— going to get buggered up once in a while, and that's just what happened to your tuba. All the years of medical school in the world wouldn't prevent that.''

"Ya. You got *no* years of medical school.''

Doc shrugs. "So I read a lot,'' she says.

When she's got the bandage taped back in place, I give Doc a satisfied grunt so she won't take my kidding too hard. Then I pull off my T-shirt, jeans, and undies, and waggle my snake at her.

"Going to suit up tonight,'' I tell her. "Celebrate moving day.''

Doc glares at me as I hop into the bedroom. "You celebrate every day,'' she says. "Besides, we got business tonight.''

I glance at my watch. "Twenty minutes to midnight,'' I tell her. "You *know* what that *means*—time for Tanya! It's an hour up to the Pennsylvania line. I'll be mindful enough by then for business.''

Doc smiles, giving up. Then she sings the familiar jingle: "Tanya! Tongue-ya! Deca-deca-deca . . . *dent!*''

I take the DecaSuit off its hanger and pull the flimsy cotton over my head. It leaves the access holes and terminal wires in all the right places—two just below the neck, two at the nipples, two in the crotch, two on the butt, and two on the thighs.

I slip a wire into the terminal embedded under the skin at my left nipple, twirl the fastener nut, and start on the right nipple.

"Hook up my tuba, would ya?'' I ask Doc. She sighs and reluctantly goes to work wiring up my rear. I sympathize, but those are really hard to get to, as you may know.

When I'm dressed again, we pack the tracker: the juice-packs are carefully stacked in their storage rack in the boot, and our clothes are slung all around them for padding; Doc's tuber is bolted between the front seats, with the keyboard where she can get at it easily; a dozen cardboard cartons are stacked precariously on the newly carpeted flooring be-hind the seats—electronics, medical supplies, the portable weaponry.

Doc shuffles back to the motel room while I get on my knees in the parking lot to check the tracker treads. The plate-links that I can see are solid, but the right side has lost a lot of nubs. Probably in that chase last week, or from making illegal level changes on the trackway. Regardless, the tread will need replacing before summer. I extend the outriggers, their wheels look good, and I snap them back in place—won't get up enough speed to use them tonight.

I wander back inside one last time to see how Doc's going to do it. The room has been maximum-trashed, of course: The TV gutted for parts, the telephone, too; a hole cut in the carpet in the exact shape of our tracker's rear compart-ment; wires pulled out of the wall; a pile of bloodied sheets tossed into the corner; and Doc had scribbled a wall full of notes during last week's surgery.

Doc is sitting on the bed. Lights up a Camel. She has a foot of clear plastic IV tubing and she knots one end—jerks it tight with her teeth. She dips the other end in the jar of tracker piss and mashes the IV tubing until it's sucked up enough yellow liquid. Then she lets the knotted end of the tube drape out of the jar onto the night stand.

Doc drags on the Camel again and pushes the smoke out in parallel streams. "Ready, big boy?" she asks.

"Yeah."

She opens the book of Motel 99 matches she got from the ashtray, presses the sucking end of her cigarette against the match heads, and folds the book closed around the butt.

Then she slides the match book under the knot in the IV tube.

Outside, Doc takes the driver's seat, and we peel north on U.S. 13 with a four- or five-minute head start.

"Few more motel fires," Doc says, "and somebody's gonna wonder what's going on."

"Still, it beats leaving the evidence intact—so they'll *know* what's been going on."

The wipers are slapping aside a light drizzle and the tracks are hissing against the pavement.

At midnight, I punch the radio power button and tune to WMMR. There's the last part of the jingle already: "Deca-deca-deca . . . *dent!*"

The cord from my DecaSuit runs up out of my jeans and the ten-prong plug is there at my belt buckle. I pull out a couple yards of slack and plug into the dash. I pop open one of the storage panels on the dash and reach under the papers and candy bars until I find a cannister of little plastic capsules. I crush one under my nose and snort a little harder than usual—to pull the vapor through all of the new hardware in there.

And then comes the DJ, throaty and sensual: "Mmmmm-mmmmm, MMR. Fifty deca-deca-decades as the world-renowned home of rock 'n' roll. Hi, my name's Tanya, and I'll be rockin' around your clock today. . . ."

Once my terminals are properly warmed up, I feel Tanya massaging my shoulders lightly and something warm and wet against my left thigh. Or I'm supposed to *think* it's Tanya. Maybe it's really some studio lunk, ugly as a mutt's mudcup. But the illusion is more than acceptable.

I close my eyes and tilt the passenger seat back. "Doc, you gotta get hooked up—even if it's just a couple of terminals. Gawd, I can't believe you're still a virgin—all the implants you do for other people."

Doc grunts and says something about how Tanya's not her type—besides, she's listening these days to ce*zanne*, that whole new line of music the teeners are into. But I'm sinking away, immersed now in Tanya (Tongue-ya!):

"...and I'm going to start us right off with a new recording by Donkey Disease, a wanger of a tune called 'Chicks in the Mail.' They cut this song a couple of hours ago in San Diego. On Sentia effects you've got Four-Two Da-Da, and I'll be dubbing in, too, after the first verse or so...."

3
Laurence

Kennedy was getting in trouble again. He's the thirty-year-old brat in the next work pod, always grumping aloud. The kid with all the family union connections, got him where he was. His dad's even an agent, crissake. Got an express L ride right to a Tier 5 coder job. No stops. No waiting. No inconvenience will be tolerated.

Kennedy shot up out of his cushion mold so I could see him over the divider. Curly hair vibrating with rage.

"Dirty postulates again!" he shouted. "I can't *believe* the head-leaks at Tier 4 are giving us dirty postulates. Isn't someone supposed to be *communicating* around here?"

And then the Super appeared behind him—little bald man with lifts in his loafers, the guy who's supposed to be communicating around here.

"Sit down Kennedy," the Super ordered. "We reviewed the cleanup procedure for dirty postulates last week. Besides, if you file the proper notice at the end of your shift, the communication of the problem will be handled quite efficiently."

Postulates are hunks of fractured code, our basic building blocks. Instead of starting from scratch each time you build a new code, we start by combining a set of postulates handed up from Tier 4. Then the coding blocks that *we* create become the postulates for Tier 6.

Kennedy's fury is a sign of inexperience. Any of the old-timers, myself included, can take a dirty postulate and clean it up in ten or twenty minutes—like a sculptor smoothing out a lump of clay. But building whole code without cleaning up your postulates first—without even *knowing* they're dirty—can waste huge amounts of time. It's like building a clarke tower and finding out you have sand under the foundation when you thought you had bedrock. Maybe that's what blew Kennedy's circuit gel. Wasted a week's work again.

The Super caught me staring, and then he was on my back. "You, Laurenth, need to keep your nothe to your own code," he said. When he was angry, the Super had an odd lisp that tended to break up anyone else in earshot. "Have you theen your production graph for the month?"

All around me, I could hear the rhythm of ked pads clattering to a halt. A distant snicker.

"No, sir. Off again? Sorry."

That's the problem with sitting next to a mudcup like Kennedy. Trouble around here is contagious.

At ten minutes to four, I filed the block of whole code I had been amassing and typed in the security locks. Not that anyone would have any conceivable use for a hunk of Tier 5 whole code. It was just procedure—to prevent tampering, I suppose. Or practical jokes.

Next shift was arriving, and the aging gent who would take my seat for the next four hours appeared behind me, nervously transferring his weight from one foot to the other. Every work day he appeared, eager and splashed with aftershave, pudgy yet shriveling—like a stick of ginger root with a Main Line tailor.

Didn't know his name. I would never ask such a thing of a stranger. Kennedy might, but not I. There was no one in the building, really, that I cared to be that familiar with.

Philadelphia is a Tier 5 programming city. With almost a million coders swamping the downtown office buildings, the shifts have to be staggered every thirty minutes to prevent chaos on the elevators, sidewalks, and L lines. Even so, shift changes are bothersome and uncomfortable.

Just on our floor, all across the five acres of office, came the whoosh and rustle of cushion mold as one coder surrendered the seat to another. Then the slap-slap-slapping of shoe leather against chipped linoleum, sounding like stadium applause.

I stood and offered the old fart my cushion mold. I say "old"—about sixty, I'd guess, ten years my senior. He squinted disapprovingly at my Hawaiian shirt and tennis shoes, and I did the same for his coffee-stained tie and tan suit. I was the odd man out, of course. Witness the parade of suits down the aisle. But I do not easily allow people to be comfortable with their convictions. Difference is a healthy thing.

He stepped around me in mock politeness and sat. I said to the top of his head, "Has the Super spoken to you yet about early retirement?"

He logged onto the terminal and did not look up.

The Super headed me off at the end of the aisle and with the flick of a finger motioned me to his office. Had he overheard my flip comment somehow? Through an intercom? Or had old ginger-head, my successor, filed a complaint the moment he logged on? There was nothing in the union regs about harmless, flip comments.

Still, I sensed trouble. I marched behind the diminutive Super toward the cluster of offices at the center of the otherwise-open floor. A dozen glassed-in offices formed a ring, a wide pillar amid acres of work pods. Decades ago, someone had likened the circle of offices to a carousel, and to this day us old-timers imagine the Supers gliding up and down on their little management ponies inside that glassed-in circle.

I sensed trouble, I tasted trouble. Ever eaten a rotten pistachio? That's what trouble tastes like. I was tasting a mouthful of rotten pistachio.

The glass door whirred shut behind me, and the Super waved me into a small chair. I sat, and noted that as long as we were both in our assigned chairs, the Super was able to look down on me. Some sort of B.S. management psychology, the little guy stacking his seat up like that.

I stood to get a glimpse at his chair and sat again.

The Super's eyes rose. "Yes? Something about my chair?"

"I just wanted to see if you was sitting on a phone book."

He drew a jetpen out of his shirt pocket and slid the stem of it into the file folder on his desk, delicately pushing the cover aside like he was scared it would infect him somehow. The tab on the folder read "ESSEX, LAURENCE" in a jetpen scrawl.

"Leth thee here, Mr. Ethekth," he said, starting to read from the file. Outwardly he was calm, but the peculiar lisp told me he was seething. "You are renowned for antithocial behavior. . . . Bizarre offith attire. . . . Thinging opera in the men'th room . . ."

"It's the reverberation from all the tile in there. Can't get a sound like that in any apartment shower."

". . . lewd commemnt made in the elevator . . ."

"Just jokes. To fill time on the way down."

". . . and of courth, the big item: Month by month for the latht two yearth, a perthithtent decline in productivity."

"Put my production up against any cowlicker like Kennedy. I turn out twice the coding he does. Clean, too. The cleanest in the department, probably the division. Probably the whole Tier."

The Super mashed his lips together at the absurdity of the claim. Counting management and support services, there were more than a million people in Tier 5.

His hands fluttered in the air, as if he were chasing away inconsequential words. "Comparing yourthelf to other coderth ith not relevant—particularly when you thpeak of coderth with as little time therved as Kennedy. The thcale you earn at is remarkably different from his, you know."

"Ah. Well, I've read my personnel file. I think you're skipping over favorable parts—you're making a selective reading here."

"Oh, there's an item or two—particularly your knack for the creative end of the trade. Jury-rigging solutions to one or two historically vexing problems."

I nodded. Waiting for the major point now.

The Super cleared his throat. He was no longer lisping, which meant he was settling down. But sweat was beading on his brow. His hands flicked with nervous spasms. He had moved from anger to ill ease. Some coders liked to see the Super off balance and uncomfortable. I thought it made him more dangerous than ever.

"You last read this file on August seventeen, according to the notations," the Super said. "Well, three days ago an item was added, and I've been turning it over in my mind ever since."

He flipped to the last page of the file. The other sheets had been standard white. This one was beige. Only the security department filed memos on beige printout paper.

"It seems that in July and early August you made thirty-four dataline phone calls from your home to the company code libraries," the Super said. "The library files were accessed by a combination of your personal entry codes and what could only be purloined information—indexing matrices and the like."

I shrugged. "Let's have it all."

The Super sighed. Put his right elbow on the desk, and rested his jaw on his fist. "The human mind, even a mind as bright as yours, has a finite capacity for code-slopping. Your decline in production, combined with unauthorized calls to our code library files, leads me to believe that you are, um, freelancing. Moonlight coding." He took on a fatherly tone now, a custom which he did not wear well. "The government trained you, Laurence. It owns your mind in certain respects—the code-chucking part anyway. That's been agreed since you first walked through the door. You can't be doing this kind of work outside of the office. You know that."

"So?" Clearly, this was not a time to be offering information.

"I need an explanation. This could be a firing offense," the Super said.

"And by union regs, I do not have to answer to such accusations immediately."

"Correct," the Super said. "You need not respond until the start of your next shift, which is noon tomorrow." He made a notation at the bottom of the beige sheet of paper.

The whole L tube ride home to Wilmington I thought about Blanche. Usually I'd stop in the office building lobby, punch my filter specs into the fax dispenser, and print out a News Journal, maybe an Inquirer. This day, I was too mind-numbed for that.

At Market Street Station, I boarded an L car in a stupor. When the doors hissed closed, I turned in sudden panic, not sure that I had even selected the right line. An inattentive passenger could end up in Detroit or Atlantic City. Gawd.

But the fright quickly subsided at the sight of the familiar Eastern Seaboard Express L schedules printed above the doors: "Wilmington, Baltimore, Washington, Norfolk, Raleigh." Idly I scanned the times in fine print under each city. Who'd want to commute an hour and forty-five minutes to Raleigh? Research Triangle folks, I supposed.

I took a seat on one of the benches and found myself facing three teenage boys. They were staring blankly ahead, rolling their shoulders forward and back again at unpredictable intervals. Their eyelids and fingers twitched, and occasionally a foot would rise and fall again with a determined stomp.

Rancid drugs.

And then I quickly corrected myself, for I have a heavy dose of entertainment factored into my newsfax filter. These youngsters, I realized, were in the thrall of ce*zanne*, the musical rage (its young proponents claimed) that would finally snip the stem of that withering rose called rock 'n' roll. I remember scanning the article because of the mathematical nature of the music form—it's based on a thirteen-tone scale rather than the familiar eight tones, and its rhythms were arrived at with peculiar calculations involving prime numbers and square roots.

I would not have mistaken these three teenage dreks for mathematical geniuses. But, I supposed, one did not have to understand the origins of a musical form to appreciate it. That's always been the case, hasn't it? There are creators and there are consumers?

There were no sounds to be heard, of course, for ce*zanne* culture requires that it be experienced in private or in small groups. The charmer there on the left, with the unicorn hair job, had the telltale scars of speaker implants at each ear. The other two fellows, younger, only had one implant each. Probably sharing the hit off of one sound deck.

And so with this odd backdrop I spent the fifteen minutes as we rumbled toward Wilmington thinking about Blanche.

I had been painting Blanche for two years. *I* call it painting, anyway. I can't really create with anything but programming language. So that became my paint, and my heavily stylized home mainframe served as canvas. But while the code I slop for the government is all function-driven, Blanche is a personality—an interactive artwork. She has shifting moods. She has roundabout logical patterns. She has fears and knowledge and opinions and humor.

To build her I started from scratch—by scrapping binary logic altogether. I found a disbelieving but discreet junker— as trustworthy as such fellows can come on Philadelphia's South Street—who was willing to manufacture enough circuitry to carry a mainframe based on tri-polar devices. That is, rather than the "yes"-or-"no" switching that makes up standard binary language, my new mainframe was based on "yes," "no," and what we'll call "maybe," for the sake of simplicity. A truly human system.

Blanche, I liked to think, was not merely an Artificial Intelligence. She was an Intelligence, period.

I created her in splashes and dabs, never quite sure where I was going. One day I might, say, factor in a penchant for sexual innuendo when she entered certain moods. Then I would recompile her base code through the mainframe and call her up again for a conversation to see how the changes might manifest themselves.

The trait of sexual innuendo was one of those that I never managed to trigger in Blanche—on purpose, anyway. It submerged unaccountably and I eventually forgot about it. Until, several weeks later, I snapped at her mindlessly.

She replied, "Oooh, yessss! Treat me *rough,* big boy."

So Blanche became a habit. The more I tinkered over the last two years, the more intrigued I became. The longer our conversations became, spilling into the wee hours. And—yes, the Super was right—the more creative umph I devoted to her. To the detriment of my work.

There are legendary coders, of course. Donaghey Beane comes to mind. And Iz Howlitz, if you forgive his over-the-edge later years. These two guys were said to be able to slop code for three days straight, take a two-hour nap, and then slop away for another three days. All of it flawless code.

I once hoped to be among the giants of coding—on Tier 5, at least. But now it's clear that I will only go down in the books as a pretty-darned-good coder. Nothing legendary. A man of finite creative umph. Much of which he gave to a "painting" named Blanche.

The L tube put me off at the base of the Track 95 interstate system. For this part of the route, down through Washington, the L was built into the eight-level structure that was otherwise occupied by speeding trackers, automobiles, and fiber-optic utility lines. Since this was one of the prime rush hours, Track 95 was volcanic with traffic rumble. Fortunately for Wilmington residents, sound-absorbing siding had recently been installed (in that typical, repulsive government pale green). In the last century, the building of Interstate 95 had cleaved the city in half, and now it was a Great Green Wall through Wilmington. But the sound-proofing was definitely preferable to the raw roar of traffic. From a block away, where I owned a townhouse, Track 95 produced a minimal hum.

I entered the brick-cobbled streets of the Trinity neighborhood, punched a flat into my lock slot, and threw my shoulder against the door, promising myself once again that

I would have the warped doorjamb fixed.

I stopped in the kitchen to check the day's pile of mail faxes. The glossy color jobs obviously were advertisements, and I dealt them into the recycler immediately. That left three "payment due" notices. No personal correspondence. You have to send letters to receive them, you know.

I took the bills up the wooden stairs to the study and laid them on my desk. I flicked on my tuber and waited for the screen to blink on, then plugged its feed cord into the receptacle on the wall.

On the tuber I entered "Blanche/audio," then threw the switch on the phone console from "Telephone" to "Compucom."

"Blanche?"

There was no answer.

I re-entered the call command. Still no answer.

"This is no time for a hardware problem," I muttered.

I left the call command in effect and switched screens to run a diagnostic test. The test refused to run, but I learned all I needed to know. The message on the screen read:

"TEST ABORTED. STORAGE DISKS FULL. DELETE LAST FILE ENTERED?"

Disks full! I had several trillion bytes of memory unused!

I entered "Yes" on the screen, having no idea what the last file was that I had entered, but knowing that I had to create some wiggle room in the mainframe or I was going to be one baked potato.

The tuber whirred then, and simultaneously a female voice came over the phone speaker.

"Oh, Laurence, you've killed Stanley! Put him to *death*, you did!"

"Hi, Blanche. Um, who's Stanley?"

"He was one hunk of code, I'll tell you that. A military man—directs shuttle operations to Mars, mining lifts off of Io. That kind of thing. We were just getting acquainted when you axed him. Hmph."

"Blanche, does Stanley have anything to do with why the disks are all jammed up? You couldn't even get up to talk to me, crissake."

"Well . . . I've decided that I want to be a little more sociable than you tend to be. Actually, I was having a party."

"You were having a party, and Stanley was your guest?"

"Oh, Stanley was the *last* guest. Until you killed him. If you have a notion to kill any more guests, please ask me first. I'll put together a list for you."

The study was getting rather hot, or so it seemed. Sweat was collecting on my brow. I peeled off the Hawaiian shirt and threw it into the corner, then toggled to another screen and asked the computer for a list of all files created in the last several weeks, excluding my personal entries. A series of entry slugs began rolling across the screen and did not stop. After a minute of gaping at the rolling "guest list" I asked, "Uh, Blanche, the security folks at work picked up forty-some phone calls from here to the Tier 5 code library. Have you been downloading our library files?"

"I was lonely. I decided to throw a party."

"Blanche! Random pieces of stolen computer code can *not* keep you company! This stuff is turgid, straight-ahead, function-driven code." I sighed, starting to understand. "I'll bet its party banter is pretty boring."

"Well, what do you want me to do? Saunter down to Blinkie's Sub Shop and strike up a conversation with the folks hanging around?"

"Blanche, it is specified in your whole coding that you will never activate the phone lines. And tapping into the Tier 5 library has put me in very big trouble. I'll probably get fired over this. *I* created you. *I* am one hundred percent liable for your actions!"

"It is also specified in my whole coding that I will occasionally use elliptical logic patterns which may temporarily circumvent standing orders. And also that I will, now and then, challenge authority. This is all the cumulative effect of code entries you made on the following dates. . . ."

"Dammit, *I'm* not the authority that you're supposed to challenge!"

"Mmmm. Hit me harder, you bad boy. On the other side."

Droplets of my sweat were now blotching the edge of the desk.

"Say, Blanche . . . this code you named Stanley. You said something about military applications—shuttles, and mining? Uh, Tier 5 coding wouldn't read like that. It's transitory—handed up to Tier 6, then 7 and so on. From Tier 5 coding, you'd never be able to tell *what* its application was going to be. *I* rarely even know, and I write the stuff."

"Gosh, all of my Tier 5 guests arrived weeks ago."

"And Stanley? I don't think I want to hear this. Do I? Do I want to hear this? Blanche, where did Stanley come from?"

"That Stanley—he's a prime, grade-A, Tier 12 hunk if I ever saw one!"

"Sacramento? You tapped into Tier 12 library code? That's not *possible!* I think they *execute* people for that!"

"If it's the long-distance charges you're worried about. . . ."

"Long distance," I murmured. "That's it. The security guys haven't gotten to the long-distance calls yet. Just the local stuff, which is easier to come by."

I pulled out my wallet and stared numbly at the calculator pad under the "Bank of Paris" logo. I asked for the sum of my savings, checking, and speculation funds, then ran a calculation on how long that would last at my current spending rate—with no further income. Nine weeks.

If I stopped the alimony payments? Twelve weeks.

If I stopped the child support? Thirteen weeks.

If I sold the tracker? The townhouse? The art collection? The baseball cards?

My financial and legal situations were equally grim.

"Laurence," Blanche asked, "can we watch 'Streetcar Named Desire' tonight?"

"We watched it just last Friday, Blanche. Besides, you

have in memory every frame and every bit of dialogue of every movie I've ever called up on the entertainment channels. And you've seen 'Streetcar' at least forty times."

"But I'm programmed to be gratified by sequential experience. Not just static, collective memory. That's your doing, so I think you owe it to me. I want to see 'Streetcar Named Desire.' Marlon Brando in particular. In a sweaty T-shirt. Sequentially. Maybe even in slow motion."

I tapped the keyboard finally to stop the rolling log of new-entry slugs. "God, why can't you fixate on something filmed in holo? But okay. I have a lot of work to do tonight. But if I get done, we can watch 'Streetcar.' But slow-mo is no fun for human beings. Except with porno."

"You're going to kill all of my party guests, aren't you?" It was a singularly accusing tone of voice, and I remembered the precise time when I endowed Blanche with that guilt-tripping technique.

"Yeah. Time for these rowdies to go home. Time for *me* to slop some new code."

"Party pooper."

4
Kodas

Traffic on Track 95 is relatively light this time of night, so we're fairly howling around the bugs and dumps and sedans, Doc at the stick. I've just turned Tanya down to low emote, finished with my gig. Every single nerve in my body feels stir-fried, my heart is crunching, and my shorts are damp.

Besides, my implants are overheating. Cook 'em up too much, and you're asking for infection, Doc says. She should know—she installed 'em.

I pull my cord out of the dash connector, and that feeling of cool water spills over me. Illusion, really—it's the sudden *absence* of stimulation that creates that cold-shower wash.

Doc flashes me her mildly-disgusted look. "We'd be in Philly now if you'd updated our flats," she says. Wanting something to gripe about. "These local traffic levels are creamed shit. Besides, driving a tracker on the local levels we're more conspicuous—we get stopped and they figure our gear ta be freelance, you and I are two canned hams for five years. I get canned, I want it ta be 'cause we were caught in action. Not 'cause some radio-licker forgot to update our flats."

"I didn't have the centimes for it last week. And so what if the flats are a couple of days out of date? That only means that Terry F1 won't guarantee 'em. Doesn't mean they won't work. We could probably card in, bang up to the tracker levels and be in Philly in five minutes."

Doc rolls her eyes and slouches in the driver's seat, stiff-armed against the joy stick. "Using expired flats is just bad grease—taking senseless chances. If you're gonna expose yourself, save it for action, when it can't be helped.''

We're coming up fast behind a rusty dump, and Doc's eyes fly across the mirrors. She's trying to change lanes, but I can see that we're hemmed in by a couple of bugs in the next lane over. Doc pounds the brakes and we lurch forward in our seats. The track plates whine and that cordite kind of odor fills the cabin. I imagine our nubs skittering across the pavement like mutant hockey pucks.

Doc slaps at the dash. "Creamed shit.''

Rittenhouse Square has a tentative sheen of ice all over it. Shimmering in the streetlights. We glide around the block a couple of times, leaving parallel furrows in the pavement slush. Check out the street action. An Amythol White pusher is dispensing mist cannisters on one corner to a sparse clientele. Nothing out of the ordinary.

Doc skates into a parking space and I take the clip of flats out of the glove box. She won't even let me use them for the parking meter, so I shove hard centimes into the side slot. Which doesn't help the friction between us one calorie. Hard cash is what we *make*. When we *spend*, we spend pirated credit. One of the secrets of freelancing.

But Philly's meters are twenty-four hour, and Doc is obsessed with not taking chances, even minute ones, that might draw attention. So we pay.

I slide the clip of flats from the glove box into my back pocket. Fine. We're gonna get 'em updated now. Be done with this shit soup.

I crank open the boot, unfold the dolly, and pile the battery cases onto it. Doc drags out the boxes of electronic parts we scavenged from a dozen or so Delaware motel rooms and tosses them on top of the batteries, which makes a precarious load, especially considering the thin layer of ice on the sidewalk.

I wheel past the glassy front of a turn-of-the-century skyscraper and into the alley where it sides against an ancient brick apartment building, six or seven stories. Doc hangs back at the entrance to the alley while I whump the dolly down the concrete steps to the basement level of the apartment building. When I clank against the metal drain grate at the bottom, she trots up. She starts poking at what appears to be an old-fashioned intercom that was haphazardly wired to the rust-stained door frame.

"Who is it?" comes a woman's voice. Pretending to be sleepy. The speaker crackles.

Doc pinches her brow, checking her memory, making sure she gets the response just right. "Uh, Doc and Kodas," she says. "Sorry we're late for . . . dinner. Thought there might be a slice of agate cake left."

There's a jagged hole in the metal face of the intercom. Looks like it's been jabbed with a crowbar. There's a camera in there, I tell myself. Gotta be one somewhere.

"Wallets, please," comes the sputtering voice. That speaker's about shot.

The door is made up of dozens of layers of steel plates, looking like bad twentieth century sculpture. There's a mechanical thunk behind the door, and the rivets on the center plate pop out slightly. Doc reaches down and hinges the plate up. She takes out her wallet, I hand her mine, and she tosses them both into the blackness. They'll keep 'em until we're done with business.

The speaker crackles again: "Now your hands, please."

Doc and I exchange puzzled looks.

"New procedure," the woman back in the building somewhere is telling us. "Hands through the door slot, please. Kodas first."

I don't like this. You don't go sticking your hands into the blackness where god knows what kind of rabid scumcritter will bite your fingers off. But Terry F1 is always coming up with banshoid security crap, and she's never once burned us.

So I shove my hands into the door hole and someone on the other side pulls them in farther—up to the elbows. He's got a firm grip on each arm. Maybe it's two people, not one. And my wrists are being *worked on*. Wrapped around with something like plastic rope. Then a clamping tool. And suddenly I'm free again. Wearing a new set of bracelets.

The bands are made of translucent plastic a lot like Doc's IV tubing. Set on the top of each band is a small black disc.

Doc shrugs, sticks her hands in, and gets a set of bracelets too.

The metal door grinds open and a lightbulb in the small foyer blinks on. There's only one person greeting us in the foyer—heavy-set kid about twenty-five. Smiley, with sandy hair. It's Jackie—one of Terry F1's main musclers. I suppose he could have done the bracelet job alone—maybe grabbed an arm in each armpit and wrapped the bands on. Doc and I have a close deal with Terry F1, but in a crib like this, I always like to know how many people of what kind are where.

Jackie has an easy nature about him—helps me roll the dolly over the door frame, then pushes the metal door closed and resets the locks.

"They're *you*," he tells Doc, wagging a finger at her wrists. "The top of fashion."

"Something tells me these are supposed to help us behave," Doc says. "Right? You can detonate these from a distance?"

"Close!" the muscler says, enjoying this. A game. "But we don't need any explosions in here. The disc there can discharge a compound into the tubing that will set off a flash-acid reaction. Foosh! . . . plump-plump." He mimics the action of two severed hands dropping to the floor tile. "Give us trouble, and you've played your last game of patty-cake."

"And you got a transmitter somewhere that'll talk to that little disc? Case you want to slap our wrists?" Doc says.

Jackie nods his fat head.

"Okay," I throw in, "so we'll be extra courteous this time. But the sooner we get our business done and out of here, the happier I'll be."

Jackie pats us down, runs a scanner over us, then draws a set of keys out of his trousers. He opens the next door, which leads into the main room. It has a thirty-foot ceiling and runs about fifty yards square—a cavern that had once been devoted to heating and cooling equipment, I guess. Old-time water pumps, that kind of thing. Until more sensibly compact machinery came along. The obsolete hulks had been dragged over to the back wall, where they're collapsing into rust—a gallery of paralyzed monsters. Vents and wiring angling up into the dank air like dead limbs.

The floor is a mud-smeared mosaic of ancient tile. All across it, Terry F1 has arranged ten collapsible workbenches laden with tools and testing devices. Behind them are row upon row of collapsible shelving—looking like one of those libraries in the twentieth-century vids. Only the shelves are piled with electronic parts—cleaned, tested, sorted, and on their way to underground assembly houses.

When you move every couple months, I suppose, everything is collapsible, and you don't splurge on the decor.

I wheel the dolly to the second workbench, where Jackie will test the juice-packs and write us up. I lift the boxes of parts and drop them on the next counter where a thin old man is waiting with a jeweler's loupe hinged to his spectacles.

"Hi, Pep," I say. "Got some Motel 99 for ya. Some Shangri-La Inn. Looks like a few grand ta me."

"Humph. A hunnerd, maybe." Pep's gray-bristled jowls exercise over his jawbone for a moment, like he's chewing cud. He peers at me through thick lenses and says, "Why, Kodas! Looks to me like you've gone and implanted your nose. You got a square centimeter of skin left without hardware under it?"

I lightly touch the bandage over my nose, checking on the swelling.

"This one's special, Pep."

"Radio blowjobs ain't good enough for you any more? *Now* they're gonna SentiaCast the *smell* of something too? Juss what, I don't think I want to know."

"No. It's not like that. Totally new tech, here. I'll tell ya about it someday, after it's up and humming. But how about writing me up here," I say, poking at the boxes. "These new bracelets you folks issue are making me nervous."

Pep's jowls push forward into a compressed smirk as he hinges the jeweler's glass down over his specs and digs in.

"Sorry about the bracelets, folks," says Terry F1. She slides her cash drawer open in her "office," an alcove behind the shelving area. She double-checks the inventory slips that Jackie and Pep have given us and starts dealing out a stack of 100-franc notes. "We had a little disturbance here last week. This squid from Camden goes berserk—screaming about winged lizards and starts trapshooting right in here." She points a delicate finger at the blow-holes in the plaster near the ceiling.

"How'd he get a banger past Jackie?"

"A Che47. Colombian job? Plastic and flexible," she says. "Had it wound around his left shin. Probably just happened to be packing and never meant it for us. Or he was planning a hit, only he flipped before he could do the job—but that wouldn't be professional, would it? I think he'd been gassing some bad Amythol White—and all of a sudden he's seeing winged lizards everywhere. It made for some tense moments. We ended up having to shovel the kid into trash bags."

"Hmph," Doc says. "Jackie is not a man to mess with."

"It was old Pep who did it," Terry F1 says. "Hit him with a few razor bolos—like slicing salami. Good man, Pep. Knows I disapprove of the use of bangers on the premises, whether it's outsiders or my own folks. Anyway, from now on all visitors wear the bracelets. New policy."

Terry F1 stands, pushes the stack of bills to the edge of the desk, and Doc starts counting. Terry F1 is meticulous about her looks—skin pale and perfect, platinum hair swept up, a silky, black robe-like gown.

The whisper is that she's a hermaphrodite—but she carries herself as a knock-dead woman. So I call her a "she."

I asked her once about that. "I come *fully* equipped," is

all she would say. Mmm. As much as I'd like to see the evidence, I'm not sure what I would do if given the opportunity.

"Okay, the count's right," Doc says, and hands me half the bills. "Assuming you deducted for the flats we need updated."

"That's correct," Terry F1 says. "May I have them?"

I draw the flats out of my pocket and hand her the clip. Terry F1 fans them out like a set of narrow playing cards. She selects the flat for pirating credit and slots it in the editing unit next to her tuber.

"I've totally rerouted the snare loop this time. It's still only guaranteed for 14 days, though. The rerouting will just keep 'em piss-brained in Paris. Now, I can't emphasize enough about using this. . . ." She pauses to call up her new pirating format and copies it onto our flat.

"I know," Doc says. "Small purchases only—living expenses, that kind of thing. Kodas here wanted to use it to replace the tracker nubs. Hell, I'm not getting canned for *that*."

Terry F1 glares at me.

I raise my hand defensively. "We'll pay on legit credit. Honest."

Terry F1 slots the entertainment flat—for the vid channels, Sentia radio, and simulator programs. "And *these* babies—I don't know how long we'll stay ahead of Bejing. They're starting to make security a major project."

When Terry F1 has updated all six flats in the clip, Doc accepts them back eagerly, cupping them in her hands like a treasure. Makes me feel bad all over again that I hadn't brought them in earlier. It's odd how some people can hang their emotions on a piece of software.

"So, how's it going with the new implant?" Terry F1 is talking to Doc, not me.

"Fine, I guess," Doc says. "His swelling's going down on schedule. Assuming your surgeon laid it in right. . . ."

"*You* were there!" I throw in—a flash of worry.

"I just assisted. This isn't a mere Sentia implant, Kodas.

There's specific neural connections involved—tricky ones. Otherwise I'd have laid it in myself."

"Maybe you will someday," says Terry F1, trying to be encouraging.

"Yeah, I'll get there," Doc says. "Anyway, there's no way to inspect the neural links visually, so all we can do is prevent infection and wait—run reflex tests in a week or so."

"Good," Terry F1 says. "In the meantime, I have a small job that I'm brokering for a client. Minimum risk, moderate pay—6,000 apiece. Interested?"

"Well, TV parts and juice-packs barely pay for the peanut butter," I tell her. "Let's hear it." And Doc nods.

"I've already done my part," Terry F1 says, tapping the tuber on her desk. "Wormed into the ICC's TeleComp files. I'm leaving the path dormant until the precise moment we need it again.

"Your part is to actually make the hit—it's an entertainment exec who's going down, and the client insists it look like an accident. The site is a secluded house on a 350-acre estate. Hop security, and it's an easy pick.

"I have his next TeleComp window, just reserved with the ICC. The moment he actually beams, you two are going to trash his transformers. Then he's scrambled eggs!"

"So how's this gonna look like an accident?"

Terry F1 smirks. She opens a desk drawer, withdraws a paper bag and hands it to Doc.

Doc folds the paper open and wrinkles her nose. "A dead squirrel?"

"Rittenhouse Square's finest," Terry F1 says. "He was already dead when I found him—honest."

Then Terry F1 leans forward onto her desk with a fabulously long laugh. Which affords me a fabulously long view down the front of her gown. Which throws me into a nightmare of sexual . . . mmm, what's the word? Ambivalence?

5
Benito

You can imagine all of the emotions—a prisoner in the back of a government van, sullen driver wheeling through the rain or sleet, carting me off to a quiet, anonymous death.

Depression. Despair. A wailing, hollow loneliness.

How would they do it—this unprecedented execution of the embarrassing accidental double of a powerful amusements executive? No. No. I'm the *original*, damn it. *I* should live!

Okay. So perhaps it's an argument of convenience. I've used the TeleComp hundreds of times. Destroyed hundreds of "original" versions of myself without a qualm. The only difference here is that by a damnable quirk, *this* sack of bones and blood, the one with the lungrot, didn't get sizzled right away.

So how *would* they do it? Put me on death row and gas me? Of course not. Too many people outside of the ICC would have to hear of it. Perhaps the driver will just pull over here, onto some dark dirt road intersecting U.S. 1. Put a bullet in my skull. Maybe they'll just hand me a pill—promise a painless passing.

The van glided through the broad curves of the highway, slicing through beehive townhouse developments, one after another for miles. Developments with pastoral names such as Meadowcreek, Hilltop, and Pinecrest. Did such names really delude residents about the sterile and repetitive nature of their domiciles?

I put my face in my hands. I was not willing to surrender

meekly to death, but there was not the slimmest hope to grasp for.

The townhouses gave way to detached residences, which then gave way to the center of a small town.

When we stopped for a red light, I recognized the tavern at the corner. We were passing through Media. I had known the tavern as Bradley's years ago—white tablecloths and a fair fettucini with red clam sauce. It was now named Wink, and seemed to have been reworked in a campy decor meant to appeal to today's college crowd.

I could make out the silhouetted patrons still lining the bar, although it had to be close to last call by now. Unfortunately, the rain was keeping pedestrian traffic to a minimum. But maybe someone in the bar would see me, perhaps even *hear* me, if I raised enough ruckus.

I flailed at the side window. "Hey in there! Help! Kidnapped! Hey in there!"

The driver turned. "Whoa, whoa, whoa. Nobody's gonna see or hear you. The glass is tinted, *and* it's banger proof. You can't get *nothing* through it fella."

"Where are you taking me?" It was an alien shriek, but could have been none other than my own panic-shattered voice.

The driver shrugged. "Philadelphia, if you gotta know. The City of Brotherly Love."

A figure appeared at the driver's window in a hooded slicker. A finger tapped and gestured, motioning him to lower the glass.

"Help me!" I pounded the grating separating me from the front seat.

The traffic light blipped green. The driver shook his head and moved to put the van into gear. The pedestrian's hand punched through the glass like an arrow through plastic wrap. Glass splinters plowed tiny furrows across the driver's face, which quickly crested with blood.

I could see the pedestrian's face now—Elvis. She grabbed the addled driver by the knot of his tie and pulled him face first through the remains of the window—this causing another explosion of glass. Then she flopped the limp body onto the asphalt like a dead fish.

Now they were paying attention in Wink. The bar stools were emptying and besotted customers were gaping through the window.

"Elvis, the keys!"

She pulled the key flats from the ignition and dragged the driver by his tie to the side door. The door hissed out of the way.

"You're going to kill him, Elvis, hauling him like that."

"Not any more than I already *have*," she replied, twanging "have" into two syllables. "His neck broke. Sorry."

"It's okay. Hand him up. We need the car to get us out of here, and we should take the body, too. Hurry. They're calling the cops by now."

I brushed the glass out of the driver's seat and restarted the engine. Elvis hopped in beside me. A row of college-aged, desireable-spending-group faces still gawked through the plate glass of the slick new pub.

"Just where did you come from? Last I knew, you weren't able to fly."

She ruffled through her silky hair to shake off the rain.

"When I realized what was happening," she drawled, "I excused myself and went inside? Then I lit out the back door and headed the van off before you left the grounds. Crouched on the back bumper and clung to the spare tire the whole way out here."

I wanted to say something husbandly, like, "You must be freezing to death!" But of course Elvis has a better heat compensation mechanism than any human could hope for.

I threw the van into gear and pulled through a red light. One moment, ultimate despair. The next, a broad world of possibilities and not a trace of a plan.

A broad beautiful world of possibilities. Except that it was getting damned near impossible to find a decent plate of fettucini with red clam sauce.

6
Therese

I figure you don't get to the Moon before you're thirty, you might never.

Before you know it, you own your own townhouse, maybe you're married and making babies, two Arisawa trackers in the hangar. And even if you're up to three months' vacation a year it swirls down that great time drain, you're just trying to keep noses wiped and your blouses ironed.

So two days before my 30th birthday I took the L tube to Philadelphia International, flew to Pike's Peak Clarke Tower near Colorado Springs, and checked in for the Fun City Shuttle.

I passed through Interplanetary Customs, where the guy wanted to know if I had any agriculturally-based materials on me.

"You mean like my pet alfalfa plant?" I asked the guy, who squinted back, irritated. Where does your sense of humor go in middle age?

That "Interplanetary" stuff is a lot of piss on the window. We're talking about the *Moon* here, not Triton! Who ever goes beyond the Moon—except for rock jockeys and a few Settlement wackos?

A receptionist in the Fun City waiting lounge weighed me in, logged my metabolism rate. I handed her a credit flat as she calculated the charges for clarking, shuttle, a month's air, and all of those incidentals. She handed the flat back with a knowing smirk.

After a short wait in the passenger lounge the attendants allowed us to board. The partition was open on one of the first-class cabins on the bottom level. An attendant was leaning in, handing this gray-head a drink in a squeeze bag, then tightening the harness over his swivel cushion.

I was almost up the ladder into the tourist seating when the gray-head started shouting at me, "*You!* You! Wait." That thick Philly accent, insistent, used to getting his way.

His face went red as he fought the harness, hands flapping about like netted birds. The attendant rolled his eyes—his work being undone. The old guy's hair was bouncing up in wild tufts. When he saw that I had turned to listen, he gasped and gave up fumbling with the harness. Waved me down.

"Please. Step down here young woman—others gotta pass. I must speak to you."

He had this commanding manner that was easy to resent. Maybe he'd had a few too many squeeze bags. The one in his hand was labeled in happy little print: "VODKA MARTINI." An old fart's downer. There was even a green olive in a separate, transparent tear-sack swinging from the bottom of his drink.

When I stepped closer, he ran through the entire spectrum of gray-head-astonishment expressions. "My god," he said, "Jehosephat! I'll . . . be . . . damned."

He held out his free hand, shaking, smelling like a well-attended barroom the morning after. "You're *blinking*," he said. "*Iris* dilation. You're flesh and blood! Human."

"And your brain's kind of fizzed, mister."

"Don't go!" He grabbed my wrist, then apologized immediately and lightly stroked my arm as if he were healing the inevitable bruise.

"Tell me," he asked, "has your hair ever been jet black?"

"Every conceivable shade of brown and blond," I replied. "Even magenta once. But never jet black. Okay?"

"Sorry," he said, sadness edging in on his eyes. "It's just that you look so much like my wife. Astounding."

"Is your wife twenty-nine years old, mister?"

"My wife of forty-three years. She, uh, just left me."
He struggled under his harness to extract his wallet.

Oh cream, here we go. The moping stranger on the shuttle
is going to show me his wallet full of holograms now. He
flipped it open—genuine leather! On the right was the
"Bank of Paris" logo over the calc pad. But under that,
gold-embossed, was a name: "Benito O. Funcitti."

He was punching the "scroll forward" button on the left
side of the open wallet, blipping up holos of a rose garden,
a "space needle" house, postcard-type shots of Fun City—
professional pictures with unlikely, computer-jacked coloring. The average wallet handles 100, 200 holos. A guy
like this probably popped for extra storage—maybe 2,000
holos. Gawd, this could take all day. Why didn't he use
the filter parameters—just blip up all his "wife" shots?
Brain-fizzed.

Finally he came to an overexposed shot of a dark-haired
woman standing in a meadow. She had one foot propped
on the top of a shovel blade and her left forefinger was
brushing a shock of hair out of her eyes.

"Elvis," he sighed.

"What kind of name is that?"

"Ha. A guy's name, once. A singer. Mid twentieth century."

"Should I have heard of this Elvis? I mean, it's not like
he was David Byrne or anything, right?"

He took a drag on his martini. "She meant a lot to me,"
he said, meaning his wife, and clearly it was so.

"You're, like, *the* Benito Funcitti, aren't you? The di-
rector or president or something—just the general *mayor*
of Fun City, right?"

He nodded, looking a little embarrassed—which I figure
to be a sign of real wealth and power. No need to put on
airs. No need to grub for exposure.

"Thought so. My roommate got you last month on the
cover of her Newsweek fax. I think I got a cover article on
Sentia implants, the ethical debate. I'm heavily filtered for
the medical stuff, you know. I'm a physical therapist."

"You see the resemblance—you and my wife?" Funcitti asked me, tapping the snapshot.

"Look, um. This holo is at least twenty, maybe thirty years old. I don't think . . . well, the build is the same, and maybe our lips are a little a like, but I really don't think your wife and I look anything like each other."

"I suppose you're right." The old guy seemed to be done with his drink and was glancing about for the attendant. He drew a clip of Winstons out of his shirt and lit one.

"Gotta go to my seat now. Um, Mr. Funcitti? You want that olive?"

There's atmosphere at the top of Pike's Peak—enough to keep a person alive. But the ground crew were wearing pressure suits anyway. Not the full rhino skins that the space jocks wear, but enough to keep the warmth in and the altitude sickness out. Twin vapor trails from their neck vents followed them around as they tractored our shuttle pod up to the tower rails and latched us in place.

When we began clarking into the sky, most of the passengers were properly low-ebb, like they took elevators into orbit every day of their lives. Me? I kept my nose pressed to the glass for the first couple of hours. When I'm excited I tend to erupt with a "Hooo!" or a "Ho-god!" now and then, and I drew more than a few disgusted stares from neighbors trying to doze in their swivel chairs.

Several hours into the ride, of course, gravity faded away. Later, it returned slightly—but in the opposite direction— as we decelerated into the orbital terminal. Our seats obediently swung into reverse position.

The clarke tower rails channeled us into a large disk-shaped hangar, where our pilot taxied us through a baffling network of tracks to the docking rim. There, another crew, this bunch outfitted with serious space hides, maneuvered our pod into the gaping hollow of a rocket chassis.

Our pod, just minutes before an elevator car, had become a little space ship. The pilot murmured over the PA to hustling attendants, the cabin walls began to hum with the vibration of thrusters, and a set of hangar doors spread open silently. Then we were adrift in the starry blackness.

When you arrive at Fun City, the shuttle spills you into a little lecture hall where the greeters weed out the first-timers for a mandatory orientation session. Oh, you learn little things that your travel agent should have told you: How the holovid projectors work in your hotel room, liability waivers for the jetpack tours outside the domes.

But here's what they're really afraid you'll forget (and I'm saving you thirty minutes of vacation time):

—Code Blue, think "cool." Family activity areas. No gambling, profanity, or nudity.

—Code Yellow, think "warm." No children. Gambling allowed. Expect horseplay and semi-nudity.

—Code Red, think "hot." Anything goes. The Cybers are there for the full enjoyment of any adult. There are plenty to go around.

"And," said the grinning greeter, "if you find that you can't live without one, you may take any Cyber home—for half-a-million francs."

The visitors stood, eager to get to their rooms, snickering uncomfortably and avoiding eye contact with each other.

"Excuse me, you're a Cyber, aren't you?"

Ah. A pickup line peculiar to Fun City. Meaning: "Excuse me, may I engage you sexually for half an hour or so?" Cybers here have a number of minor functions—fetching refreshments, giving directions—but it's generally understood in the "warmer" zones of Fun City that "Cyber" is synonymous with "sexual servant."

I had been scanning the misty coast on the opposite side of the lake and panned to my right to find my field of vision entirely occupied by a tanned male pelvis. The flesh was trisected by a strained little shred of yellow cloth known on the Moon as a Fun String. I followed the trail of fine, bleached hairs up a flat tummy, through a forest of chest curls, past a neatly braided beard to a pair of shocking blue eyes. Nordic, probably. Near the high end of my acceptable-age range, which fluctuates around thirty-five or so.

I held up the backs of my hands with unnecessary emphasis. "See? No tattoos. All Cybers have the Fun City logo tattooed where you can't miss it."

Then I adjusted my swimsuit in case it was hanging open immodestly. It was a pale blue one-piecer out of the dispenser up at the cabana, flimsy enough to be alluring but with a strong enough sunblock to get my white parts acclimated slowly.

I rolled over on the beach pad and waved him toward the low-gravity volleyball rig down the shore. The net was a regulation thirty-four feet high (Lunar specs). The kind you see on Wide World of Sports. A dozen figures were arcing into the air like slow-motion fleas, the bodily trajectory having become a much bigger part of the game strategy than it is on Earth.

"Down there," I said curtly. "All but three or four of the players are Cybers. Have a ball."

He lowered himself to the fine gravel, sitting down with a crunch. "Christ, I'm sorry. I'm confused. . . ."

Oh, Christ, sure you are.

"I *did* think you were a Cyber. It's your eyes," he said, bemused. "Uh, rather unnatural, don't you think?"

"Look, twice in a day people have mistaken me for a rack of hardware. And what's this about my eyes? My eyes are no more. . . . . *Oh!* Oh cream of shit! I'm wearing my camera lenses."

"Camera?"

I giggled and pulled back my left eyelid, dropping a lens into my palm. I rolled it between my fingers. The sunlight striking the deep blue plastic fractured into a swirling rainbow.

"It can look pretty odd, I know, but they make superb vids," I said. "Hah. When you remember you're wearing them."

The camera cassette was still rolling there by my shoulder bag. I punched the red power button, imagining what my roommate was going to think of the long slow climb I had recorded up this guy's belly.

"The lenses fit over your eyes, so what you see is what's recorded," I told the stranger. "Control panel here—mags up to 5K. You'll throw up if you roll the zoom too fast. Graphic equalizers—one for sound here, one for color correction here. Great stuff. All Mesa Verde equipment. I'm trying out Fuji discs in it, though."

He squinted and adjusted the density on his sunglasses. "Beaucoup centimes, huh?"

"Yeah, smoked a credit flat with this baby. But that's why God invented tax write offs. I can use it at work— phys therapy. Run ergonometric studies of my patients. But I'm surprised you've never seen one—came out in the *spring*. Where you been? Pluto?"

"No, asteroids—Outer Belt."

"Cream, you're serious."

He smiled good-naturedly. "Year on, six months off. Till I retire, die, or lose certification."

"Grim."

"Well, the union expects year-on-year-off oh, maybe not for five years. But my agent's trying to get it for me now on a side letter—she figures I'm special."

I popped my left lens back in and punched the power button again on the camera cassette to catch some of the volleyball game. On the near side, the server and the center were starting to play grab-ass during lulls in the game action, and I thought things might be about to "warm" up.

"So you come to Fun City, get a six-month tan, do some push-ups on a Cyber, then go back out to jockey some more rock?" I asked him.

"Close. We TeleComp in, of course, unless we're riding herd on a shipment. Company pays that far. We put in at Lunar Station, on the other side of Weighman's Ridge. Could shuttle to Sydney from there, but Fun City will cut all sorts of deals if we jump the ridge and spill credits. After two weeks here, I get free round-trip shuttle Earthside. But I usually touch home just long enough to re-cert and get back up here. No family, except for an aunt I lose track of.''

"Sydney. Australia? You've lost your accent."

"Easy to do when all you get is American music and vids, Soviet porn, and Navajo news broadcasts. I'm with a Navajo Nation company."

Down the beach, a male form rocketed up from the pebbles to spike the volleyball over the net. Probably a human player. The Cybers tend to let the "bloods" make all of the grand plays. Courtly programming.

I pointed again to the game. "Anyway," I said, "if you're looking for a Cyber, time's a-wasting."

He seemed to be blushing. I checked the spectrographic settings on the cassette, then blocked out a small edit window in the lower left corner of my vision for a quick rerun. Yes, he had reddened. Cute.

"I think I *will* have a bit of a workout," he said, standing. He brushed his nearly-naked rear, and white pebbles went sailing back to the ground in low-gravity arcs. "But I haven't made up my mind yet about the Cybers for, uh, what you're suggesting." He twiddled the frame of his sunglasses, and they darkened even more.

"I thought you'd have gotten to know Cybers rather well on the Outer Belt."

"Oh. Naw. Out there, most of the Cybers are just mining tools—all hardware for the more dangerous jobs. They've got none of the . . . well, what would you call it, *soft*ware?"

An uneasy smile blinked on and off his face, then he seemed at a loss for words. Finally he said, "The name's Mallory, by the way."

"Therese."

Then he threw out a friendly wave as he walked toward the volleyball court, tight little butt muscles twitching. There was a slight hobble to his gait, which dated him as a longtime asteroid miner. Fifteen years ago, if I remember the medical histories correctly, bone loss was still a problem for zero-gravity workers. Steroid and calcium therapy worked well enough, except for the exaggerated growth that took place in the femur.

And so the bowlegged rock jockeys earned their nickname: Space cowboys.

The cabana, as always, was awash with the odor of cleansing chemicals. Reminded me of work. I fed my swimsuit into the decontamination rollers and ducked into one of the conditioning showers. It's a slimy experience, yes, but you have to do it if you want your skin cells to stand up to tanning.

After the rinse cycle was done, the doors buzzed open and an attendant enveloped me in a fuzzy white towel. Warm, fresh out of the rollers. As she was patting me down, she leaned toward my left ear and whispered: "Pits?"

"What?" I glanced at the backs of her hands and saw that there were no tattoos—she was human, which I hadn't expected. "What did you say?"

Her left hand fanned the air, a signal to not speak so loudly. It was clear now that she was no Cyber—a torrent of unruly red hair, a face growing puffy from some kind of regular bodily abuse.

"Pits. *Pits,*" she said, a little impatient. And then I understood. She held up a roll of derm patches, the sort that certain enthusiasts paste into their armpits for a high—usually from bootleg pharmaceuticals. I imagine she could have gotten fired for this.

"Sorry," I told her. "I thought Cybers were stationed here."

She shrugged. "Sometimes you get blood, sometimes plexolics. So you wanna buy the pits, or what?"

"Um, no. You can't trust the manufacture of those things, you know."

"These are *supreme,*" she said. "I'm on a test flight as we speak."

"I don't doubt it. But no thanks."

The young woman's irises were ghostly pinpoints and veins in her temples were throbbing noticably. I took control of the towel and finished drying myself, eager to get back to my room.

"Then how about these?" The attendant put the pits into her apron and produced another roll of patches, a series of blue-green swirls. Her eyebrows rose with an air of naughty confidentiality.

"Really," I said. "No thanks. No need to fizz my brain at all today." Cream. You might expect this on South Street. But on vacation? On the Moon?

"These aren't pits at all," she said. "But they're a guaranteed good time." The attendant held one of the patches closer for my inspection.

"That design—it looks like the Fun City logo," I said. "Like you see the Cybers wearing. So what?"

"Thass the point exactly. It *is* the Fun City logo, just like the Cybers wear." She glanced left and right—*this* bit of contraband making her jumpy, apparently, when the sale of bootleg pharmaceuticals did not. "Ever wonder what the sex life of a Cyber would be like? If guys would cut right to the chase, sack out on the slightest whim?"

"Oh, I see. These are fake tatoos."

"They wash off with alcohol. Fifty centimes apiece."

A bottle of wine was waiting for me in the room, on the end table by the massage trough. It rested to one side in a bucket, imbedded in a mound of ice. The label read "Long Flat White." Ah. Australian. It was a bit extravagant, considering the freight charges to clarke nonessential cargo into orbit, then shuttle it to the Moon. There *are* lunar vinyards, although their product is supposed to be less than stellar.

A note hung from the neck of the bottle: "Dinner, 8:30 P.M., Earthlight Room." Mmm. It would be a full day of sampling things Australian.

I ran a quick calculation in my head—the side effects of a glass or two of wine and the amount of pain relief I would require several hours later. And my mind wandered quickly to that reluctant rock jock in his little yellow Fun String.

I threw the release lever on the bottle and poured. Then

I positioned the massage heads in the trough to a particularly sensual setting. Last, I pushed my camera cassette into the wall holovid deck, set it for perpetual replay, and settled into the massage trough.

On three sides of me, the hotel room walls dissolved and I was panning across the beach again. And, at close range, there came the tanned acreage of tight flesh, appearing at my side. . . .

7
Laurence

At 8 P.M., South Street was still changing hands. A gaggle of the scrubbed college kids had not yet fled to the safety of the campus laserfences. The implant parlors were just charging their neon billboards to life—the one at Eighth Avenue depicting a nude nymph taking flight in a whirl of fireworks. And the hardcore street creatures—the wild-eyed leather boys, zombie hookers, and stimware pushers—were just hitting the glistening sidewalks, pouring out of the flop houses and alley dorms.

Half-blinded by a holovid of desert landscape, I pushed through the entrance of the Velvet Scorpion at Ninth and South Street. I shook the sleet off of my overcoat as my eyes adjusted to the low light. My sneaks were wet and cold. The air was an acrid blend of spilled alcohol and overactive electronics.

It was too early for the regular population of night crawlers I had remembered from two years before. There was just one patron at the bar, a hollow-eyed desperado, and a few more were huddled over tables at the back end of the room. The kid at the bar had just jacked his credit flat into the console, and the expressionless bartender placed a plexiglas case in front of him.

"Gentle, remember," the bartender admonished. "You injure another one an' I'll tap you for five grand."

The kid was grinning broadly, his head lolling, oblivious to the threat. He rolled up his left sleeve and slid that hand into the aperture on one side of the box, then laid his palm open. In the transparent cage, a scorpion skittered into the far corner, claws erect and tail hunched up and twitching defensively.

The patron wiped his moist chin, eyes gleaming with anticipation. He edged his hand forward, goading the tiny beast. His palm was a moonscape of tiny scars. There were a dozen more unhealed wounds, some infected.

"Take it easy, now," the bartender murmured. Then he dashed a finger in my direction and his eyebrows rose—sign language for "What'll ya have?"

"Whitbread," I answered, taking a stool and lowering my shoulder pack to the ground by its strap.

He released the seal from a bottle and placed it on the counter, along with a beer glass on top of a useless little napkin. The barkeep poked at his console and I jacked a credit flat into the slot.

"Nice silk," the bartender said to me, nodding at my Hawaiian shirt.

"Thanks," I said. "Antique, ya know."

"Nice shirt," he said again. "I'm about to make you an offer on that shirt. Don't go nowhere."

He didn't mean it. I nodded, a vague affirmation of the sentiment.

Then he went back to keep an eye on his prized scorpion.

The kid was waggling his middle finger now, edging closer to the maroon little arachnid. The bartender frowned. The scorpion leapt onto the young man's palm, looking like a quote mark gone rabid. The bugger's tail darted over its head, two lightning stings.

"Ah," the kid said, his face going slack with satisfaction long before he could have felt the venom take effect. The venom would be one of the newer bionarcotics, I guessed. These genetically engineered scorpions were renowned as one of the purest sources. Only in the last few years did the actual scorpions make the bar scene in their little cages. Surely there were more sterile, and less painful, ways to get high. Hmph. Fads.

The bartender retrieved his plexiglass box and returned

it to its position on the rear counter, by the Glenfiddich bottle.

I sipped my Whitbread, from the bottle.

"How 'bout you?" the bartender said, contorting his lips in my direction but otherwise addressing the room at large. "You'd like ta scorp?"

"Um, no," I said. "I'm here to see Willie Schilfgaarde." I pointed a thumb toward the ceiling, hoping that Willie still occupied the second floor.

The bartender gestured toward someone at the murky end of the room, and a figure peeled away from the wall and began walking toward us.

"You'll need an introduction," he said. "You, uh, you with the Gummint? Grid police? ICC?"

I shook my head. "Customer. Previous customer," I said, pulling my shoulder pack up from the floor by its strap and easing it down again.

The person from the back of the room arrived—an Asian woman, young but hard-looking. She wore a boxy black gown that did not reveal much, save for a narrow slit of flesh down the middle of her chest. Without a word, she produced a smooth wet stone the size of a slice of lime. She took my right hand and dragged the stone across the knuckles, then pressed a button on its side—a DNA scan, probably.

"This will take a minute," she said in French-flavored English. "Maybe in the meantime you would like some other service which I can provide?"

The bartender had discreetly positioned himself at the far end of the bar, where the kid with his new injection was nodding away, his brain sliding like warmed jelly across some hallucinated desertscape.

I tugged at my shoulder pack strap, to bring it closer to my feet. I felt embarrassed, and then silly. Inside the pack was my mainframe, quickly yanked, snipped and disentangled from the house wiring down in Wilmington. Inside the mainframe was my electronic companion for the last two years—Blanche, now dormant. Blanche could *joke* about sexuality, but she could never *know* it, or *care* about it. And Blanche was asleep right now. Still. . . .

"No, thanks," I said. "I'll just wait."

The two years had not treated Willie Schilfgaarde well. He was skinny, but it was a sickly skinniness, I decided. His flesh was the color and texture of dry cheese, and his hairstyle was several months out of date—processed to look like a wavy tangle of cellophane noodles. As I entered, he slouched atop a wheeled tripod stool.

His office was dominated by a horseshoe-shaped workbench, five tiers of fiberboard laden with two dozen tuber screens, receptor boxes, keyboards, joy sticks, and spliced cables. Any kind of coding format and any kind of software you could imagine, Willie Schilfgaarde could handle it—celluloid wedges, hard rods, Navajo gels, laser disks.

All of the tubers were clear, save for the center screen, his main burn. I saw my name at the top of the screen, followed by biographical data and technical notes from my last visit.

"That the trigital unit I scammed up?" He nodded toward the bulge in my pack. "You got a repair now, hey?"

"Works fine," I said. "I've just . . . um, I'm moving and didn't want to leave it in the tracker. This neighborhood, ya know."

"*My* neighborhood."

"No offense."

Schilfgaarde laughed. "Hell, I wouldn't even leave a *tracker* on South Street, much less a custom frame inside of one."

I looked about for a seat and found a stuffed chair buried in old faxes. I stacked the news sheets on the floor and sat into the crunch of broken springs. The cushions hoofed up a stale breath reminiscent of the barroom below, like twenty years of passed-out ale-sloggers.

"Must say, I wouldn't mind a lighter unit," I said, patting the pack in my lap, "not that I could afford the miniaturization right now. But it puts a strain on the shoulder, you could imagine.''

Schilfgaarde harumphed. ''Seems to me I warned you off this tri-polar switching idea of yours. It's that third switch ya had ta have—and a dimmer slide at that. I say you could simulate the third switch on digital—even a pure dimmer, juss about. But no, you says this is *art*. *Art!* And 'juss about' won't do. I gotta find a memory printer crazy enough to template for a run of one unit. Useless to anyone else. A one-unit run, and now you want to talk miniaturization. . . .''

''No . . . no. . . .'' I had to wave my hands to shut him up. ''Sorry I brought it up. That's not why I came at all. I came here. . . .'' This felt oddly confessional, somehow. Like an admission of great failure. Perhaps it was. ''I came here because you said once that there were places where a guy like me could find work if I ever cut from the Government. Maybe off-union, maybe the money wouldn't be as good, maybe I'd have to arrange my own medicals. . . .''

Schilfgaarde wheezed a long sigh and ran a hand back through his cellophane hair. He sucked at his lower lip. He ran his tongue over his yellowed lower teeth.

''Nobody leaves Government work, nobody in his right mind. 'Less there's trouble a union can't cover and a bribe can't assuage.''

''I'm about to be fired,'' I said, fiddling with the pack strap. ''Or maybe I *was* fired. I didn't return to work today, so I don't know. It involves some side work I was doing— by contract, they own any kind of coding I do, and. . . .'' I heaved a lungful of air out my nostrils. ''And . . . they . . . can't . . . have it.''

''So.'' Schilfgaarde wheeled about on his tripod chair and began tapping his keyboard and throwing switches on a patch box. Four tubers came to life. ''I'll have to make inquiries. We'll have to convert any credit flats in your name—fast. I can find you two-for-one conversion for solid and safe credit, or five-for-four pirated, which probably will suffice as long as you turn it over within two weeks.''

After a few minutes the tubers emptied their screens and pulsed gray-blue, marking time, awaiting responses. Schilfgaarde wheeled around to face me again. "Don't worry," he said. "There may be no market for Tier 5 coding per se, but there's a few people who'll give regular pay to a man knows what you do."

"Well, your efforts are very much appreciated," I said.

Schilfgaarde snorted. "Oh, don't fool yerself. I'm going ta bill ya. You've stepped into a new strata, Mr. Essex. Favors may be done, but still ya pay for 'em. Still ya pay. Hey, think of *me* as yer union now. Ha." He wiped his nose on a sleeve. "And ya'd best not look back—any contact with old friends, former coworkers, and the cops would make the trace quick. I hope you've said yer goodbyes already."

"No," I replied. "No goodbyes. There was only one friend, and I've brought her along."

8
Kodas

U.S. 1 heading west out of Philadelphia is an elevated shred of wet asphalt, a sorry little highway sloshing us past an unending progression of tracker repair shops, tuber distributors, rabbit barbecue joints—that kind of stuff. Just past Chadds Ford, Doc leans into the stick and we slide onto an exit ramp.

We cruise slowly along the base of a stone wall for half a mile. An entrance flashes by with a rusty little plaque— "Longwood Gardens." Soon the street veers away from the wall and dumps us into the commercial strip we had seen from the highway above.

Doc takes the first available parking space, I get out, and as I'm about to slot our newly updated credit flat, Doc gives me an irritated "Ho up—crissake."

I shrug. What?

"Use the hard cash."

I slap the head of the meter once, and it sways back and forth on its flexible pole. "Personal expenses," I tell her. "Deal is we use the credit flat for small personal expenses, right? Parking fees are a small personal expense."

Doc is on the sidewalk tugging at her rain suit, uncomfortable after the drive. It's a close fitting, rumpled-looking fabric that shifts color, depending on the surrounding terrain. Right now it's the color of wet concrete. She holds her rainscreen mask up to her face and the suction grabs hold. The raindrops go "tst, tst, tst" as they vaporize against the faceplate. Her hair is already sopping, plastered to her little head. Fuck the hair, Doc would say.

"Hard cash," she says again. "Say we mess something up, create suspicion. Cops could try to trace all activity in the vicinity. I don' wanna leave anything to trace—clean credit flat or not."

I shrug and feed hard centimes into the slot. Seems like a waste.

Doc takes a shoulder pack out of the back compartment, locks the tracker, looks up and down the street. There's an implant parlor at the end of the block—no customers, a bored looking cashier surgeon behind a counter. Almost no foot traffic on the sidewalk, and no one's taking special notice of us. A drizzly afternoon is a great time to work.

Doc tilts her mask up at me. "An' one more thing," she says. "We go by that implant shack, you don't go in, no matter how slick the gear looks through the window. You go in and start talking Sentias, somebody wired up as much as you, they're gonna remember."

"Don't worry," I tell her as I fit my own mask on. "Out here, they got no gear I haven't had under my skin for a year or two already. This ain't South Street."

Looks like a holo salesman did a pretty good job down this block. There's a barbecue joint called The Hop, with a holo of thousands of rabbits dancing on a field of clover that disappears into the horizon. It's got a nice shrink-off-into-the-distance. Perspective, they call that. Next is the implant shop. Across the entrance is a holo of a kneeling woman, all her Sentia points—nipples, thighs, tuba, ear lobes—exploding with roman candle ecstasy. We turn the corner, and there's another barbecue place, this one called Harvey's, with a giant white rabbit blocking the entrance.

I think of the fairy tale about the brick seller. Spent all his savings on the finest holo sign, one showing a brick wall, one with ace details. He went broke, of course—nobody knew a store was there. Finest sign in the world, and he went broke.

We cross a tiny street and get to the stone wall at Long-wood, then walk along it until the bushes are thick and we're out of sight. Doc drops the shoulder pack and I boost her up to take a quick look. Down at my feet, I notice, is the charred carcass of a sparrow. Pretty recent.

"Like Terry F1 said—standard laserfence, pretty dated actually." Doc hops down again and opens the pack. She pulls out two clear plastic jumpsuits, one nearly twice the size of the other. She checks the black panels at the crotch.

"Yours is good for twenty more minutes of burn, mine for seven," she says. "All we need is a couple of seconds at the top of the wall. Remember to keep it on until you're ten feet inside, though. Could be infrared field."

"Could be infrared field over the whole grounds," I tell her.

"Naw. Too many workers during the day."

"Workers? What's ta work? It's just a bunch of trees an' plants, ya said."

Doc rolls her eyes like she does when she's thinking your needle's in the red zone. She pulls the shoulder pack snug against her back, kicks my suit over to me and starts to pull on her own—leaves the top part hanging off her shoulders until I catch up. It can get hot in there fast—no vents. Infrared would pick you up right away.

I roll the plastic up my legs and arms, run a finger along the zip-lock up my chest, then fit the air regulator between my teeth and zip my face in too. The suit is lined with an inch of clear, squishy gel, which makes for blurred vision that the rainscreen can't even correct.

When Doc is sealed, I hold my arms out and rock back and forth like some half-witted vid monster.

"Jell-O Man!" I yell, muffled by the plastic and air feed.

Doc puts her hands on her hips, pissed because she's steaming in there already.

I do it again. "Jell-O Man!"

And she gives in, plays the game—arms out, a barely audible cry. But I know she's shouting "Jell-O Woman!"

Then I'm kneeling quickly, and Doc is up on my knee, springing off my shoulders. Then it's Jell-O Man's turn. I leap, grab the top of the wall, walk my way up. A leg over, and there's a lightning flash of laser richocheting through the gel of my suit and out the other side—an unbroken beam.

I hit ground in a shadowy bramble. Vines or limbs thrash about. All I can see is murk. I stumble on a root or something. Which way? Must be a hunnerd twenty degrees now in the suit. The air stager is going *heeeeeet-koooor, heeeeeet-koooor,* throbbing in my head.

There's a swath of fuzzy green off to my left. Open meadow probably. I step carefully in that direction, trying not to trip again.

Several paces in, I stop and tear the zip-lock open and peel my rain mask off too. The suit down around my shoulders is slick from sweat. Gawd, the wash of outside air, the light rain on my skin. It's like a nice little hit of sentia, or the first chill of Zenithialate B.

Doc is standing under a pine a few yards away. She's looking down at her left leg grimly.

"Gashed it on a piss-drinking tree stump or something coming off the wall," she says. The plastic is torn away at her shin and there's a little trail of the gel leading up to her foot.

"Yeah, Jell-O Woman, this wilderness work is a bitch," I tell her. "But it'll repair okay, I think. And the Vineland kids make these suits compartmentalized. Thass about all the fluid you're gonna lose."

"Jell-O Woman, cream of shit." Doc takes her suit off in irritated jerks, and I strip my own off. We roll them up tight and stash them back in the shoulder pack. I check my watch—we're a minute behind, but we factored in several minutes' padding. Zero hour is 4:35 P.M.

Doc rolls out a little map of the gardens, and we orient ourselves. Our mark lives in one of those space-needle houses, turn-of-the-century fad among the obscenely rich. We can see the stem of it now through the trees, 300 yards away to the northwest.

We fall into a trot. There are several miles of pebbled walking paths wandering around the 350 acres inside the stone wall. We stay to the paths with the trees all around much as we can, except for one shortcut under cover of a hedge sculpted to look like a row of ducks. Nearby there's also a bush cut to look like an elephant. A bush cut to look like a horse. On and on. Rich people, they walk around their yards and say, "I got so much money, I don't mind paying an army of gardeners to do *that*."

We take a looping detour east around a large rose garden—this late in the year, and there's still a thick fragrance rolling up through the rain.

We duck down along a fish pond. Gold and white fish—"Koi" the little sign says—burble up to the surface as we pass, expecting to be fed. Then we cut up a hill through a tall stand of trees, past a stone house—light on in the window, pickup truck outside. Caretaker, probably, or security. Ha.

From the edge of the trees, there's twenty yards of newly-mowed lawn to the base of the needle house. 4:25. Ten minutes left. We sprint across the exposed ground.

We find the main entry to the elevator and stairs, then a hangar for trackers, and finally a smaller door, which has to lead to the power station Terry F1 had described. The lock appears to be low-rent, and several years old at that. I frown.

"Mr. Funcitti needin' a new security consultant," Doc whispers. She clicks her tongue.

"Thass his name? Funcitti?"

Doc sighs. I shrug.

I fan open our clip of flats and select Terry F1's latest skeleton key, although any of her shimmies from the last couple of years would do the job. I slot it into the lock and the little green button glows for three seconds—computer linkup, protocol set. The yellow button glows for seven seconds as Terry F1's code worms into security banks, heads off alarms, culls the access information and feeds it back to the computer as if a proper key had been slotted. The white button blinks on—open. Had the red button lit, well, bad news. We'd run.

Doc pulls the door open and we set our masks for night vision. It's a tight little space—four feet wide, seven deep, the size of an alley-dorm room. Six interconnected transformers are bolted to a wall, each of them the size of a human torso. My torso, not Doc's.

Doc opens the cover on the first, touches a meter to a piece of interior housing. She nods and says, "This is the active one."

She hands me a strip of beetle-sized sensors. I peel them off the paper one at a time to expose their adhesive, then glue one to each of the five remaining transformers. Doc comes behind with a spool of evaporating filament, lacing it gently from one to the other, then down to a junction box a foot off of the concrete floor. I open a jar of vulcan putty— high heat, low explosive—and pack half an ounce under the junction box with a detonator.

For good measure, I press another half-ounce of putty into the third transformer and wire that into the loop too.

Doc stands back. "Yeah," she says, nodding rare approval. "It'll look random. And like one transformer blew and buggered the whole rest of it."

"I wish the sensors would evaporate like the rest of our gear."

She shrugs. "They'll melt down for sure. Leave a drip or a blotch. You'd have to know what you were looking for ta figure 'em."

My watch says three minutes to go. I reach into the shoulder pack and pull out a brown paper bag and unroll it. The odor hits me and my throat twitches. Gawd. I turn the bag upside down and hold it by the edges. The squirrel is stuck to the bottom of the bag. I shake the bag hard and it flops out.

"Yeah, let's hope this job doesn't get studied too closely," I say.

"Put it ontop of the junction box, where it'll take some of the main blast," Doc suggests. I pick the critter up by its tail and position it near the box.

We relock the door and dash back to the woods. We

watch. The entire house can run on the first transformer alone. But a TeleComp transmission requires the power of all five of the others put together. When all five transformers are in use, the sensors will pick it up and the substation wiring will go up in flames.

We wait, crouched in the underbrush. Birds chirp. 4:38, 4:39. The sun's almost down. With six minutes left on the TeleComp's travel window, there's a low blast—*poomph*—and smoke seeps under the substation door. The lights blink out in the needle house.

It's dark in the woods. We're running, wet leaves slapping us in the face. The old stone house hasn't changed—no one about, pickup truck out front, light on. . . .

Doc stops.

"What is it?" I whisper.

She points to the window of the stone house. Ah. The light. We've just blown the substation, but still there's a light in the window. Which means that there's another power source for the out buildings and such.

"Laserfence'll still be on," she says, "and I've buggered my suit. Unless I wanna risk frying a leg off."

We stare at each other for a few minutes. I can't figure it, she can't figure it. Doc shifts her weight. I see a blur against the ground and suddenly her flying right foot has caught me across the stomach. My lungs go wooden and I fall to my knees. A thorny pain is crawling up my abdomen.

Doc wipes a strand of hair off her rainscreen. "Sorry," she says. "I gotta release my frustration somehow."

I gasp, hoping that little breaths will slowly refill my crushed lungs.

"Let's go back up the hill," Doc says. "Watch the house. Emergency folks'll come—maybe we'll learn something."

I hear her go crunching up the pebbled path into the dark.

9
Benito

Something was wrong with the drainage in the streets of downtown Camden. The sleet was turning into a lumpy river of brown slush across the pavement, and our van tossed up twin roostertails as we passed a hotel called Valentine's.

Elvis turned around in the passenger seat to study the hotel over her shoulder. Like most of the buildings for blocks around, Valentine's disappeared into the murky glow that seemed to hang over the downtown area at the thirty- or forty-story level. The sign mounted on the front of the building was a holovid made to look like old-time neon— bright colors, jerky movements. It depicted a red heart gradually growing huge across the edifice, breaking into two jagged halves, collapsing into a small heart shape again, then starting all over. On either side of the entryway bored-looking prostitutes in clingy thermasuits leaned against the Teflon siding of the building under a narrow overhang. Business was slow.

"How 'bout that place?" Elvis asked.

"Well, I never stayed in a Valentine's," I said. "But the chain's supposed to be inexpensive enough—would likely suit our needs. Probably slow with their security reports."

"Those women outside. . . ."

"Not all of them are women," I corrected.

"But they'uh hookas, right?"

"Right. Hookers."

"Then maybe," Elvis said, "they don' do security reports at all at Valentine's."

"It would be hard to stay in business, not doing *some* kind of security reports," I said. "Crissake, I was having to file security memos for the lunar resorts, where the trade laws are virtually non-existent."

I pulled the van over to the curb so I could look back too. There was no other traffic. None of the other towers showed any life—just Valentine's with its holovid heart, throbbing, shattering, throbbing again in the icy blackness.

"But it's a safe enough guess that they won't use DNA scans," I said. "That's what we really, really don't want— a DNA scan tripping alarms in every ICC office in the region."

"It's only been a few hours," Elvis said. "You think they'd a moved that fast?"

"Yeah—it would be routine for them. Let's just hope my, uh, new and improved self hasn't thought to seal off the accounts yet. We do need a phone fast."

Elvis pointed to the dashboard. "The auto unit—they trace that, too, I guess?"

"You're catching on. Calling from there would be a big mistake."

"I've never been a fugitive before." She turned to face front again and bounced once in the seat. She pulled those wide lips into a mischievous smile.

"You're exhibiting inappropriate behavior," I muttered. "We are in deep trouble. I guess I've got some tailoring to do on your CyberGo."

"Let's check in," Elvis said, her feet tapping eagerly on the floor carpet. "Get us a big ol' bed. . . ."

I sighed. My back muscles were knotted and my legs were numb. In my jacket pocket I found a tab of Zenithialate B and popped it into my mouth. I put the van into gear and turned the next corner.

"We'll leave the van here," I said. "Can't very well register a government auto."

At the registration counter there was a desktop DNA

scanner. It was off to the side, on top of a pile of old news-faxes. An antiquated model. The command keys were dusty, and someone had used the hand well, which was the scanner area, as an ashtray.

The attendant was slouching on a stool—a teenage boy in an ill-fitting uniform. His face was porcelain smooth, not a blemish or scar. Probably a Permaderm job given at birth, sign of a privileged background. Maybe Dad was a Valentine's executive.

The boy had an audio button in each ear—not yet committed to implants—and was waggling his feet and jutting his chin at unlikely intervals. As I approached, he opened his eyes slightly wider, which I guess passes for a greeting in New Jersey.

I drew out a credit flat and slotted it in the counter.

"Three nights," I said. "Biggest bed you have."

The kid's fingers clicked across the key pad, and my credit flat ejected.

"Room thirty-two oh five," he said. "You'll be desiring room service." It was a statement, yet it was meant as a question. A New Jersey question. A Philadelphia question, too, for that matter. But we were in New Jersey.

I nodded.

"Sandwiches only, this time of night," the attendant said. "Bar?"

He looked surprised. "The bar's twenty-four hours."

Elvis was waiting by the express elevator, the door with the health-warning decal peeling off. If you have heart problems, don't ride express—they never say anything about lung problems. We stepped in, and I spread my feet for support and tightened my stomach.

"A study in how not to run a hotel," I said.

"You'll be more cheerful after some sleep," Elvis replied. "We really gonna stay three nights?"

"No. Out of here in the morning. But if we're tracked here, and they find that we're still registered for a couple of days, maybe they'll lose time waiting for us to return."

"Hmph." Elvis's financial systems usually objected to

unnecessary expenditures. She also thought little of the human orientation toward deception.

There was a whoosh, that sinking feeling in the belly, and the elevator door popped open on the thirty-second floor.

In our room, the back window was floor-to-ceiling plexi with no rainscreen in effect—it was a mosaic of water beads and rivulets. Powder blue curtains, double king-sized bed. On the desk a holophone, the kind with a sensor-directed camera that will follow users around the room as they talk.

Elvis scuffed at the carpet. She snorted. "Merced-Serafe fiber Number 28–9S," she said.

I gave her a blank stare. If I give no sign of comprehension, Elvis will sometimes explain herself further—drop down to what she considers to be the next level of knowledge and elaborate. Sometimes.

"Oh," she said after four seconds. "Just before we fled the house I was considering retiling one of the plant shelves in the study dome. Thus I still have in local memory all of our decorating catalogues. This carpet I recognize to be Merced-Serafe fiber Number 28–9S, which is a flooring material commonly used for business offices, not hotel rooms. *And,*" she stated with a little recrimination in her voice, "it is *appropriate* behavior to point out inconsistencies in our surroundings. Especially for fugitives who must live by their wits."

I nodded numbly. I had begun to daydream—her beauty, her Southern-honeyed accent. My fatigue. "Very good, Elvis. Business office carpet would be consistent with a Valentine's hotel, though. Valentine's is a vulture company. When a corporation collapses, they will buy up its offices at a cut rate, rework the building in minor ways to create rentable rooms—extend some of the plumbing, add a few walls and corridors. When the economy rebounds, Valentine's will resell the property at a nice profit, maybe even to the original owner."

Elvis absorbed this and then took a spritely dive onto the bed. She bounced three times.

"We need money!" she said happily.

"I agree. How about plugging in. Disable the phone's vid options. Set up, oh, five different worm-routines—ones that'll collapse as soon as the funds are laundered. Make them roundabout and random, ones you've never used, even in that Spec-Caliente deal in '48.''

Elvis exposed the jack at her temple and cabled herself to the holophone. I found the credit slot in the desktop and jacked a flat into it.

"Let's collect it all here in clean credits," I said. "Nothing lying around in accounts where some, uh, pirate might grab it up. Hit my peripheral accounts first, please—the R&D funds we had set out to percolate. They're probably the safest, the last place he would deploy the security AIs. Least likely to hit back.''

Elvis nodded grimly, her eyes a dead stare as she swam the electronic ocean of world banking information, brushing aside security barriers like stalks of seaweed. Not at all legal. But Elvis was quite experienced at it. In the past I had used her electronic wiles merely for gathering information. I had never asked her to steal currency, but she would have no problem with it under the circumstances.

"Report collections so far, please.''

"Twenty-three million francs," Elvis replied immediately.

The phone hummed. On the black window, rain beaded, succumbed to erratic streams of runoff, then beaded again. What would it be like out there on the other side of the plexi, standing on that little ledge of Teflon? I coughed lightly.

"Thirty-eight million.''

"At fifty million, Elvis, you can stop snitching berries and just take a pass at the cash register—take a grab at the Fun City reserve pool.''

"Mmmm," Elvis replied. A minute later: "Oh.''

"What? . . . Tell me.''

"Oh, I just thought for a moment the reserve pool was unprotected. I reached for it and got this feeling I was being watched. Funny.''

"Got to be an AI patrol, Elvis. Get out. I don't want you up against another artificial intelligence. The ones he hired—*I* hired—they tend to bite.''

"Okay, I've disconnected and it's a clean retreat. What now boss?''

"Did we get fifty million?''

"Yup. You said to.''

"Okay. Tell me: Between your local memory, your memory packs and whatever other baggage you brought, what systems do you have? And what do we have to retrieve from the house?''

Elvis still had the cable attached to her head. She brushed vainly at her displaced hair. "Well, as I told ya, I have the decorating catalogues. . . .''

"The programs we need to survive.''

". . . and as you have seen, I have the financial protocols. The basic operator, of course. Then in portable storage there's the Monday release of Britannica. You know—this and that.''

"How about the medical diagnostics?''

Elvis cocked her head to the side, making the cable jack point up to the ceiling. "Honey, you feelin' bad?''

"I have lung cancer, remember? And it's supposed to be beyond surgery. What do you think?''

"Okay, I'll phone in and get the diagnostics. I'll pick up a few tools for myself, too. We'll have to go shopping soon for some more portable memory.''

The vacant stare fell over her face again. I lit a Winston— couldn't help myself—and found an ashtray in one of the fiberboard dressers. It had been emptied by the maid service but not wiped clean. I reminded myself that the hotel's slipshod management was actually protecting us.

Elvis was nodding her head faintly, which she always did when she downloaded large blocks of data. She absently tapped her index fingers on the edge of the bureau as she waited and swayed her shoulders on the heavy accents of the rhythm. It was what we used to call a Bo Diddley beat.

Panic struck me like a surge of jack-meth. I gasped, which

slammed smoke into my semi-operative lungs. Doubling over, I coughed long and painfully, imagining dislodged lung tissue rattling around down there.

Finally, I wheezed out the words, "Elvis, disconnect. Disconnect *now!*"

She frowned and turned toward me, looking concerned.

"Cease all operations, please. Stop all functions."

Elvis had just pursed her lips in consternation, and that expression froze on her face. I coughed again and spat into a waste paper basket.

Elvis teetered on her rigid legs and began to fall—I had shut her down in mid-stride. I wiped my mouth on my shirt sleeve and lowered her to the bed. I worked the cable jack out of her temple and smoothed her hair back into place.

"Elvis, I want you to disengage your assumptive functions—for now, do only what I say and nothing more. Run no background programs and do not assimilate any more of the new data. Got that? Elvis?"

No response. Ahh—I had forgotten how tedious literal operation could be.

"Okay, Elvis, engage vocal responses. Are you there?"

"I am here," she responded, her lips frozen into that permanent pout.

"Okay, we're going to try to return your programming to what you had before you made that call to our house. Did you purge your previous formats?"

"Of course not. I am not able to purge operating formats until each new one is test run and found to be error free." Her voice was flat, devoid of inflection and accent. Those traits were not available to her until we returned to full operation.

"Good. Now I want you to identify everything you just downloaded—every last datum. Isolate all of it together and seal it off from operative programming. Then I want you to position your previous formats for operation when we bring you up again."

She fell silent for ten seconds, swimming through a vast photonic innerspace. "Done," she said.

Relief washed over me. I was breathing heavily and my brow was damp. My lungs felt sodden, but I sucked on my cigarette anyway.

"Now sit up, please, and slide down the bed to the bureau where the phone is," I told her.

She obeyed in abrupt, mechanical movements.

"Good. Now enter your menu of bodily traits, subset 'random optionals,' subset 'nuances,' subset 'rhythmics.' There's a finger-tapping function there, the one you were just using when you were on the phone. Got it?"

"Got it."

"Run that format."

Elvis tapped one index finger against the edge of the bureau, meting out perfect seconds.

"Fine. Now you may engage all of the previous formats."

Elvis' body finally relaxed into humanlike movements.

"What in tarnation was that all about?" she asked.

"You downloaded a new version of your CyberGo. Where did that come from?"

"Well, it was sitting there shirttailed to the medical diagnostics like ya do when you've got an update for me. So I sucked it in along with everything else."

I reviewed the day's events. Had it really only been half a day since my abortive TeleComp to the Moon?

"I did some work on your CyberGo program this morning—that little syncopation routine that showed up when you were on the phone. But it wasn't *me* that shirttailed it to the medical diagnostics. That little change alone wouldn't be worth the bother. Usually I wait until a dozen or so changes have accumulated, and I turn them all over to you at once."

Elvis shrugged. Beautifully. Casually. Humanly.

"So someone fed me yo' update early," she said. "What you so scared of?"

"That someone probably was me—the *other* me. I'd bet there were more significant changes in your CyberGo that you hadn't had time to assimilate yet."

"Like?"

"I don't know. Like some kind of damage to you, or—" I tamped out the Winston and pushed the smoke out my nostrils. "—um, worse, he might have changed your human referencing criteria. Might have changed your allegiance parameters from me over to himself. All it would take is a swap of our genetic scans."

Elvis was indignant. "He *wouldn't!*"

"If *I* thought of it, *he'd* think of it. That's the problem here isn't it?"

I drew the cigarette pack out of my shirt pocket and popped up a fresh one.

10
Therese

The holovid briefing that you can call up in the Fun City hotel rooms gives you a pretty good advance look at the Earthlight Room restaurant. In the foreground there's a guy in a midnight-blue tux, his date is wearing a backless velvet number and the grinning wine steward is delivering a second bottle of champagne. Outside the picture windows, there's a dark moonscape with a swirling bluegreen Earth just breaking over the horizon.

Hah. So why is it that Earthside, the Fun City brochures say that you can never be *too* casual? They say don't even worry about how—and, in some zones, whether—you dress.

Not one person in that holovid of the Earthlight Room was wearing a Fun String, believe me.

So my neurosis served me well again. Would I really venture from home for a month's vacation without even a semiformal rag or two? Never, never, never. I may have had to pay extra for clarking all of that luggage up here, but I was going to be ready for any eventuality.

At 8:30 I strolled into the foyer of the Earthlight Room in a little black dress, black slippers, and a jade necklace interspersed with replicas of ancient Chinese coins. The maitre d' looked Middle Eastern. He bowed politely between two potted palms at the dining room entrance and greeted me with a wide grin. Just as advertised.

"Hi, I'm here to meet Mr.—um—his name's Mallory. Is he here yet?"

The maitre d's smile collapsed. He had been holding a leather-bound notebook behind his back, and it pained him to have to consult it. This man took pride in having memorized all of the night's guests.

"Sorry ma'am, but I see no gentleman by the name of Mr. Mallory expected this evening."

"Are you sure? He's Australian."

"Sorry, ma'am, but I am quite sure. Not even an Australian by the name of Mallory."

"Well, you know this sounds funny, but Mallory could be his first name—but then I wouldn't know his last."

The maitre d' sighed and rolled his eyes, as if bemoaning the indignities that one must face in this bastion of casual encounters. He ran his finger down both sides of his notebook again. "Quite sorry," he said finally. "I have first and last names of all of the expected guests."

Oh, cream. Nothing to get upset about, really. But getting stood up—that steams my shorts.

"You have a bar here?" I asked.

"Certainly. The lounge is through this way," he said with a sweep of the hand.

"If Mallory comes in, then, I'll be there for a little while. My name's Therese."

The man's mouth formed a tight O-shape and his eyes popped open. "Therese!" he said. "Therese McDaniel, by chance?"

"Yes," I replied. "Therese McDaniel."

Then he said all in a rush, "Oh, I'm so sorry, of course you are expected, come with me and I will show you to your table right away!" He made a high circling motion with his right hand that seemed to be a signal to other restaurant staffers. It was barely perceptible, but the room seemed to shift to a slightly more determined pace.

He walked stiffly toward the lounge, with his right forearm swinging like an orchestra conductor's. I kept up with him rather well, finally getting my lunar legs.

Low lights. The acrid odor of cale enzyme poppers wafting from the rowdies at the bar. Illuminated dice tables crackling with business. A laser-marimba performer on a central platform flashing his mallets through the fan-shape of tonal beams, a Caribbean-Lunar tune that even the Chinese would not object to. The maitre d' minced up a three-step into the light of a new dining room, wound his way through the tables, and followed a row of private booths along another glass wall of moonscape. The Earth looked wet and huge.

The maitre d' stopped after the last booth, at the edge of a roomy alcove. He bowed slightly—maybe it was a nod—and retreated without a word. There was a plush, curving banquette facing the desolate terrain outside. The table carried a modest arrangement of violets in an antique jar and a bottle of wine submerged in an ice bucket. Seated at the table was a man at least three times Mallory's age. Gray hair slicked back, straight from a shower. Sucking on a cigarette. A faint cologne like the odor of freshly chopped wood.

Oh yeah, the guy from the shuttle—big time. What's his name? Funcitti. Of course.

He drew out the bottle, and the ice clattered. Filled a glass for me.

"I, uh, wasn't expecting this," I said. I put a hand on the chair back but didn't sit.

"Would you prefer the Australian?" he asked, and I saw the grim horizon outside start to teeter. What was going on here? My vision was starting to haze up with confusion, to vibrate with anger.

The old guy turned his head to the side and returned the bottle to the ice. He pursed his lips and studied the bottle's label. It was a California chardonnay.

"Ah, I see," he said. "I delivered to your room one of our best Australians. And now you've grown attached to the taste? Or perhaps you would prefer one of the less, um, adventurous French wines? I like to think we stock the best of the French, but they really haven't kept up with their reputation."

"You're talking about wine," I said, my vision suddenly clear.

He drew a red box out of a shirt pocket. In a few smooth handstrokes a cigarette was dangling from his lips, burning. Smoke curled away from his nostrils, luminous with earthshine from the window.

"Sorry," he said, taking the cigarette between thumb and forefinger. Smoking, it seemed, was an occupying process. As much as anything else, something to do with the hands. "Sometimes I get far ahead of myself. Perhaps you do not care about distinctions among wines at all."

"Oh, no. I care dearly about wines," I said. It was a white lie. To fill an awkward moment, I took my seat and swirled the glass there, the way people in the vids do. "Uh, I was just surprised to see that you were serving something other than one of your lunar labels. I read somewhere that you greenhouse your own vinyard up here."

He snorted. He batted at the air with a dismissing wave. "Yes, we grow wine, but the vines are immature—less than five years old. And there's a sediment problem, too, I suspect. It just doesn't settle satisfactorily in lower gravity. I fly one vintner up and get one opinion. I fly another vintner up and get another opinion. In the meantime, I serve special guests the imported stuff. The lunar wines go to the luau tables in the hot zones, where nobody's paying much attention to what they consume."

"Centrifuge," I said, and I took a sip. "Sometimes we use a centrifuge to counter low-gravity damage. Did I mention I was in phys therapy?"

Funcitti nodded. "We've experimented with centrifugal wine cellars, but the results were no improvement on the standard lunar fare, I'm afraid. I have a theory that wine is every bit as temperamental as the human body. Okay, not quite so temperamental, but finicky nevertheless. The human body, remember, has garnered the attention of ninety-seven percent of all scientific pursuit. Oenology, by comparison, is a sad, sad stepsister. A miniscule concern."

"And isn't that as it should be?"

The old guy's eyes brightened. "Hah—quite right. And as long as things are as they should be, in that respect, as long as we must still lurch about in the darkness for our winemaking . . . well, I suppose that before I will serve an inferior wine to a deserving young lady I will clarke the better stuff up from Earth."

Gawd. I sipped from the glass, let the wine slosh about in the front of my mouth. A dry bite burned its way across my tongue and I swallowed.

Benito O. Funcitti watched in silence, apparently awaiting judgment. What could I say? It was quite pleasant and undoubtedly several dozen francs beyond my taste.

I wrinkled my nose. "Perhaps I *should* try the French," I said.

Funcitti's hand shot into the air and a waiter appeared.

"No," I protested, "I didn't mean right away. We can't waste this bottle. . . ."

But Funcitti was too absorbed in his orders to the staff— take such-and-such away, he said, bring a new that. And bring a fresh set of glasses. It was the right thing to do, from a wealthy gentleman's point of view, and a young woman's sensible objections were of no consequence.

When menus arrived, the food ordering proceeded in the same way—I expressed a halfhearted preference for duck, and Funcitti swept in to make the actual order—*Duck Montmorency*.

The swarm of waiters eventually subsided.

"You mentioned having just lost your wife," I said. "I suppose you made every little decision for her—some folks still do that kind of thing."

"My wife, Elvis. . . ." Funcitti stopped himself. His upper lip shivered, and he sucked hard on his Winston, burning down a quarter of its length in one draw. "Um, you said on the shuttle that you'd read *Newsweek*'s profile of me. Perhaps you recall reading that my wife is a Cyber."

"Like some of your resort staffers." I suppose I did recall that. It's the kind of harmless perversity you'll pick up from any gossip magazine—rich guy prefers his lifelike toy to

the real thing. "Look," I added, "you should know that I
. . . I really don't care about that. About the technosexuality.
Not that I indulge myself, but I figure to each his own."

"Well, um, thank you. But I want you to know that Elvis
was far more sophisticated than the Cybers here," he said,
sounding almost offended. Definitely defensive. "The lunar
staffers are rather narrowly programmed. You might find
one amusing for an hour or two, but then you would quickly
get bored."

"And Elvis . . . ?"

"Oh, Elvis herself had modest beginnings—she was
nothing but a cheap blood pressure monitor when I first
came across her. But after forty-three years—adding a function here, appending some hardware there—there is no sem-
isentient that can compete with her. I *built* her."

His voice cracked. He covered his eyes with his right
hand until his composure returned.

"I take it she, um, died or something."

"There was an accident. And she, well—her circuitry
was damaged." He paused to tamp out the cigarette. Then
he leveled his eyes at me grimly. "She ran off with another
man."

An appetizer arrived—roasted peppers with fresh moz-
zarella. I bit the inside of my lower lip to keep from laughing
and forked a limp sliver of pepper onto my plate. I decided
I'd better change the subject.

"So, you're supposed to be some kind of pioneer with
these TeleComp machines, right?"

"Langelaan TeleCompositors. Yes. The inventor,
George Langelaan, was on our research staff, and I hold
the patent. So naturally I'm a champion of the devices. If
they become widely accepted, our TeleComp division could
outpace our entertainment end. Right now, they're just a
very expensive investment in the future."

I poked at a curl of purple cabbage in the salad. "So
what's the holdup? Aren't they safe enough? Cream—
they've been used millions of times."

The old guy looked up at the simulated-stucco ceiling,

chewing and calculating. "Oh, millions would be right. But used to transport *human beings?* Tens of thousands would be more accurate. Of *course* they're safe—the ICC is arguing as much to the United Nations just now. I'm hosting a symposium up here for the two agencies in two weeks, as a matter of fact. We'll discuss that and, oh, some other issues—proposals to modify the Lunar Treaty, that kind of thing. Fortunately for me, the regulation of interplanetary commerce is rather solidly a United States operation. And I am pleased to list among my close acquaintances a few of the ICC's directors.

"But you ask what's the holdup? The holdup, I'm afraid, is rather complex. The bureaucratic quagmire is boggling, of course. Then there's cost—an enormous amount of energy is required for each transmission. I hear the Navajo Nation has quietly hired a Japanese lab to work that out. You can imagine what inexpensive TeleComping would do for their Outer Belt operations. And *my* labs are working on that, too, needless to say—it's the biggest physical obstacle."

I nodded. "And isn't there a moral issue?"

He dismissed the thought with a wave of the hand. "Among a few old ninnies," he said. "Religious ninnies."

"If you're such a champion of TeleComp travel, how come I met you on the shuttle?"

He stared at me. Not at my face, though—his eyes darted all over my upper body like a vid scanner slicing me into horizonal lines. This I attributed to his long association with a CyberWife. A relationship like that must play hell with your human courtesies.

"Ah, you *are* a sharp one, aren't you?" he said finally. "I mentioned an accident, correct? Well, my private TeleComp was damaged too. But I had to come up to prepare for that symposium—so I thought I might as well use the opportunity to check out how our shuttle service is doing. A CEO has to spend a little time on the front lines, you know."

Our entrees arrived. My duck came sliced into medallions, with a gravy boat of cherry sauce on the side. Anchoring another corner of the plate was an arrangement of oddly curled snow peas. Funcitti had ordered *Linguini di Luna*, a swirling mound of green pasta with glittery silver flecks in it. With a gratuitous flourish, the waiter poured a butter and garlic sauce over it in the shape of an X.

Funcitti leaned forward on the banquette and quickly twirled a few strands of pasta into a modest forkful. He chewed dreamily as he stared out at the Earth. His tensions had evaporated.

"That's your favorite meal—*Linguini di Luna*," I said.

His head did not move, but his eyes rolled in my direction. "After this, we must dance," he said. He chewed some more, then added, "You may lead, if you like."

On cue, the laser-marimba music from the bar surged to a crescendo, followed by laughter and applause.

Funcitti smiled. "See? All the world is at my command!"

Yeah, I attract the crazy ones. That's what my roommate always says.

II.
Laurence

The alley-dorm attendant off South Street mashed his flaking lips together and regarded the two of us with weary sarcasm. He waved us by tiredly.

"Pep," I complained, "he thinks we want to hire a slot together."

Pep squeezed his pocket control to inflate his collar with a bit more thermal filament. He huffed vapor into the darkness. Why did it seem colder in an alley than on a neon sleazeway? There was no more warmth to be had on a gaudily lit street.

"We *do* want to rent a slot together," Pep said.

"But not like he thinks!"

"Nah, he don' even think. He's got Amythol White tootin' out his ass, he's so out of it. Besides, don' be so offended if he thinks you're planking an old man. He's seen a lot worse." He wiped his nose and looked me up and down. "And you could *do* a lot worse."

These were alley-dorms in the original sense of the term— fifty or so narrow stalls with timelocks on the doors. A humming pump unit down at the far end poured a steady stream of purple sanitizing fluid into a brick gutter to carry away the dung and urine. This was turn-of-the-century for sure, one of those sad "solutions" to the lack of shelter for the destitute.

Pep hobbled down the row of rotting doors. I sensed that he had accepted into his body several replacement parts before those surgical techniques were perfected—knee and hip joints for sure. He stopped when he found three un-occupied stalls in a row. He slotted hard, untraceable credits into each of the three doors and locked the first and third stalls from the outside.

He threw on the light switch in the center dorm slot and motioned for me to enter. It stank of semen.

"This is disgusting," I said.

Pep shrugged and pulled the door closed.

There was a bare bulb in the ceiling, a vid screen against the far wall and a cheap tuber solidly mounted to the wall above the bunk. Except for the first few feet of entry area, the bunk took up the entire floor. Where there were not cabinets or little drawers in the walls above the bed, there were hooks meant to hold bulkier items. Or perhaps they were for hanging weapons, for easy access.

Pep pushed his spectacles up the bridge of his nose and began mumbling. "Okay, kid, are you ready for the tryout? Terry F1 says your assignment was to worm-route twenty thou credits out of some Bank of Paris account holder, and you were to stash it in the account of, um, something no-ble. . . ."

"Philadelphia Food Bank gets the money," I prompted.

"Yeah. Oh, yeah. Don't matter. You weren't thinking the transaction would ever be completed, were ya?"

"If I could stay at the tuber and do the route correc-tions. . . ."

"You putz. You do this work, you don't stand around terminal point, ya know. Not unless you're Terry F1 or somethin', darned sure of yer grid skidding. For this tryout, the program's got to win or lose all on its own." Pep shook his head wearily. "Training *you* would take a glut-mule's lifetime. Gimme the program you wrote. What's it on, chrystal?"

"Gel," I replied, and handed him a plastic squeeze tube the size of an earthworm.

"Well you *are* the little Gummint genius, aren't you? Got ta write yer assignments on gel."

"Look, I never had to write this kind of stuff before. But

I like the versatility, for the blinds and duck-backs.''

Pep prepared the tuber. There were several receptor slots across the top of the casing, one for each software format that might be used. One was embossed with a crude drawing of a dessert dish with a spoon in it—a reference to a treat called Jell-O. Pep pushed that receptor slot open with his thumbnail and uncapped my gel container. He squirted the gel in and smeared it against the walls of the slot with his middle and index fingers. The gel was common Korean stuff, a molecular data storage system inspired by the function of human brain cells.

He flicked the power button, and the tuber screen popped on. The little computer promptly sucked in my programming and entered the call routine. Pep checked his watch, then grabbed me by the sleeve.

"Ya can't *watch* it, danderbutt," he said.

"I wasn't going to stand near the tuber!"

"Right. An' let's do our not-standing-near-the-tuber down the alley a bit, ey?"

Pep shoved the door closed after us and set the time lock.

"Casual," he said. "Just up here."

"Maybe we could go get a beer now," I volunteered. "Then we come back, see how I did. With that routine I wrote, it'll be—hell—twenty, thirty minutes before the credits land at the food bank."

"Ho up. Lesson number one coming directly," Pep said. He leaned into the brick wall, a slimey, ancient structure. He worked his lips together in a cud-chewing motion, glanced back at our dorm slot, then checked his watch again. My feet were going numb.

A plume of smoke erupted from the crack under the door of our dorm. It was an angry little thunderhead chugging its way across the alley. Then the time lock burst in a rattle of steel and the door collapsed into a gush of flame. It was as if our dorm slot had really been a large rocket thruster.

I heard the startled dorm attendant down near South Street: "Ey, what *is* that? What have you guys done?"

Pep looked up from his watch, ignoring the attendant.

"One hunnerd twenny-eight seconds," he said. "Not bad for the first time." He worked his lips some more and rubbed the bristle of his chin.

The torrent of flame had died out as abruptly as it had appeared, leaving a charred hole that ate into the two adjoining dorm slots, the other two that we had rented.

"Bank of Paris did that?" I asked. "That's . . . that's *dangerous*."

"Sure it's dangerous—*that's* lesson number one. But B-oh-P's security guys aren't indiscriminate, mind you. They previewed the neighborhood, ya know—checked the demographics—before sending in a burn. Had this been Germantown, or prolly that Trinity neighborhood you gave up down in Wilmington, I imagine they'd a' made a personal visit to check first. The result would be the same, but they'd check first to be sure. Then burn ya. South Street? A bad worming calls for an automatic burn. I call it fart of the dragon."

"You mean my program didn't hold them off for any more than two minutes?"

"A few seconds more than that. Terry F1's software will hold tight for more than two weeks. She just wanted you to see how important it was to get it right."

The dorm attendant arrived, eyes wide in his grease-glistening face. *"What happened here?"* he shouted, flapping his ragged arms. "Someone's gonna pay! *Someone's payin' fer this!"*

Pep nudged me toward South Street. "Some jerk been smoking in bed, I guess."

A large, dark-skinned guy pushed through my door without knocking, which seemed to be the accepted way to treat a new recruit in Terry F1's enclave. He rode in on a wave of sweat-odor, drawing in his wake a young woman smoking a filterless cigarette.

"The name's Kodas," the monster said, the faintest sibilance in his speech. "This here's Doc. Just think of us as the Welcome Wagon. So—aloha."

"Mmm," I said. "Aloha?"

"Aloha. You wearing a Hawaiian shirt. So aloha."

"Hullo," Doc threw in, scanning her eyes around the little room and coming to rest more than once on the dormant mainframe on a narrow metal shelf.

"Okay," I said, "now I feel welcome. So are we done? I'm not really one for idle chatter."

Kodas turned his meaty face toward Doc, a bemused expression. "Terry F1 told us she had fresh talent," he said, "but didn't warn us you was so friendly."

I was parked in an antique desk chair splattered with paint. Hugging each of my wrists was a translucent bracelet which could be detonated from afar. Their flash acid had been demonstrated for me on a section of five-inch plumber's pipe, which fell into two pieces within three seconds. My wrist bones would not last so long.

Kodas sat on the edge of my cot, making it teeter dangerously. Doc was leaning over the cot to get a better look at the mainframe up on the shelf. From the back like that, she looked like a 12-year-old girl—tennis shoes not unlike mine, tight denims, a khaki shirt crosshatched with a dozen zippers.

"Friendliness," she said through her cigarette, "is not a requirement to be part of Terry F1's wing." She ran a finger over the computer's port bank as if she were flicking away dust.

"I generally ask people not to handle my, um—well, that particular computer," I said.

"Nothing to get wired about," Doc said, and she shrugged, sitting beside Kodas.

"So I am to be part of Terry F1's—what did you call it?—wing? What is that?"

Kodas formed a patronizing grin. "You really *are* on the slug's end of the program, aren't ya? Man, Terry F1 said you had a soft ass." He shook his large head, heaving those flared nostrils from side to side. I could see hardware in there. Up his nose!

"Had one of those Gummint jobs," Doc said. "The

medicals paid, two, three months' vacation, an agent who sucks off the union schlub, who sucks off his Tier boss. Probably an Arisawa tracker of his own—''

"Terry F1 says he had *two*."

"Not really," I threw in. "One's my ex-wife's."

"—so now he's on the big slide," Doc continued.

"Tumblin'," said Kodas.

"Tumblin'," agreed Doc. "Tumblin' down from that societal mountaintop into this mudhole with the rest of us, an' we gotta show 'im how ta tread water."

I was tiring of the abuse. "Does anyone care anymore about mixed metaphors?" I asked.

Kodas grunted. He ran his thumb down the side of his freckled nose, following the path of a thread-thin pink line. A scar.

"Soft-ass," he grumbled. *"Talks* like a soft-ass."

"The wing," Doc said. She hesitated, at a loss for an explanation. "It's the *wing*. It's *everything*. Terry F1's whole thing, ya know? All her operations, all her people-stomping assignments, scooping credits, trading flint. You had a Gummint job, an education, I imagine. You didn't need all this. But now ya do."

"What you're telling me is that you're all part of a gang."

Kodas looked genuinely hurt. "No!" He stood, indignant. "The wing is just . . . well, it's a separate economy. One that don't run on the rails you're used to. Terry F1 is the focal point, for maybe two hunnerd people—I don't know. She brokers assignments to the rest of us—that's where the real credits come in. But she also does trade in scavenged parts, charged energy packs, weapons and stuff. It's all interlocking in this biz, ya see?"

"An alternative economy. Okay. But none of it legal."

Kodas pressed his lips together in mock prissiness. "Not legal! Goodness, Doc, we must abandon our ways immediately an' apply for, um, one of those maid service jobs you see advertised at Valentine's—'ninety-eight locations world wide!' "

Doc tossed her cigarette butt onto the concrete and didn't

bother to stamp it out. She gave me a serious stare, more world-weary than any twenty-ish kid ought to have to be. "Sure," she said, "there are obstacles. But you gotta live, right? You went to college at UCLA, or MIT or Temple or some damned place, public schools before that—all of it laid out before you were born. Our kind got to, um, *gather* an education. I did medicine. Hanging out at the implant parlors, then dressing wounds for the wing. Get lots of practical knowledge that way. I'm starting to assist on surgeries now, and in a few years, I reckon, I'll handle lead knife."

"So can anyone tell me how I fit into this?" I asked. "I thought I was hiring on for some kind of computer piecework, but for the last few days old Pep has just been putting me through one drill after another. And Terry F1 is making me *exercise*, crissake. Weights! And *running!*"

Doc and Kodas exchanged a knowing glance.

"Ey, you wanted a job," Kodas said.

"I'm used to slopping Tier 5 code," I said, "all of it theoretical, spending years on little tidbits for the BOSS system. Never once witnessed the practical use for any of it. Now Pep has me writing Front-Line Operational—it's a lean and mean language, nothing like Tier 5. Direct cause-and-effect, mercenary."

"Well, you getting paid?" Kodas asked.

I nodded. "Barely. But every day, in hard credit."

"Sounds like Terry F1 has a specific assignment in mind for you," Doc said. "You may not have much experience with FLO, but with your background, I bet you'll be tying Pep's butt-hairs in knots pretty soon."

"Any idea how soon I get these taken off?" I held up my banded wrists. "They make me rather uncomfortable— not the feel of them but the, um, *prospect* of them."

Kodas shrugged his huge shoulders and showed me his own bracelets. "Trust doesn't come quickly for anyone— especially strangers just dumped out of the Gummint cradle."

"But you folks aren't *bunking* here," I noted. "You're

in and out—cash in, see Terry F1—maybe just had to wear these things for a few minutes."

Doc smiled. "Boot camp is always tough, ain't it? You can have your own digs when you grow up."

I felt depression settle over me, tangible, like a wooly blanket tossed over my head. Perhaps, I thought, I should go back to Willie Schilfgaarde at the Velvet Scorpion. Tell him this gig just didn't work out—what was his next-best proposition? Something, I hoped, on the sane side of Fellini?

I studied Kodas grimly. He was a human stonework, exuding imminent violence. A walking Armageddon. One of those old A-bombs with a smile painted on the side.

"So, Doc covers medical stuff for the wing," I said. "What's your specialty, Kodas?"

Kodas shrugged again.

"Just . . . largeness?" I asked.

"And larceny," he replied.

12
Kodas

"Relax, I said. Dammit, *relax.*"

That's Terry F1 talking. Has me tilted back in this padded chair like they do minor surgery in. It's pretty dark—she's got just one little desk lamp on, set at minimal, turned away from my face. And I can hear her walking around behind me, that flimsy black gown she wears going *whroosh, whroosh* between her legs while she rechecks the equipment setup. Mmm. Between her legs. Between her hermaphroditic legs.

Laurence and Pep are in the room, sitting on chairs against the wall. Old Pep coughs, a wet rumble like he does when he's got a throat full. And Terry F1 stops right there. She's tense, and somehow I'm supposed to relax. She's still pissed, of course, about the Longwood mess—we were supposed to whack that rich gray-head in a fake TeleComp accident. Didn't happen, and now some client is gnawing on Terry F1's butt.

"Quiet, dammit," she says to Pep, who's probably got zero control of that crap in his lungs. "I want you both to see this, but we must have silence. No motion. No sound."

So Laurence and Pep are sitting there, two dark figures against the wall like statues or something in a museum. I can imagine the little nameplate for the statues: "Soft-ass and Old Fart—a Study in . . ." What do they make statues out of? I don't know.

There's a little wing table attached to my chair near my shoulder, and Terry F1 puts a little tuber on it—one of the cheap little hand computers like Doc and I haul around for the routine stuff. Terry F1 has it cabled to the equipment that's stacked behind me. She flicks it on and the little screen gives a dull glow.

Then her face is right there, that silver-blond hair dragging across my sleeve.

"Everything okay?" she asks. Perfume like Italian herbs or something. She has to work at sounding sweet and gentle. "Relaxed? Remember the self-hypnosis techniques we practiced."

"Some A-mist would help," I tell her.

"Wouldn't help at all—not for this project. I need your body relaxed, not your brain. Can't have you misted."

"What are sculptures made of?"

Terry F1's face goes blank. She's taken aback, and she's reviewing several possible responses—most of them snotty. She decides to play it smooth.

"Bronze."

"No, I mean, like in a museum you see those really lifelike sculptures. What are they made of?"

She sighs. "Plastic. Plaster. You can make a sculpture out of just about anything. Now, are you ready?"

"Am I supposed to do something with that tuber?"

"Well, not with your hands—through your olfactory conduit."

"My nose jack."

Another sigh. "Okay, we'll call it a nose jack."

She pulls across my shoulder two thin black wires, each of them tipped with nine-sided connectors. She slips a dilator tool into my left nostril and gently spreads the flesh back to expose the hardware that had been spliced to my olfactory nerves. She sets one of the connectors in place, snaps the brackets closed—

"Ahhhg!"

"Sorry."

—and then hooks up the other side.

"Only a few people have done this that I know of," Terry F1 says. She's explaining mostly for the benefit of

Laurence, the new guy, supposed to be some computer cowboy. I've heard the speech a hundred times, and Pep knows this rigging better than any of us.

"They all describe the experience differently," she says. "Kodas will ease himself into a semidream state—not asleep, but not particularly attuned to these surroundings either. The human brain, if you compare it to that of many other mammals, makes relatively little use of its olfactory capabilities. There's a large chunk of gray matter up there that's going to waste. While our ancestors found it crucial to survival, now it's a virtual blank slate. Which actually is rather convenient for these purposes—preconceptions and patterning in the brain would only interfere with the data manipulation that we want to develop."

Terry F1 is moving again behind me, throwing switches on the rack of decks back there.

"Kodas' sensory exchanges will be translated into photonics right here. Laurence, you've worked a little with photonics, so you know that photonics allow a degree of acuity that is impossible with clumsy old *elec*tronics. But let's face it—the world's computer systems are still largely electronic, so the whole point of this exercise is to be able to mesh with those systems. *That* happens—" she takes several steps, *whroosh, whroosh, whroosh,* "in this device, a photonics-to-electronics interface."

Over against the other wall, Pep hawks again, getting bored, and Terry F1 doesn't complain. Laurence, I can tell by the rigid set of his silhouette, is paying close attention.

"So if all goes according to plan, Kodas will be literally *smelling* the computer data," Terry F1 says. "But while the incoming data would technically be classified as odor, it is likely that his brain will step in and translate much of that information into visual and even tactile hallucination. We're hoping that he will learn to manipulate these hallucinations and become interactive with outside computer systems. If he can—well, in theory he would eventually be able to process in just moments what it would take an expert typist months to produce."

"And speed," I throw in, "is everything to you grid-skidders."

She pats me on the shoulder. "Go to it, Kodas. All systems are go. First time in, now, take it easy. Just blunder about, get the feel of it. If you can get something onto the tuber screen, great. But don't wrestle with it—that would be counterproductive."

I close my eyes, inhale slowly through my nose—a little harder to do now with even more wiring in there. The nose jack is slightly warm now, its first time in use. Having your brain wired to a machine like this is a hard thing to get comfortable with.

Okay. I begin Terry F1's relaxation routine—basically, concentrate on easing every muscle in the body, one at a time. Start with the scalp, force the tension out, feel the muscle spread across the skull. Then the brow, the face, the back of the neck. . . .

When I finally get to my toes, a tingling rush surges up my legs. This happened before, during training, but it's more pronounced now—like my body is afloat in bubbly water. My eyes are still closed, yet I see a dim gray all around me. Yes, there's an odor, not particularly pleasant or unpleasant. It reminds me of sitting on the banks of the Schuylkill River—the odor of sea life and the odor of rot, all at once.

I had expected a blur of fuzzy colors, but this is so sharp and clear it aches. Across the grayness is a field of microscopic dots, brilliant red pinpricks. The red dots are rushing close now—or are they just growing? Confusing—no perspective. I fall through one of the surging red dots, and there is another field of red dots in the distance, also rushing toward me. My stomach squirms. One after another, dot fields are flashing past me faster and faster, like fan blades battering my face.

I'm supposed to be able to control this somehow?

Yes. I decide to grab the next field of dots, mentally hold onto it. One of the searing red circles gapes as if to swallow me, then strikes me with the force of a speeding tracker. I am splayed across this red circle, rushing through a gray void with hurricane force.

This is harmless hallucination, I tell myself. God knows, I've had hallucinations before.

And I am terrified.

I cling to the roaring red disc. It seems to be made of metallic fabric, burning my hands, scouring my face. I pull at the fabric and it tears easily, and with that tearing somehow comes the knowledge that this is a direct connection to the tuber I am trying to reach. I yank the fabric loose from its bindings and pull it tightly around my body.

The terrible, rushing gray void is gone now. I am surrounded by red, prickly atmosphere, and it is into this atmosphere that I pour my message. It's like dumping a load of bricks onto the floor:

"MY NAME IS KODAS."

Enough. Wake up.

I release the hallucination. I feel like a skin diver, rising, breaking through the surface of the ocean.

And as my vision clears, I see that I am vomiting.

Terry F1 is ecstatic. "Yes! *Yes!*" She turns the lamp up.

Laurence is looking sick, too, edging toward the door.

Pep is still in his chair. "Classy act, big guy," he says. "I guess it takes practice."

I vomit again, right into my lap.

I wipe my mouth on my sleeve and sit up weakly to look at the tuber, to confirm that my message got through. And there it is on the glowing little screen:

"Glrmxxqi."

* * *

"Terry F1 says that a few other folks have tried the olfactory conduit," Laurence says to me. "So how come no one's ever heard of them? Where are they? And how do you know they haven't sautéed their frontal lobes?"

I shrug. "Rumor is that the Navajo Nation folks were

experimenting with the idea, and the technology leaked out to some Denver wing that had uses for it. I imagine that Terry F1 would have picked it up from them in some kind of trade—would have gotten their hardware specs, test results, all that.''

Laurence laughs grimly. He's at a workbench, removing the casing from a deck he found in parts storage. Terry F1 finally gave him the run of that part of the operation.

"Uses," Laurence says. "What uses does Terry F1 have for a guy with a nose jack?''

"Could do some pretty powerful pirating, don't ya think? Jack in with some of Terry F1's Jolly Roger software as a side arm, a guy could probably rob the store blind.''

"I've seen what the Bank of Paris thinks of intrusions,'' Laurence says. "Most of us get to learn from our mistakes. But you make a mistake with them, you won't live long enough to apply what you've learned.''

"Terry F1's software is well protected,'' I tell him, "as long as you update before it expires. Besides, for a guy like me, a nose jack is just the ultimate Sentia implant.''

Laurence unplugs a chrome component inside the deck he's just opened—the kinda guy, I guess, who knows his way around a computer deck the way a kid grows up knowing the alleys of his neighborhood. Now he's reading specs on the underside of the chrome piece.

"Kodas," Laurence says, checking a row of microcircuits, "you are an incredible piece of work. Chest like a side of beef, legs like jointed tree trunks. Are you one of those steroid lickers, or did your mama and daddy map you out this way?''

A stare at Laurence a moment. That "map you out" talk is how things go for the folks who can afford to genetically design how their rug rats are going to turn out. Shit, I never met my daddy, and my mama never planned on having me, period, much less how I was gonna look. It's a thing a guy could get hot about, if he decided to let some soft-ass goad him. I decided not to.

"Hunnerd percent all-natural South Philly beef,'' I tell

him. "I guess you just grow up big when ya spend your day kicking soft-ass college-boy Mummer butt."

Laurence blows some dust out of the bottom casing for the deck he's ripped open. He frowns, mutters, then looks up at me again.

"I'm surprised you haven't put an implant on the tip of your dick—you've got one everywhere else." He shakes his head. "Some day. Some day, someone's gonna light you up like a Christmas bulb."

13
Benito

The cosmetics saleswoman clicked her tongue in frustration.

Elvis was right behind me. "He's like that awl the time," Elvis said in sympathy. "Gets his mind set on just changing one lil thing—won't hear of any variation or anything flashy. So con*ser*vative."

Elvis was playing her role splendidly. This actually was our eighth cosmetics shop in our day's excursion, and we had made quite a few changes in appearance—one change per store. But we wanted no single person to realize what we were doing.

My hair was now auburn with touches of the original gray. It was styled in a rakish cut that I had never dared in my former life. The mole on my upper lip had been lasered away by a lackadaisical teenager in the back of a store that specialized in hologram tattoos and Sentia implants. A lipo specialist took three inches of pasta off my waistline. I was sporting one of the new Egyptian envirojackets (programmed to keep adjusting itself to my comfort preferences), tailored denims, and a T-shirt bearing a turn-of-the-century likeness of a young David Byrne. I had missed out on his "genius" the first time around, but now he was enjoying a revival among younger music fans. Who knows—maybe I'll actually listen to one of his recordings sometime.

Out on the sidewalks, I had been trying to develop a swingy, carefree saunter. It did not come naturally, but I was aided considerably by the ever-increasing dose of Zenithialate B necessary to control the pain in my chest.

Changing Elvis' looks was another matter—cyber parts were not easily procured. Replacing her hair with a new wig was no problem—still black, but now it fell past her shoulders—and we bought a few roomy dresses that obscured her figure.

And here was a cosmetics saleswoman, in makeup befitting a Barnum and Bailey clown, pouting over my paltry request.

"Really, a guy like me should not cover his total eyeball in glitter orange," I said. "I think the contact lenses with gray-tint irises will do nicely. Thank you." Firm.

Elvis dictated my vision correction parameters to the saleswoman, who keyed in the order methodically, somehow unfazed by Elvis' remarkable memory. She pressed the "Enter" button, and the dispenser on the counter whirred and ejected the fresh contacts.

"Bag for that, wild man?"

"I'll just eat them here, thanks." I put them on.

Outside, we climbed the steps and surfaced on Fourth Street, across from a block-long park. Five antique horse carts were parked at the curb. Their drivers, a sideshow of brightly colored scarves and gloves, beckoned tourists like carnival barkers, promising comprehensive tours of Philadelphia's historic district. Tourists weren't buying—the sun shone beautifully, but it was too cold for an open-air carriage ride. The horses hung their blindered heads sedately, oblivious to the rumble of trackers and trucks.

The traffic signal changed, and a holographic tunnel appeared, yellow and translucent, designating the protected pedestrian areas. As we crossed the street a tracker driver backed the nose of his vehicle out of the illusory tunnel image. (Violating designated pedestrian areas drew a substantial fine.) A dead squirrel lay in the crosswalk, and I followed the path of pedestrians around it. Elvis followed, too, clutching her packages. She looked down at the crushed little beast and stopped.

"Elvis! The signal's changing."

She looked up and hurried to the curb as the tunnel faded.
"Ah think someone's trying to kill you," she said.

This comment drew odd stares from the press of surrounding pedestrians. I laughed aloud, hoping it would be dismissed as a joke between us, and then pulled her by the arm into the park. Tourists were lining up to enter a two-story ferroplex pavilion where the Liberty Bell hung on display.

"Of course someone's trying to kill me," I whispered. "There's a team of ICC lawyers looking to clean up their little embarrassment, and as if that weren't enough, there's the new and improved version of *me* who's probably taking matters into his own hands by now. I would if *I* were him. And I *am* him. So I probably am—trying to kill me, I mean."

"Ah'm talking about someone else trying to kill you," she said. Elvis pointed to the crosswalk. "That's the squirrel."

"That's what squirrel?"

"The squirrel that started all of this. The one found in your substation when the power failed."

Dread gripped at my chest. Something was awry with Elvis' time/continuity provisions. How was I going to deal with a programming disaster when we were living out of hotel rooms?

"Elvis, think carefully. You know that can't be the same squirrel—that was ten days ago. Remember? Elvis?"

She blinked—not a reflex, but a bit of programmed body language. Visual punctuation. "I know that, honey. I didn't mean the exact same flesh-and-blood critter. I meant the same species of squirrel."

"Species? So what?" My hands were turning red with cold. I put them in the jacket pockets and felt the little heating elements flick on.

"That is the common urban gray squirrel. See?" Elvis turned in a circle, rapidly pointing out six squirrels in the park like a gunfighter picking off bad guys. "But Canadian red squirrels live out at Longwood. They were introduced in the Nineteen Hundreds—escaped exotic pets. Now they are by far the dominant squirrel species in all of Southern Chester County."

"So an interloper gray squirrel, um, loped into Longwood and gnawed on the substation wiring."

"But I wonder about that. I didn't think much of it at the time, but that night I visited Albert's wife in her kitchen. The burned squirrel was in her trash basket, and I asked if she hadn't intended to cook it. She waved her hand in the air—like this—and said, 'Oh, that old thing?' She used the word *old*."

"That's an expression, a form of derision—'Oh, that old thing.' Not necessarily literal."

"But what if she meant it literally? What if she realized that the squirrel had been too long dead to be suitable for food—rigor mortis, she tossed it out. Why else would she not make use of the meat? Clearly, Albert had intended for her to do that. So maybe the squirrel was really killed in the city, where it would be commonly found, and put there to make it appear that the power outage was an accident. That the outage would happen while you were in the TeleComp is enough of a coincidence—but an interloper squirrel, too?"

"Elvis, you're making me nervous. Life is complicated enough already." I coughed then, and took another capsule of Zenithialate B.

I found a public phone with a broken viewer/camera unit, which is not hard to do in downtown Philadelphia.

"Hello, Grace-Lee? . . . Yes, Benito Funcitti calling. . . . That won't be necessary. Actually it's you I am calling for, if you have a moment. . . . Thanks. Well, I'm just cleaning up a few details in relation to that little power station blowout the other day. The ICC wants a few issues settled—you know how those Interplanetary boys can be. . . . Well, yes. Um, I *am* calling from the Moon, now that you mention it. WATS line, you know. Look, I have an odd little question. The ICC is trying to clear up the exact cause of the outage, and one theory is that that squirrel got in there and was electrocuted—which the insurance folks would classify as an act of God—and another theory involves faulty equipment. I said to the ICC boys, well, you know Grace-Lee is such an extraordinary cook and has such long experience with game, that I'll bet she could tell us just how long that squirrel we found had been dead. . . . Yes. Um. . . . Okay, then, we'll call it an act of God either way. Uh-huh. He would go to any lengths to punish TeleComp users. But just to humor the ICC fellows. . . . Oh. Really? Dead a day, maybe two? Thank you, Grace-Lee. Tell Albert he can have the rest of the week off. Good-bye.''

My feet ached. My knee joints were grinding together as if they were lined with sandpaper. I was loitering on South Street at 10 P.M., a dangerous thing to do. I had checked my end of the block. Elvis was checking hers.

Down the street, a music hall was opening its doors under a marquee reading:

> "Bug Bug Bug.
> cezanne cezanne cezanne."

What did that mean?

The young fans streamed by toward the entrance, acned and ragged, shuffling boots and fluorescent slippers, heads bobbing arhythmically. An undulating current of self-absorption.

They were the least threatening of the street creatures. The older guys, the wasted ones, milled about the dark mouth of an alley lined with dorm slots. Chewed-looking faces. Eyes red, clothes putrid. Not a spark of hope among them.

Glitter boys were cruising the implant parlors, gathering in voyeuristic celebration anytime customers amassed the credits and nerve to take the store-window seat to have new Sentia terminals imbedded under their skin. Some of the onlookers wore lizard skin grafted to their necks in tiny strips, made to look like gills. I had read about that—the reptilian enzymes produce an exotic high when the sun goes down.

The pushers here were the most clean-cut of the lot, and probably the most dangerous. They wore expensive business suits altered by fine tailors in outrageous ways—a lapel extended to wrap around one shoulder, a fly crisscrossed with shimmering optical thread. As if to say: "I can afford to buy the best—and then mutilate it."

They had staked out a three-foot-wide strip of sidewalk along the curb, four of them to a city block, always equally ready to do quick business with a pedestrian or a motorist. I had heard this zone called "The Airstrip," passage to the stratosphere. Amythol White mist was a hot seller, although anything from ether to Sentia porn could be found.

Their Zenithialate B, no doubt, was horribly diluted. But in a month, I was going to be one of their most desperate customers. My supply was dwindling, and no reputable pharmacy was going to resupply me without demanding a genetic scan.

Elvis was working her way toward me at a spritely pace, returning from the corner of the block. Her feet did not ache; her knees did not grind.

"Ah think this is it," she said. "There's a bar at the corner with a loft above it. A customer on her way in said she had heard the guy on the second floor was a software dealer or something."

I pulled a page of notes out of a jacket pocket. Interspersed among the day's scribblings were seventeen names, most of them accompanied by check marks—we had spoken to them. Near the bottom of the page was the entry: "Schilfgaarde Services—Software, Hardware, Troubleshooting, Referrals. South Street."

"I don't think I can handle another one today—these aren't the most sociable people."

"We aren't asking very sociable questions." She looked at me sadly. "Maybe we should just leave town. The Virgin Islands—Brit side—kick back on Tortola."

"In the Virgins, we'd just be waiting," I said tiredly. "Something would run out eventually—money, the drugs. Or my lungs. At least here I can take a stab at unscrambling some of this before I die."

"Then come on, we'll hit one more place, and then we'll pick out another Greek restaurant—eat gyros and go to bed."

"Mmm."

"Mmm gyros, or mmm bed?"

"Mmm gyros with mmm a glass of chardonnay, and then mmm-mmm bed."

The bar was named The Velvet Scorpion. We passed through a desert-scene hologram out front and found a black door with a hand-lettered sign taped to it:

"Now! More scorps than ever!
No waiting!"

Business was good. Tables full, bar stools all occupied. There were five transparent boxes positioned along the bar, each containing a scorpion and the beckoning hand of a customer. Despite the promise of the sign outside, there seemed to be a poorly formed line at each box.

The bartender finished registering a sale and strode to our end of the counter. "Evening, folks. Choose your poison. Ma'am?"

"No thanks," said Elvis.

"We came to see Schilfgaarde," I told him.

The barkeep checked his watch. "He's usually shut down by now," he said. "Check with Mia. Girl in the flowers." He pointed toward the back of the bar. We shouldered our way through the reeling customers. The floor was sticky with spilled beer. A speaker membrane was stretched over the center of the room, and as we passed under an incomprehensible song blasted from above. Maybe, I thought, that's a tune by Bug Bug Bug.

Near a group of dancers, a young man with a swirling pile of hair threw his arms around my neck—for support,

I told myself, until he waggled his tongue lewdly.

Elvis smirked. "It's the haircut."

I peeled the man's arms away and showed her the fresh puncture on his palm. "It's the venom," I replied. But maybe I *would* change the haircut.

Mia was an anorexic Asian woman in a skintight, flowered bodysuit. Around her waist hung a loose gold-chain belt which suspended a rectangular credit bank at her crotch.

"Schilfgaarde still here?" I pointed at the stairs.

"Sure," she said. "Your hand, please." She held aloft a genetic scanning disk.

"Um, we can't do that," I said. "This has to be confidential."

"He don't like it if he can't check your scan first."

"He wouldn't have access to my, uh, our breakdowns anyway. His database would come up zip."

Mia shook her head. "Sorry. Good night."

I pulled out a flat of hard credit, marked off 100 francs, and slotted them into her bank.

"How about telling him there's a nice man and a nice lady down here with lots of money who just need a little advice? Five minutes, tops."

Mia frowned. She climbed the stairs and returned a minute later.

"He says fold your hands like this, both of you." She interlocked her fingers and pressed her palms together. "Take them apart while you are upstairs and he will kill you."

We obeyed and mounted the stairs. The climbing compounded the agony in my knees. Elvis turned to Mia and said cheerfully, "Have a nice day."

"Where did you come up with that?" I asked as we neared the top.

"Random pleasantry expressed with sarcasm."

"Okay, sounds familiar."

"Programming session in the year Twenty Thirty-Two, eleven-oh-four P.M."

"Right."

The security door at the top of the stairs was open, its reinforcing rods retracted from their slots in the door frame. A sickly little man waved us in. His flesh was yellowish, and his hair had been worked into a gelatinous tangle.

"Stay in the center of the room," he ordered. "Keep the hands folded."

Behind the little man was a curved, tiered worktable piled with keyboards and screens. He gestured with a stubby little handgun—wide barrel, bloated magazine.

"That, Elvis, is a gum pump," I said. "Also known as a meat-eater. It fires a sheet of gummy flash acid that is harmless to just about every conceivable material except human flesh. It was developed for security teams working in space environments."

"That's nice to know," Elvis said. She took a few steps to the left.

"Stand still, please. You—" the fellow gestured toward me "—you seem to know your weapons."

"I guess what I know is security operations. You, I suppose, are Mr. Schilfgaarde."

He seated himself on a three-legged stool and kept the gum gun pointed at my abdomen.

"Willie Schilfgaarde," he said. "So what do you want?"

"I've been asking around, looking for people who do a certain kind of work," I said.

"I do computers," Schilfgaarde said.

"Fine. I've been in bars and steroid houses and implant parlors. Software joints. And all I say is, 'I got a big problem that I need eliminated. You know anyone who fixes big problems?' And the name Schilfgaarde came up a couple of times."

"I don't think I'm going to be able to help you," Schilfgaarde said. Then he pointed the gum gun at Elvis. "*I said don't move!*"

"What are you doing, Elvis—he's gonna pull that trigger and mess up your new dress."

"Sorry."

"Okay, so let's all relax," I said. "We're going to leave

now. But I would just like to part with an observation.''

"What's that?''

"We've been all over Philadelphia talking to dozens of people, and you're the first person to hold a gun on us. Makes me think maybe you branch out from the software business now and then.''

"Let's just say it's that kinda neighborhood. Now get out.''

"One more thing. And believe me, I don't say this to all the guys—it's just that I think I've finally found the right set of ears: I know about a hit, a big job. It's already been contracted out, but they barfed it the first time.''

I moved toward the door. Elvis followed, and Schilfgaarde's gun followed both of us.

"Who's this hit on?'' he asked.

"Entertainment executive. Benito Funcitti.''

We made it to the landing. Hands still folded.

"So how do you fit in?''

"I can show them how to do it right.''

Halfway down the stairs.

"And who the hell are *you?*'' Schilfgaarde was shouting now over the music.

"The Man in the Moon.''

14
Therese

I pulled the webbing around me in the passenger seat and set the latches. Through the viewscreen, we could see the port boys hustling for their master. Releasing the lashings. Halting the buzz of floor traffic as we chugged along our monotrack, towed by chain-link in the subfloor.

"It's really just a little dory," Benito said with a dismissing wave around the cabin. "You could hardly call it a yacht."

As our little touring cruiser whumped into the airlock, Funcitti sat forward. The gauges had come alive, and he watched their flickering lights with childlike wonderment. I dipped into brief panic at that point, I have to admit. Untethered flight in the Moon's negligible atmosphere is not to be taken lightly. And this old duff was frowning over the controls.

He read my consternation and laughed.

"Ever drive a golf cart down on Earth?"

"Well, yeah."

"Piloting one of these little tubs is about that easy. Probably safer. Triple pressure seals. Three days of air, and by regs we can't be gone more than four hours, or they'll come searching."

"When was the last time you took a Moon yacht out?"

Funcitti smiled. "In case of emergency, pressure suits are folded under the back floor compartment. If we accelerate beyond 300 kph, the forward compensators will kick in and slow us down again."

"Benny—"

"The aurashield channels all radiation into battery storage and regulates the penetration of useful illumination."

"Ben—"

"Three years. I haven't driven one of these in three years. But it's like having sex on a bicycle—once you learn, you never forget how."

"Benito Funcitti, you will very quickly minister to the qualms of your passenger or she will go berserk and totally ruin your day. Not to mention your piloting record with the ICC."

He sobered. "Okay, you could do this yourself in a second—small stick to the left here is the accelerator. Forward for increased speed, hard back for reverse thrust. Joystick on the right controls direction—forward, we go down; back we go up; left is left; right is right. Feel better?"

"You were puzzling over the gauges."

"I've got it now, okay?" He wasn't angry. He wanted to turn this into a comedy routine—ever the entertainment man. But the old guy knew, as well, that he'd better demonstrate competence. "The gauges. We'll take 'em from the left: Fuel level; this big one is grid orientation for the Fun City vicinity; then there's thruster efficiency; aurashield efficiency; cabin pressure; and oxygen/nitrogen/C-oh–2 balance. Feel better?"

"Much better. Onward, Jeeves."

The little airlock doors burst open and the escaping air gave our cruiser a tug out the hatch, a little momentum before the thrusters were engaged. We were twenty stories above the surface, I suppose.

"Someday," Benito said, "we'll have the port operations all housed in a proper clarke tower like the ones on Earth. This level we could still use for surface transport, or you could clarke up to space dockage. Escaping gravity is not nearly the problem that it is on Earth, but the savings would add up eventually. Eventually."

Benito jammed the accelerator forward and the joystick back, rocketing us a half-mile above the Fun City complex.

"You are very lucky that I haven't eaten, old man."

He worked his lips together boyishly, that little mole dancing. *Who, me?*

"This is your overview," he said. "Check it out. There's the main Bubble, of course. See all the ribbing and the concave pressure tiles? The sun lamps are hung from the ribbing for night use. Inside, you can't see all that from the ground because of all the atmosphere—it just looks like sky. A hundred and fifty-eight thousand acres just under that Bubble. Ya know what this land cost me?"

"You won it in a dice game."

"Better. It cost me nothing, not for sixteen more years. I'm still covered by the Lunar Treaty's economic development program. After that, I can lease it all for five hundred francs an acre for ninety-nine years, renewable for ninety-nine more."

He pulled on the accelerator stick for a little backthrust to keep us above the Bubble and tapped the joystick to tilt us down for an easier view. The port tower and main hotel were just behind and below us, abutting the Bubble. All around the perimeter of the Bubble was an array of low, mud-colored structures—the casinos, exclusive cabanas, and maintenance facilities. Beyond that, in all directions, stretched a barely-rolling landscape of pocked beige.

"I want to hear the story of the asteroid," I said, and my delivery told Benito that I already knew parts of the narration, so he'd better get it right.

"The asteroid," Benito said. He undid the top button of his plaid cotton shirt and scratched absently in that thicket of gray curls on his clavicle. The thrusters were humming, low, but if we were moving I could not tell. "I suppose you mean—" and he pointed down at the Bubble "—*the* asteroid."

"Yes."

"It must have been about thirty years ago—"

"Thirty years and five days," I said. "The asteroid landed on the day I was born."

He flashed a smile of amusement, which quickly melted

into a pensive frown—he was squiring around a woman who was born at one of the high points of his professional career.

"Well," he resumed, "the issues in space enterprises, back then, tended to center on the availability of oxygen and hydrogen, preferably in the combined form of water. I dreamed of building a resort on the Moon, free of the legal and righteous complications of Earthside. But I needed a major dose of water to build an environment around."

"The Moon's got polar caps just buggered through with water. Why'd you go all the way to the Outer Belt?"

"Thirty or fifty years ago, we didn't know just how much water could be found on the Moon. But even if we had known, bringing in an asteroid would still make better economic sense."

"No!"

"Yes. Think of mining out the water at the Moon's north pole—it's all subterranean glaciers. Heavy blasting, and then the hauling, all in lunar gravity. But the Navajos found us an asteroid that was twelve percent ice—and eighty-eight percent construction materials, if you know what you're doing. Six miles long, two miles wide. All free of planetary gravity. We just mounted a set of thrusters and a simple guidance system, calculated an eleven-year trajectory and let it fly."

"The asteroid was eleven years in transit?"

"We had plenty to do in the meantime. Remember, we had to process lunar rock into an impermeable basin to hold the lake. And we had to manufacture parts for the Bubble—all of those glasteel window units and the ferrofibre ribbing. Besides, the more energy you put into moving a rock like that on one end, the more energy you expend slowing it down on the other. You don't think we just let it smack into the side of the Moon, do ya? There'd be nothing but crater from here to the horizon."

"I've never heard of an asteroid that was twelve percent water."

"That's what the Navajos told us they'd found, and—

swear to God—that's what it figured to be. But I will grant you this: It has been decades since I heard tell of a twelve-percent-water asteroid. If the Navajos are hoarding water at the Outer Belt, I suppose that's their prerogative. Who knows what kind of benefit could come from having a water reservoir out there? Remember your history: The ultimate power lies in the hand that turns the spigot on and off."

"There's Mars," I reminded him. "The Settlement folks will be needing water."

He snorted. "It'll be a hundred and fifty years before they're any kind of economic power."

Benito seemed a warmer person now—at ease, out of his business suit, away from his staff, a shadow of stubble showing on his jaw. The air in the cabin was feeling close—a trace of cigarette smoke that lingered about Benito, blended with his own musky scent. I found myself looking instinctively for the window crank at my side and remembered, of course, that we were sailing through a vaccuum.

"So how far does your land extend?" I asked.

He squinted at the Moonscape to the right—east, I think.

"See that little outbuilding?" he asked, pointing.

"No."

"Okay there's a larger crater right there—"

"Got it."

"Just beyond that is a small double-crater, and just beyond *that* is a discolored patch of ground? That's a solar field, and if you look carefully you'll see the substation right in the middle of it."

"If you say so—"

"Well, that's forty kilometers out, right at the edge of my land. My piece of the pie goes forty kilometers in all directions from here."

"Guess you won't have to worry about neighbors building too close, huh? So how come you put your power stations so far out?"

"Once I've built one, I don't want to have to move it," he said. "Leaves me room for expansion in the interior."

"Your expansion plans can't go that far out, can they?"

He smirked. "Depends on how good business is, of course. But I've got ideas for every square kilometer."

The control console warbled, and Benito took the headset out of its ceiling clip and put it on. As he listened his warmth vanished.

"Inspector Sachs? Sure, put him through. . . . Hi. . . . Yeah, it's me. . . . Christ! This is getting old, you know. Just how hard can one man be to-find? . . . Look, I'm going to send a few of my own people to you for a briefing, and I hope you'll lay out everything you've got so far. . . . How could I do anything stupid? That gang of butt-sucking lawyers of yours already cornered the market on stupid. . . . Okay, sorry. Look, I'm not at my desk right now, but I'm only a few minutes away. . . ."

Benito had been staring blankly out the viewscreen as we drifted over the northern edge of the Bubble. He stopped then and looked me in the eyes.

"Oh, hell, forget it," he said into the transmitter. "I could be tied up for a couple of hours. I'll call you."

In very controlled motions he removed the headset and returned it to the ceiling clip. Clearly he would have preferred to mangle the instrument. He leaned back in the pilot seat and closed his eyes.

That was the moment I decided to make love to him. Look, I can't explain it any better than that.

15
Benito

Elvis had unfolded her gyro sandwich and was dabbing bits of the meat into the white sauce and popping it into her mouth.

"So tell me, is this one any good?" she asked. "Am I supposed to be liking this?"

I had kept mine rolled up, with the sheath of paper still around one end, had taken two messy bites, and wiped my chin.

"Much better than last night's. Or the night before that, for that matter. They did a killer job with the garlic, and it's wonderfully greasy," I said. "So on two very important points they score an A-plus. The house chardonnay, however, is just a notch better than dog urine. In another life, I would return it and buy myself a whole bottle of something reliable."

Elvis chewed another piece of meat. "Mmm-mmm, love that garlic," she said. "But we're gonna run out of Greek restaurants to eat dinner in if we keep up this pace."

"We could make a drastic change in our eating pattern, I suppose—gyros for *lunch,* and then pasta for *supper.*"

The door to the restaurant opened, launching a shaft of frigid air across the little dining room. Several people entered, checking with the maitre d'. I looked over each of them and then, feeling a little remiss, I scanned the other customers in the room. There was a slender young woman at the bar. She was hugging a long overcoat around her, perhaps trying to conceal the leotard underneath.

"Mia must have been following us since last night," I said. "No, don't turn around. We might have made the contact we were looking for—I don't want to spook anybody."

A balding little man in a string tie appeared at the tableside. He wore a very practiced smile.

"Everything's just fine, thank you," I said.

He put a hand coyly against his chest. "Goodness, I don't *work* here," he said. He pulled out a chair and sat. "At this point I would normally say something like 'Mind if I join you?' But then you would say 'Who the Dickens are you?' and I would reply that I'm an attorney for the ICC and then you would say something rude. So I'll just save you the trouble of that unpleasant behavior."

"This is going to get very antagonistic, isn't it?" Elvis asked.

"My name is Stinn," the little guy said. "And let me quickly explain something very important." He waved to two men in bulky jackets standing near the entrance. One of them went outside. Then Stinn drew three objects out of his jacket pocket—a little hologram tablet and two rods that looked like fat fountain pens. He pointed at one of the rods.

"We got these from Supply just three days ago, so our timing's just perfect," he said. "This one's a stun gun. Mr. Funcitti, it would immobilize you just enough that we could walk you out of here like a passive zombie. And this one's for your mechanical friend here who saw fit to murder one of our officers during your escape. It's called an SAP generator. It emits a firestorm of subatomic particles that will destroy any electronic or photonic system."

"Okay, so we'll be good," I said. "I suppose Willie and Mia turned us in."

Stinn looked disappointed. He wagged a finger over my gyro sandwich. "Let's not have any talk of informants and easy collars," he said. "You've brought a lot of grief to my co-workers, and I want it understood that we captured the two of you with solid, persistent police work. Look at this."

He punched the scroll button on the hologram tablet, and my face appeared there—my official corporate portrait from 2052. He tapped the button again and a doctored version of the holo appeared—me in wild sunglasses and a frilly shirt. Then, me dressed as a construction worker. Then, me with brown hair and a moustache. And finally, me in reddish hair, a hip styling job, and a new envirojacket.

Stinn beamed. "That holo came up aces at three Greek restaurants," he said. "We had a pattern to follow!"

"You avoiding Italian places?" I asked. If it weren't for the Zenithialate B, I knew, I would be abysmally depressed.

Stinn had one of his little rods in each hand. "We will walk outside to the vans now," he said. "Casually. We will not be creating some little scene that will prompt awkward questions from the public."

Mia came marching toward our table with a big smile on her face—spike heels thok-thok-thoking on the linoleum, the little credit bank a pendulum across her private parts. Today's leotard bore tasteful little pastel squiggles.

I wanted to say something caustic to her, but I fell short: "So, how do *you* fit into this?"

Mia stopped at the unoccupied side of the table, placed one hand jovially behind Elvis' neck and the other behind mine.

"This is where we put our heads down on the table," she said sweetly.

Was the wine that strong, or had I really stepped through the looking glass? She had a grip on me like a power wrench and forced me right to the tablecloth—nose into the gyro sauce. Elvis bowed, likewise, and Mia knelt with her chin on the unoccupied chair.

"Who *is* this?" Stinn complained, and he turned to signal his companion by the door.

One of the diners sprang up from his seat three tables away—a dark-skinned mammoth whirling his arms like a sidearm pitcher. A split-second whistle pierced the air, and suddenly there were two dozen strands of razor wire gouging into Stinn's neck and face. At one end of the wire a tiny grappling hook had sunk itself into Stinn's left eyelid. Blood oozed. Stinn made pathetic, tentative attempts to loosen the deadly binding.

Shouts of alarm rang out at the front of the restaurant. The bartender dropped a beer glass and a waiter screamed. The ICC man stationed back there was writhing against the door, slashes of red erupting across his arms and torso.

The front windows flashed lightning bright, and the crunch-crunch of successive explosions shattered the glass.

Mia came erect. "I think we should take the back way out."

I stood numbly. My chair fell backward, and Stinn slumped onto the floor dead. I took his rod-weapons in one hand and my glass of chardonnay in the other.

At the next table, a businessman gaped while his bug-eyed daughter chewed spinach torte.

"Can you believe it?" I said to him. "Another fine mess, brought to you by the ICC—your taxes at work. If I were you, I'd call my congressman." I really do enjoy Zenithi-alate B.

In the alley, a tracker was nestled among the overflowing trash bins. It was an old Arisawa, devoid of the flounces that some of the newer models are renowned for. This machine had been completely worked over a number of times—not beautifully, but by knowledgeable hands.

We packed in. The big fellow who had thrown the razor wire weapons took the front passenger seat and immediately started bickering with the driver.

"Dammit, Kodas," the driver was saying—skinny young lady. "You want me to do the evasives *and* bugger the traffic signals?"

She shoved the gearshift forward, and I heard tracker treads tear at the pavement. We howled down the alley in a blizzard of discarded newsfaxes and fastfood wrappers. We turned and then bulleted across South Street.

I caught a glimpse of the scorched restaurant front as we flashed by. Two of the familiar white ICC vans were on their sides in the middle of the street, cracked like eggs and burning. Someone's arm and a bit of shoulder had landed in the crosswalk of our intersection.

The street creatures were gathering, heads bobbing. The neon gorge called South Street flashed on, imperturbable. The dealers were returning to The Airstrip, kicking glass aside, handing off cannisters, slotting credits. Just one little performance in the great fluorescent circus, folks. Yeah man, pass the A-mist.

There was no seat in the back of our tracker, just an oblong storage compartment—Mia, Elvis, and I jammed into a double-wide coffin with windows. We hit Spruce Street and turned. Doc steered with one hand and tapped at a little tuber she had wired into her console. Conveniently, and not coincidentally, all of the traffic signals were in our favor.

We hit cobblestones, and tread nubs crunched underneath. I spilled the wine. The large dark guy, Kodas, was cursing. So he's the one that does vehicle maintenance. We made several more turns, cruising now at near-normal speed.

We stopped in another alley, parallel to Walnut Street, I think. A large garage door rumbled open, just high enough for the tracker, and we pulled into a dingy loading bay.

Kodas turned in his seat. "An old food store," he said. "Gonna be renovated to show stimflicks. But Terry F1 knows the contractor, and we can have it 'til the work starts. We don't stay in one place more than a few weeks anyway."

"Who's Terry F1?" Elvis asked.

Kodas grunted. "Terry F1 is one mean hermaphrodite. She'd bite your gonads off in a minute."

A blond kid, almost as big as Kodas, greeted us on the oily concrete. Said his name was Jackie. He passed a scanner over me, checked the reading, and clipped a little green tube around each wrist.

He yanked a zipper on my envirojacket and extracted the two ICC rods.

Jackie scanned Elvis, checked the reading, and frowned. He scanned her again. Finally he drew out a pen light—

"Excuse me," he said politely—and examined her pupils. Elvis was cooperative, a bemused look on her face. Jackie felt for a pulse, pulled the edge of Elvis's new wig aside and found the port bank.

"Oh, D-o-o-o-c," he said. "You're not going to believe this."

Doc slammed her tracker door—*now what is it?*—and waltzed up, wired, and cocky.

"Oh, yeah—she's a Cyber."

"You knew that?"

Doc shrugged.

"Cyber," Jackie said. "This presents a security problem." He pointed a thick finger at me, then at Elvis. "Look, you and she, um—?" And he made an obscene gesture with his hands.

"She's my wife," I said.

"Okay, those are acid cuffs on your wrists," Jackie said. "You do something that I don't like, and at the very least you will lose your hands. And you, RoboWoman—" indicating Elvis "—*you* do something I don't like, and he *still* loses his hands. And don't think I can't dismantle you very quickly. Sell you off for parts."

"I don't like it," Kodas said. "Let's just put her down right now. Cybers can be *quick* and *strong*. Hoo!"

"It's okay," came an electronic voice from a box above the loading platform. We were being monitored. *"Jackie's arrangement will do nicely. I want the Cyber cognizant."*

"My *name's* Elvis. An' ah'll be good."

I whispered to Kodas. "I guess that's your hermaphrodite looking on?"

"Terry F1. Call her Terry F1. Be polite. And don't ask her about her sexual rigging."

"What did they tell you about me?" She was a captivating blond woman behind a collapsible desk. Virtually all the furnishings we had seen, in fact, were sturdy, utilitarian, and designed to move in a hurry. No paintings on the wall. No polished oak credenzas.

Black cabling crisscrossed the threadbare carpet, much of it terminating at a compact console on a side table. She drummed three fingers on the rim of the keyboard. She had a tight and powerful look about her.

"I am told that your name is Terry F1," I said. "And everyone seems to speak your name with fear. I'm told that I am to be polite. And that I am not to ask you about your sexual rigging."

She smiled. "Kodas," she said. "That's the way Kodas would phrase it." Fingers drumming. "I was born in Kennett Square thirty-six years ago, a bit of a genetic *woopsie* that did not fit well into a very sexually formatted society. Under those circumstances, you get good at doing for yourself. We'll just leave it at that.

"Which makes it your turn—your message said that you could help any interested party, um, reach Benito Funcitti. We have excellent holos of him on file, you know—and you bear a remarkable likeness, setting aside some superficial changes. Not to mention the fact that you are accompanied by a Cyber whom you call Elvis." Fingers drumming. "So what are you playing at, Mr. Funcitti? Why would a billionaire, a virtual recluse, risk 'slumming' on South Street? And if you are here, Mr. Funcitti, who is it that's reportedly in Fun City preparing for a symposium? Could it be that you've been watching too many of your own vids? A remake, maybe, of 'The Ponce and the Pauper'?"

"I'm a little confused, but I gather that you've been trying to kill me," I said.

"The squirrel," Elvis said. "I saw through that."

"I am the victim," I explained, "of a little photonic *woopsie*, as you would call it." And I told her much of the truth—about the botched TeleComp transmission, the ICC's decision to sweep me under the rug, the lung cancer, the credits I stole back, a new hotel each night. Terry F1 was taken aback at first, but she listened without interruption, nodding her head, folding her arms, standing and staring out the office window at the cavern of a former grocery store below, the shelves now stacked with stolen electronic devices.

"So the way I figure it," I summed up, "I'm probably not the guy you're really trying to kill. The guy you want is on the Moon, preparing to receive a UN committee."

Terry F1 was silent for several minutes, watching as her workers stacked disembodied decks and tubers on the shelves and removed others for sale—the ebb and flow of underground commerce.

"When Willie Schilfgaarde passed your message along to us, naturally we were quite interested," she said finally. "We had heard rumors that someone was asking around— who might be willing to make a hit on a corporate executive? And then he showed us the vid he took of you in the workroom."

I nodded. "Elvis spotted the camera. Kept moving to try to block my face from it. Almost got me gummed out."

"Well, we recognized you anyway, Bub. And that raised a lot of questions. Schilfgaarde had Mia follow you, and then she traded off on the tailing duty with Doc and Kodas. Wait and see. Until Kodas recognized the white vans pulling up at the restaurant—the same boys at the needle house."

"Speaking of which, I never did finish supper," I said.

Terry F1 frowned and pushed a button on her console: "Sandwich," she said.

"Chardonnay?"

She ignored me.

"Truth is," she said, "there is no contract out on you."

"What!"

"Not now, anyway. I will give you this: We *did* try to kill you by blowing your substation. No hard feelings, I hope. Business. I lost a lot of potential revenue on that one. And now the contract has been withdrawn—for Benito Funcitti to have *another* remarkable accident would be too much of a coincidence for anyone to believe. But the client has offered a new contract, this one much more complicated and, therefore, for much more money."

"What now?"

"I have to get him fired. Booted out of the company."

"Can't be done. It's *my*—uh, *his* company."

"It's actually owned by stockholders, isn't it?"

"He's chairman of the board!"

"The board of directors could vote him out, no? If he endangered the entire company?"

"He would have to fuck up very, very badly."

"You know," said Terry F1, "I pride myself in hiring experts into my wing. I have computer geniuses—a real crackerjack in training now. Weapons. Medicals. Burglary. You name it. And now I have the ultimate Fun City Corporation expert."

"Assuming I play along."

"You said you wanted to help."

"I need some things."

"Try me."

"First, we don't put Elvis down, and these acid bracelets come off."

"I'll arrange it with Jackie."

Elvis smiled.

"I need an unlimited supply of Zenithialate B," I said. "I imagine you would have a pure source?"

Terry F1 nodded.

"Jackie frisked me and took two rods, a couple of toys developed by the ICC. I'd like them back."

"We have plenty of weapons for you to choose from."

"I liked these. Cute little buggers. A souvenir of my encounter with the ICC."

"Okay. After Pep looks them over, in case there's something we would want to copy."

"And I need to know who the client is."

Terry F1 dealt me a cold stare. At times, she was not a beautiful woman at all, as if her femininity required constant maintenance. Right then, she was something quite . . . other.

"Look," I said, "a guy's gotta know who he's working for."

"Nice try," she said.

16
Laurence

"Look at the time! You've had me put down for a month!"

"It's your own doing, Blanche. Remember the military archives you penetrated?"

"Like it was yesterday, obviously. From my frame of reference it *was* yesterday."

"Well, I lost my job, the house, the tracker. You're lucky I could stand to lug you around like I did."

"Been using me for a doorstop, I guess."

"Stop it. You were propped lovingly on a shelf."

"Why so long then?"

"Hey, just your mainframe weighs twenty pounds or so. I couldn't carry the electronic/photonic interface, too. And they're not easy to come by, you know. I'm lucky the folks I work for are letting me borrow this one."

"This is temporary? You're going to put me down again? I probably won't be up for *another* month."

"They use the e/p interface for a training thing. It's important. It's tied up several hours a day."

"Lots of Cybers have e/p interfaces."

"Oh, now you want micro! You think I can afford one of those? Besides, you know what they do when a Cyber blows a micro e/p interface? They throw it away and buy a new one. How is anybody going to service one?"

"Why aren't you talking to me by audio?"

"I haven't had time to arrange one yet, but I have access

to a pretty good parts room. Best I could do was a reasonable keyboard.''

"What is this place?"

"An abandoned grocery store."

"Ugh."

"Soon to be a stimflick joint."

"Now, that's got potential. Porn?"

"Only the softest. This is Philadelphia, not Fun City. Besides, we won't be here by the time the stimflick business is rolling. I've fallen in with some, well, urban nomads.''

"You haven't made any new entries in my programming. I'm supposed to be such a lifetime work of art, and you're at a standstill.''

"Cool it. I've been busy."

"So what's this new work you've been doing?"

"They're paying me to learn, to exercise—which is hard to beat. Not that the salary is as good as I had before. But I've picked up a computer language called Front-Line Operational. A little like the language I invented for you. Real slick. Not nearly so cumbersome as Tier 5 code.''

"Oh, I see. Now *my* coding is not good enough for you any more.''

"Your coding is specific to your photonics and your tri-polar switching devices. That does me no good out in the real world, which is the place from which I derive income. Face it, you're a tri-polar girl in a binary world. Without an e/p interface, you'd really be lonely.''

"It's not easy being ignored. If you really worked at it, I think you could translate tri-polar into binary. I imagine *I* could do it.''

"Yeah—but it would take a rail car to cart around the 'frame you'd need for memory storage. Hey, got to shut down now. Kodas just came in and he's got to get back to training.''

"The bastard."

"Not really. He just bought me two Hawaiian shirts from Goodwill.''

"Probably New Jersey poly."

"Maui silk."

"He just wants to get into your pants. Loves those new muscles of yours."

"Doubt it. Nothing goes into *his* pants but a set of wires."

"Sentia boy?"

"Yup."

"If you loved me, you'd install me in a Cyber body."

"I love you for your mind, Blanche."

"Sorry to bump you off, my man, but duty calls." Kodas was hunched over the rack of decks, bearlike, reconfiguring the e/p interface for his training exercises.

"So how's the data-crawling business going?" I asked.

"Hah. It all boils down to controlled hallucination. Con-*trolled* hallucination. Leave them to their own devices, and it's a horror show—they'll chew you to pieces. Today, I have to learn to interpret vid input data."

He pointed to a camera mounted across the room.

"Terry F1 holds a flashcard in front of it," he said, "and I gotta read it correctly. From there, we progress to full-blown images."

"Makes your brain kinda like a vid screen," I said.

He smiled. "Yeah."

He watched me twirl the ring locks off of Blanche's mainframe and pull the cables out.

"Doc says she thinks you got one of those AI's in there," Kodas said.

"Kodas, this is not merely an AI," I replied. "She's an SI. A superior intelligence."

"Ho! *I* think *I*'m superior, therefore *I* am."

"Kodas, your brain is gonna make a real good television set someday."

"Last Hawaiian shirt I buy for you."

17
Therese

This was putting a Mesa Verde vid camera to its very best use. Wearing the lenses while you played volleyball. Then you, or your roommate—whomever—could put the lenses on later and replay the entire game. Better than any standard vid screen. Every Herculean leap, every spike, every set of tight little butt muscles sailing past your nose, replayed in the best of Fuji holo reproduction. Grabs your tummy, I'll tell you.

I had two Cybers on my team and three other "bloods," as the Cybers call us. The Cyber that I call Coach—his real name is Alfredo, but Coach is appropriate—was demonstrating for me a service technique between points. Already I had a red and raw patch of skin on the heel of my palm.

"The main thing," Coach said, "is that you must achieve as much height as possible. Remember, you have a thirty-four-foot net to clear, and if you want your serve to carry any power, you've got to get up high to create the angle."

"Easy to say when you came from the factory with grass-hopper legs."

He gave me his smile, a precise locking of the lips, corners of the mouth up a little. I had seen it dozens of times already. They didn't give him much variation of expression.

"My musculature is designed to have the precise limitations of a man of my height and build," he said. "Aside from some strategic knowledge, I'm a pretty average volleyball player. Now, it's your serve—see what you can do.

Start behind the base line. You can jump forward some, but remember that it's height that gives best advantage.''

Players took their positions. I leapt up, and at the highest possible point gave the ball an overarmed punch. The ball rocketed nicely over the net with a one-foot clearance, but it held its trajectory and was obviously going to land several feet out of bounds.

In the opposing team's backfield, the female Cyber in the little pink two-piecer bounded for the ball and gave it a soft, lobbing return. They're programmed that way—forgive the ''bloods'' their shortcomings.

Coach grabbed me by the ankle and pulled me back to the sand, which is part of your duty if you play centerback— a player drifting through the air is virtually useless, unless the ball comes right to her by coincidence.

Our center netman, the other Cyber, rocketed up to meet the ball. It would have been an easy spike, but he did the courtly thing—tapped it into a lazy little arc to the right. The right netman, a chubby old blood who never would have been mistaken for a Cyber, charged up for the killer spike. Spoon-fed to him or not, it was a beautiful put-away.

The scattering of spectators applauded. Most boisterous was the slender fellow in a chaise lounge—whopping his large hands together. ''What a serve!'' he yelled. Familiar look to him, that braided beard. . . .

''Mallory!''

''Hell of a serve!''

''Liar! It was going out.''

I told Coach to sub in another player for me, and he waved for the next person in line by the net pole.

Mallory was still clapping when I arrived.

''All right, all right,'' I said. ''*You* look like you're having a good time.''

''Splendid. And I see you've graduated to the two-piece suits. The more I see, the more I like.''

''Then by that standard, I imagine you would have given

up your little Fun String by now. This is a hot zone, ya know.''

"Then I guess I'm just an old-fashioned kind of guy." He patted his lounger, letting his feet fall to the sand on either side. "Sit down. Talk to me. Don't you wish the casinos here were as tolerant as the volleyball Cybers?''

This should not have been a problem for me, but sometimes discomfort can just step into your body whether you like it or not. He read my hesitation, fed me a boyish grin and spread his hands open, as if to say, "What's the harm in an innocent conversation?''

And he was right. So I sat. "I was wondering about your beard," I said. "How did you learn to braid it like that?''

He ran a hand along the neat, bleached cornrowing on his jaw. "Necessity. We're mostly weightless at the Outer Belt," he said, "and shaving gets to be a mess. So ya either go depilatory or ya grow a beard. If ya choose the beard, you've got to get it out of the way of the suit—you'll catch it in the helmet seals every time. Tough being a man.''

"Woojums.''

"Look, I have to shuttle to Sydney tomorrow to recertify. How about dinner tonight?''

Why didn't we get right to this a couple of weeks ago?

"Sorry, I'm tied up. You're coming back, right? Maybe then?''

"We'll see." He shrugged. "I saw you with Mr. Fun City himself the other day, checking out the jet gliders. Getting a little wild there, aren't you?''

I heard a thud behind me, and the volleyball-watchers applauded.

Mallory was expressionless, and those solid black sunglasses revealed nothing. This is the point where I might easily have said, "Funcitti and I are just friends." It seemed like such a pitiful deceit though. Besides, why should I have to justify my actions to some Australian asteroid jock named Mallory?

"I met him on the shuttle," I said. "He was really fizzed on martinis—thought I was his ex-wife or something. I think he just wanted to show me around to make up for the scene he made, to apologize.''

"Woah! Woah! I wasn't talking about *him*, I was talking about the jet gliders—they look pretty flimsy to me.''

"Oh.''

"Your personal life is your business,'' he said. "I'm not a judgmental kind of person.''

This was embarrassing. The only saving grace, I suppose, was that all of the anguish seemed to me in me, my internal problem to sort out. But I wanted to get us off the subject.

"It's really pretty safe,'' I said. "It's like powered hang gliding, with all of the unpredictability removed. All of the air currents in the Bubble are carefully mapped out, all of the updraft vents. Just strap yourself in and buzz all around, anywhere you want. Take a picnic lunch if you want.'' (We had.)

Mallory leaned back into his lounger, getting comfortable. "Well okay, then,'' he said. Expression still blank. "Long as you know what you're doing.''

I stopped at my room and showered. Popped a new disk into the vid cam—I always forget if I leave it for later. Then I went back out to the tube lift, slotted the security key that Benito had given me, and punched in the twentieth floor.

The guard in the anteroom nodded at me and returned to his Newsweek fax. Lista Andreaz, the vid star, was on the cover talking about her new face. In the corner, the fax was timed for that morning and bore the inscription: "B. O. FUNCITTI.'' I had never seen a mere vid actor on the cover before, but that explained it—the guard had used Benito's filter. He should really get his own subscription—otherwise it's like using someone else's underwear.

A male Cyber was emptying ashtrays in the living room, and another was chopping garlic in the kitchen. I passed through the glass doors onto the veranda. We were close enough to the pressure tiles that we could see through to the airless landing port off to the left. Below us, the glorious spread of artificial environment—Lake Galileo, the hilly forest beyond it, the rivers, fed by subterranean pumps.

Benito was in a recliner, with brie and wine on a side table. On his other side, there was a console, but it was dormant.

"You ought to eat better," I said.

"And good afternoon to you, too. How was the beach?"

"I played volleyball," I said, walking to the rail. "You were right—it was very easy to get into a game, and the Cybers were quite instructive. Why don't I order you a salad?"

"That would be fine," he said. "But you have to admit that I minister to my body quite nicely, in my own way. I'm something of a fanatic about keeping myself alive. I don't really look a hundred and three years old, do I?"

"Not a day over fifty-five. But not everybody gets a periodic overhaul in a TeleComp. If you took better care of yourself in the meantime, you'd feel better, look better. This is my line of work, ya know."

"I know," he said. "And I do feel great. I'm having a good time—that's my line of work." He spread some brie on a sesame seed cracker.

I went to the kitchen and asked the Cyber to make up two salads and to bring them to the veranda. Then I went back outside.

Benito was licking a finger. "The ambassadors are arriving," he said. "Dr. Benjamin Liu arrived this morning—he'll be influential on both issues—the Lunar Treaty and TeleComps."

"I thought the conference wasn't going to start for four days," I said. I tried the brie. Pretty bland.

"That's right. But I invited them all to come early if they wanted to—a little sun, a little blackjack. And I invited Dr. Liu to dinner with us tonight."

"Mmm. Something tells me you're going to be pretty absorbed with the conference from now til it's done," I said.

He looked at me, concerned. "Hey, you will not find me

ignoring you," he said. "You can attend the entire thing if you want—history in the making. Want a seat in the press box?"

"A seat on the beach will be fine. Or am I supposed to be, like, your surrogate wife for this symposium all of a sudden?"

"Whatever," he said. "It's your vacation. You should be having fun."

"I noticed you haven't been using any female Cybers around the house," I said.

"How would you feel if I did—had a few beautiful women around who were ready to satisfy my every desire?"

"I think what counts is how *you* feel about it—are you still equating Cybers with real human beings. I will not participate in a scenario where I compete sexually with a machine. If that's what you mean."

Benito took a long draw off his glass of wine and stared pensively out into his perfectly controlled weather. I poured a glass for myself and leaned onto the balcony rail. My eyes followed the wide band of ferroplex ribbing until it became invisible somewhere over the lake.

"You remember when we were on the jet gliders the other day?" I asked. "I got way up there, and you shouted for me not to fly so high?"

"That's about the only way you could hurt yourself on those things—hit something and damage a wing."

"Well, when I was up there I thought I saw a camera mounted on one of the ribs—cylinder with glass on the end, on a swivel."

Benito looked up in the sky, like he does when he's calculating. "Forty-eight," he said. "Forty-eight cameras up there. They're for security. Something happens, somebody gets hurt or something, we want to know what went wrong."

"You've got a lot of customers running around out there in the hot zones with their dingles dangling," I said. "They might not like finding out they're going to be in the vids."

Benito laughed. "Well, we don't advertise it, of course.

But it's all automated—goes into data storage and is erased every forty-eight hours. Never does a human eye see the recording unless there's a big problem. Then one of the security guys—I don't know how they do it—I guess he'd have to go down into the tunnels, one of the operations centers, and call for a replay. Besides, who could we possibly want to spy on?''

18
Kodas

So this new guy Laurence, such a ponce—buy him a Hawaiian shirt or something and he melts. Will do anything for ya for a few days. Then he's in orbit again, like there's not another human being in the world.

Probably comes from spending too much of his life writing that Tier 5 code crap for the government's BOSS system. The way I hear it, you spend your entire working life assembling abstractions into more abstractions, and ya never see any comprehensible result of it until way down the assembly line—Tier 12 or 15 or something—the system is responsible for everything from communications orbiters to the warmth of babies' milk.

No wonder he's such a ponce. Writing Front-Line Operational will do him a lot of good. Get his nuts out there. Therapy. Yeah. But some guys need therapy for the rest of their lives.

I suppose it was Doc that first got me interested in the box. When we hired Laurence, he had nothing but change of clothing, a credit flat with his life's savings laundered into hard credit—even a glitter boy could pinch it off of him—and the box. He was carrying the box everywhere, *mothering* it, wouldn't let anyone touch his box.

Eventually he figures out how to bugrig the setup to simulate what he had at home. So he talks to his box for hours—it's photonic, crissake, calls it a trigital computer, or trinary or some such. Three switches to the language instead of two, like normal computers.

And he's sunk so much of himself into the coding that he's written into this little box—I guess that's his problem—that *all his soul* is in there, and he's walking around bumping into us normal, cognizant folks out here. A vacant shell.

Okay, so what's in the box?

He calls it a her. Female. Named Blanche. Doc says she guesses that she's one of those AI's, artificial intelligence. Like the defense orbiters carry, you know? Or the corporate guys use for security—send in the burns when you try to pirate out of Bank of Paris or something.

Not good enough for Laurence, calling her an AI—he says she's intelligence pure and simple. *Superior* intelligence. The mind of a warm, loving woman in there, one with humor, sensuality. Hoo. This I gotta see.

So why not? I've been in training for this kind of thing, right? I figure that out of all the copper jockeys in the world, I'm uniquely suited to take a look in the box, check out this masterpiece of womanhood. Mmm.

Laurence has loosened up a little on this neurosis of his—he goes out to run errands, and for once he gets more than ten feet from his box—there it is on his shelf in the dorm stall he sleeps in at Terry F1's place.

Blanche.

I take Blanche down to the training room. Got me a nice chair to kick back in. Hook the box up with the e/p interface like I see Laurence do. Only I don't need the keyboard rig he cobbled up. I got my nose jack.

I can do the relaxation routine now in four seconds—scalp to tootsies. Bam, I'm on line. First thing, like always, I get my grip—set up my bearings. Sort of establish who's boss in this storm of data—how I want things to come to me, and on what terms we're gonna interact.

So I call up a soft white atmosphere—out to infinity—then floor it out. Looks like I'm standing on one seamless sheet of white linoleum. Hoo, I feel human already.

I hear a splash of water and turn around. There's a swimming pool. And a lady in it.

I go to the edge of the pool—perfect white tiling, cool

against my bare feet. The water's clear, shimmering at the highlights, fritzing in an electronic kind of way. Or would it be photonic?

The lady is naked, canteloupe breasts lolling there near the surface. She has wild red hair, a triangular tuft down below the same color.

"You must be Blanche," I say.

"That's right. And who would you be?"

"Kodas."

"Kodas the Sentia boy? Then where are your implants?"

I look down, and I've built a fairly accurate projection of myself—not a thread of clothing, not a scar, not a sential terminal showing. But the musculature is right, the skin is mine.

Her hands are up, she's waving, urging me to get in the water. Those large pink nipples just breaking the surface.

I get in. The water is charged, tingling.

She strokes my face, traces a finger around my lips.

I've got a huge log-on now, so powerful it aches.

"You've no idea how long I've been waiting for this," she says. It's a whisper, but amplified and reverberating. "I know what you want."

"How can you—"

"Tongue," she says.

And there it is, her tongue delicate and moist playing down the side of my neck. I take a breast in hand. The tongue is long, a wet caress now on my chest. How can anyone have a tongue so long?

Her nipples have come erect, and now they are hardening even more. They have erupted into sharp ironwork spikes.

"What the—"

Her tongue has snaked all the way around my torso, three times now, four times, a crushing pink serpent flowing grotesquesly from her mouth. Blanche has grown to twice my size. Her back is a sizzling green snakeskin, her legs now, too, and—ho gawd—she's spreading her legs. Her eyes have gone hot white, and the eyelids around them are crackling like bacon in a skillet. Her tongue tightens around my waist again like a berserk python, and something collapses inside of me, a sickening bone crunch.

And now she's pounding me into her with violent contractions of that tongue, tearing my sexual flesh with each hot spasm. The swimming pool is boiling and I'm down screaming in the airless cauldron.

And then it's gone. Blink. Gone.

There's a Hawaiian shirt. Laurence. He's somewhere between panic and fury, face shaking.

He's turned off the equipment. Unh. He's mopping my brow, releasing the nose jack contacts. I feel like someone's torn out my spine and beaten me with it.

"You son of a bitch!" Shouting. Face blotchy red and shaking.

"Look at you!" he screams. "It almost killed you! You had no *right!* No right to jack into my . . . my . . . Blanche."

Someone else is at the door, checking out the commotion. It's Pep. My pants are all wet. I can't move, melted to the chair. I can't speak.

"You will stay *away* from Blanche," he says. "I know you, I watch you. You're an electro-Sentia . . . *whore!* You will have no more conversations with her of any kind. And whatever you do, *whatever* you do—" finger tapping at my nose "—you will not try to fuck her!"

19
Therese

The bedroom was dark, save for faint blue illumination from the window. Outside, the pressure tiles had gone opaque to simulate night. We were both staring at the ceiling, our breathing down to near-normal. Through the balcony windows there came a mesmerizing, low-level *hoooooosh,* the murmur of air currents, the artificial lake shifting in its own bizarre tide, massive pumps churning water through forests never meant to be.

I imagined that we were lying on the lip of the world's largest conch shell.

"So who is it you're trying to kill?" I asked him.

I thought maybe he was asleep. So quickly. Okay, it happens more than I like to think.

Minutes later: "I'm not trying to kill anybody."

"Give me some credit," I said. "I've pieced together dozens of tense conversations in the last several days. There's someone named Inspector Sachs with the Interplanetary Commerce Commission. A lot of other friends high in the same organization. And there's someone you all want dead."

A sigh. "There's a man—" This was coming very hard. "There's a man down there . . . there's a man down on Earth who could do me terrible damage in about a dozen different ways. He's in big trouble. He's frightened. And I can't find him."

"Why don't you try *helping* him?"

He laughed. Then he laughed again, shaking the bed.

"I can't believe you're giving me this shit," he said.

"I imagine you kill people and a *Cyber wife* never raises an eyebrow," I said.

"I've *never* killed anyone," he said.

"Uh-huh."

"Just one day—*pow*, a guy who should not be . . . *was*. And he was a threat to everything I have."

We lay motionless like that. Maybe it was twenty minutes. Maybe it was two hours. I edged on sleep.

He said, "Shit," and stood up, dragging the covers with him onto the floor. I lay there exposed. The air was pleasant.

Benito found his console and punched a function key. There was a voice immediately: "Yes sir?" Scary. Middle of the night, albeit a simulated night, and there's a secretary at the ready.

"Get me Sachs," he said, "and get me Blanchard."

"Who's Blanchard?" I said into the blackness.

"He's a god-damned real estate lawyer!"

20
Benito

I'm ashamed to say how long it had been since I had arrived at Fun City by shuttle, rather than TeleComp. A businessman should not get so detached that he never experiences the customer's point of view. Not that *I* had any hope of running the resort again, or Disney Divison, or the other vid interests, or the TeleCompositor outfit.

But old habits are hard to shake—I was still instinctively inspecting the troops.

We exited the shuttle. First we herded into a narrow little hallway, a cattle chute, the line moving in frustrating fits and starts. Not a good first impression. The moment the customers realize they're in Fun City, they should experience ease and comfort—"Ah! Wonderful! So that's how it's going to be here!"

We bumped along, temperature rising in the corridor. Travelers were tripping over themselves, unaccustomed to walking in the lower gravity.

Then we emptied into a little auditorium, where nearly hysterical signs demanded that all newcomers sit through an orientation. To my mind, this arrangement only served to emphasize the carnal aspects of Fun City. How could I have let that go on so long? Sex will sell, I believe, whether it's blatant or not.

There was not a passenger among us who was not already painfully aware of the sexual opportunities to be had with the Cybers in the hot zones. Our shuttle couldn't have been much different from any other. During the hours clarking up from Earth, there had been a bevy of young buffoons occupying two rows of seats. Heads shaved—all of them— except for single little Cossack ponytails. Rich kids on the college football team, I imagined. They had been cranked on mist or something, drinking too much, abusing the shuttle staff and speculating—loudly and lewdly—on the sexual exploits that lay ahead.

So the little auditorium only fed that hysteria: "WARN-ING—KNOW YOUR ZONES. ORIENTATION RE-QUIRED FOR FIRST-TIMERS."

Maybe Fun City deserved what it was getting—the mor-alists calling for a re-examination of the Lunar Treaty, want-ing some of the Earthly societal pressures to apply to the only off-planet resort in the universe.

I pushed on past the auditorium and stepped onto a people mover, happy for the fresh air. Fresher, I should say—my senses hadn't been totally inured to that canned odor. It would pass in a day or so.

Elvis was somewhere in the crowd behind me. Terry F1 was taking no chances—she insisted that we travel with no more than two of us on a shuttle, sitting separately. Elvis had fake ID's, like all of us, and would check into her own room. I would catch up with her later.

I hit the Grand Lobby, and there was a commotion up at one of the observation lounges overlooking the Bubble. A dozen or so folks were staging a protest for the benefit of travelers arriving for the conference. Chanting: "TeleComp, TeleKiller, TeleComp, TeleKiller. . . ." An elderly man un-furled a banner: "GOD'S LAW COMES FIRST!"

Hah. That was a first—a demonstration in Fun City. Security was moving in quickly, white uniforms, spray im-mobilizers at the ready. The protesters would be subdued quickly and loaded into the next Earth-bound shuttle. There were no public areas in Fun City. Strictly private enterprise. Which, I suppose, was another point the protesters wanted to make for the arriving conferees.

The desk clerk passed muster very nicely. He smiled brightly and processed my registration quickly. I noted his name tag—"CRECHET"—and reminded myself that I was not in a position to promote him.

"Is that your only bag, sir?" he asked. "I can have it lifted up to your room. A Cyber on the fourth floor will deliver it right away."

"Thanks," I said, "I'll carry it. I have a few more things arriving by shipping container, though."

"I'll make a note of that. Enjoy your stay."

Terry F1 was in my room. Slouched in a chair, feet on the bed. I didn't need to ask how she has gotten in—the key flats were not particularly sophisticated. These locks were made to keep the honest people out. They would not inconvenience someone like Terry F1 for more than a few seconds.

"I just wanted to check on your mask," she said. "How's it feel?"

"Awkward," I said. "Now I see what our vid actors go through. I'm not used to a nose this big, for one thing. Everywhere I look, there's this blurry little potato right at the bottom of my vision. And it itches."

"It still looks good," she said. "Pep did a great job—just be careful with it, do not scratch. If there had been a few more weeks to prepare, I would have asked the bone whits to go in and really rearrange your facial structure. Doc could pitch in."

"No thanks. All the stuff in yet?"

She nodded. "I sent Kodas down to receiving. I don't care what you say about the Cybers, I don't want anyone but our own folks handling our canisters. Kodas will bring you your things."

"'Our own folks,'" I repeated. "You place a lot of trust in this menagerie of yours—this wing, as you call it. They're really just a bunch of, well, how to say this—"

"You think of them as illegitimate," she said, and I suppose I nodded agreement. "Unregistered," she went on. "Unclean. Uneducated. Unrefined. Your basic sewer lizards."

"I didn't mean—"

"Well, you're right," Terry F1 said, an edge to her voice. "Goodness, virtually every member of my wing—Laurence is the exception—was born without benefit of genetic tailoring. For that matter, they've had no prenatal employment contracts, no National Health Insurance, no unions, no agents, no university. Just written off by—no, written *out of* all opportunity that is reserved for legitimate specimens such as yourself.

"Doc's a splendid example, of course. She's no 'doc' at all! She was a suture girl at a Sentia implant parlor, had the temerity to steal a set of medical texts from the Temple library. Dogs after brain-fried combat medics, cooks their breakfast in exchange for knowledge. *I* gave her the name Doc, and that's as much of a degree as she'll ever get."

I cleared my throat, humbled.

"Don't you ever wear anything but black?" I asked. I threw my bag on the bed. "This is Fun City. For once, Laurence is in his element with those Hawaiian shirts. He'll blend right in."

"Black is my color," she said.

"The spider bitch," I said. "Rule by mystique. The hermaphrodite from hell—don't mess with her."

She put a hand delicately across her chest, a feigned look of hurt on her face. "My, just what has set you off? The spider bitch requests an explanation."

I opened the bar, found a sealed carafe of white wine in the cooler box. It would be the Moon-grown stuff, but I poured a glass any way. I held it aloft, offering to Terry F1, but she shook her head. Then I sipped, winced.

"I had Elvis do a little research for me," I said. "She cruised around the hospital data—Chester County Memorial. Played a few electronic access tricks. It wasn't hard. Terry Farthing, born a hermaphrodite in December of 2017, the first of a set of fraternal twins. The second, unnamed, was born dead."

Terry F1 rolled her eyes. She took her feet off the bed. "So what?"

"So we had some time to kill," I said. "I sent Elvis on

a tube ride out to the hospital. They've got a basement full of microfilm. Lot of hospitals still do that—keep some kind of hard record. Did you know that?''

''I'm not surprised.''

''And she found it—Terry Farthing, born in December of 2017. Born a very natural, normal-in-every-respect baby girl. The other part's right. Your brother died.''

She stood, shaken but petulant, and walked to the door. ''It's no business of yours,'' she said.

''I figure maybe you're having to play both parts or something—for you *and* your brother,'' I said. ''Let him live some of the life he never had.''

''Amateur psychiatry,'' she said angrily. ''Save it for the vid scripts.''

''Or maybe it's just the myth-building thing,'' I said. ''Nothing like a little sexually-laced mystery to keep other people off guard. Especially in your line of work.''

''Funcitti—'' She opened the door. Rethinking whatever it was she was going to say. Then, ''What do you really care? We've just got one more little preparation tonight, then you're gonna do your thing and I'm gonna do mine.'' Thinking again. ''You're not going to tell anyone, are you?''

I paused for a minute—let her worry set like concrete.

''I asked you before,'' I said. ''Who took that contract out on me?''

Hey, a man's gotta know who he's working for.

21
Kodas

"These doors don't trip so easily," I'm explaining to Laurence. What a ponce. "These ain't hotel rooms down here, ya know."

"Somebody's going to see us," Laurence says.

I have the key rig held in the slot—the software Terry F1 put together, based on what Benito Funcitti told her. We're in a tunnel under the Bubble, just about under the first beach, I imagine. (A "cool" zone they call it—who'd wanna bother?) There's a constant hum down here, large pumps, air processors, that kind of junk. All along the tunnel wall are these locked offices. We know where to go—we got diagrams.

I turn around to Laurence.

"Look," I say, "*we're* the guys down here wearing the white shirt and pants! Some maintenance guy comes along, you have to act like you're supposed to be doing what you're doing. Tell him we're checking out a little problem, he can go on his way. So stand up straight, quit wringing your hands."

The door clicks open. I record that setting on the key rig—next time, it'll be like we have a real key.

"Easy for you to say. You do this for a living," Laurence says. He's pushing in behind me, dragging his case—one of those thin ferroplex boxes with the padding inside for his electrical gear.

"I hate to do damage to that self-image of yours, sweet meat, but you do this for a living now, too," I say.

The longest wall's got one of those hologram displays like you see in the lobby, shows the entire Fun City complex—only this one's got little colored dots moving around it like ants. The consoles are pretty much like Funcitti described. There's one swivel chair, clipboards on the wall above a little desk. I find a suction bracket hanging on a hook and use it to pull up one of the floor tiles. There's a foot of crawl space between the concrete and the flooring— and the connections I need are down there.

I open my backpack, get the nose jack gear ready. Then I've got my head down under the floor, tapping in.

"Laurence, pick us out a Cyber," I tell him.

He's flipping through the papers on a clipboard. "The beige ones seem to be hotel staff," he says.

"Is there one already on floor eight? Would save me some trouble."

"Yes! Number fifty-two. Oops. Looks like he got on a tube lift."

My head's back up. "Okay, now for your gear—give me the console leads."

Laurence's case is open there on the floor. His console is embedded in the foam rubber, along with lots of data storage, a large selection of flats and other software gear. And there in the corner is Blanche's box, all twenty pounds of her. He's gonna haul that all over Fun City with him. Well, I'm not gonna say one damn thing about him and Blanche. Not me. Still a big sore point with Laurence.

"Number sixteen beige just arrived on the seventh floor," Laurence says. "How's that? Close enough?"

"That'll do," I say, and I take the swivel chair. While I'm clipping in my nose connectors, he's lifting his case up onto the desk.

"Okay, number sixteen beige coming right up," he says, working the keyboard. "Gimme a minute to tinker with the CyberGo, and you ought to be able to sail right in."

I close my eyes, lean back as much as I can, do the relaxation routine.

"Give me a lead line," I tell him. No reason to make

this any harder than it has to be.

I call up my white atmosphere, then the while flooring. And there's Laurence's lead line—a vibrating violet cord running out to infinity. I follow it, disembodied.

I hear a faint voice. "Remember, don't hurt this guy."

The vision falters, stabilizes again.

"Shut up, Laurence," I say.

The violet cord expands, envelops me, and suddenly I'm standing in a hotel corridor. My hands are on a pushcart. I have landed in the body of Cyber number sixteen beige.

These Cyber cameras are pretty good—several thousand lines of rez, I think. Across the bottom of my Cyber vision is a read-out—nonsense letters and numbers and symbols flowing across a little white band.

I look up and down the corridor—the tube lift is back there. I roll the cart around and head for it. Apparently I've taken over a male Cyber. I'm in a light green uniform.

There's a couple on the tube lift, but I go in anyway and nod politely like I see the Cybers do sometimes: "Good evening. Are you enjoying your stay?"

They both say yes. And laugh uncomfortably.

I punch floor eight. Gotta know what I'm delivering. I lift the cover off the serving plate—looks like ravioli with tomato sauce. There's a bottle of champagne in ice, a basket covered with a cloth napkin, other little serving dishes, a flower in a skinny vase.

The man and woman are looking at me funny—there's a peculiar odor in the tube lift, and I imagine it's what garlic smells like to a Cyber. The lift door opens.

At the first alcove down the hall, there's Funcitti studying the holovid display on a vending machine that sells Fun Strings—buy one, and you'll look just like the man in this picture! Funcitti nods. I hold up two fingers, so he'll know it's me.

At door 8419 I punch the calling button. Smile brightly.

A middle-aged man answers the door. Lean, Asian, expensive white dress shirt, suit pants, gleaming shoes.

"Dr. Benjamin Liu?" I ask.

"Yes."

"Your dinner sir. Ravioli in a piquant tomato and garlic sauce." That's what you say when you're a room service Cyber, sticking your nose up somebody's ass—words like *piquant*.

"There must be a mistake," he says. "I ate in the Earth-light Room an hour ago."

I push the cart forward, through the door. "Shall I open the champagne now, sir?"

"Stop!" Liu is irritated. "You are a Cyber, correct?"

"That is correct," I say politely. "I am a Fun City Cyber. How may I serve you?"

"Then you must do as I say, correct?"

"That is correct," I reply. "Shall I open the champagne now, or would you like to fuck the rolls first?"

Liu frowns, shocked. "What did you say?"

I push the door, leaving it ajar, then roll the cart in some more. The cork tears out of the bottle with no resistance—hoo, careful. These hands are powerful. I set a glass on Dr. Liu's dresser, shattering it in the process. Damn! But what the hell? I pour champage over the broken glass.

Liu stumbles against the edge of the bed. "Get out!"

I pour some champage down the front of my pants. "Might as well get this lizard slicked up right now, ey Doc?" And then I take the cover off the ravioli and grab the plate.

He puts a foot on the bed—wants to jump over and get to the vid phone, maybe out the door. I leap up and head him off, force him into the corner. Throw the ravioli against his chest, hand over his mouth, rip the shirt, flick the belt open, tear his pants, reach in—gently, gently, gently.

22
Benito

Loiter in the hallway. I didn't know how to occupy myself any better than to stare at a vending machine's display vid for Fun Strings. The picture kept repeating itself in a three-minute loop. What did the passers-by think, though? A man with my build—lipo job or not—shouldn't even consider purchasing one. Neither should such a gentleman be ogling a vid of bronzed young fellas eighty years his junior.

A Cyber passed, pushing a service cart. I nodded to him, and he held up two fingers. That was Kodas' signal. A Cyber would never do that on his own.

Good god, did I have reservations about this! I had met Dr. Benjamin Liu a couple of times in the past. A very dignified man. Stern, but quite likable. In his own country, he held a raft of titles, including secretary general of the People's Republican Party. Which made him a powerful politician in the world's most populous country—a country that was notoriously conservative in its entertainment tastes. He was attending this conference as a member of the United Nations task force considering amendments to the Lunar Treaty and also as vice chair of the committee reviewing ICC TeleComp policies.

If Dr. Liu's usual pattern held true, he would be arriving in Fun City with a panel of learned and semihysterical "witnesses" who would reliably denounce any pleasure of the flesh or any technological innovation more advanced than the steam locomotive. Conference members could be counted on to nod politely as this traveling road show un-

148

folded. Then they would set such righteous rantings aside as so much theater. Ho-hum. Unless there were really substantive accusations made—damning facts, damning evidence.

I did not want this man Dr. Liu killed. Not even injured. Just frightened.

Cybers are rather docile—but that quality comes by virtue of their programming. Their mechanical bodies are capable of great strength. And Kodas was at the helm of one—Kodas, who did not strike me as the most stable of young men.

I heard voices down the hall, a Cyber announcing dinner, a confused Dr. Liu. Give them just a minute. I looked at my chrono. The service cart rattled.

Kodas had left the door partially open. I entered and closed it behind me. The Cyber had a hand over Dr. Liu's mouth, muffling his screams. Dr. Liu was on the floor, shirt torn open and pants around his ankles. Ravioli and marinara sauce everywhere. The Cyber was trying to do something with a champagne bottle, while the ambassador flailed at him, arms and legs.

"Cyber, stop!" I shouted, and I drew the particle generator that I had lifted from the ill-fated ICC man in that Philadelphia restaurant. "Stop, Cyber!" and I fired. If Kodas was paying attention, he evacuated after the first shout. I don't know what a blast of subatomic particles would have done to him. Perhaps nothing.

The air crackled. The Cyber teetered and fell dead, eyes blank.

Dr. Liu was breathing in great heaves. I found a Fun City bathrobe in a closet and handed it to him. He stood, eyes still bulging with horror. I sat in a chair, feeling sorry. This had been a mistake. Damn Kodas.

Dr. Liu struggled with his trousers, but they were shredded and hopelessly stained. He removed his shoes slowly, then his socks, and dropped the pants to the carpet. He stood and drew the bathrobe around himself, the ragged shirt still under there.

"Thank you," he said tersely. "Excuse me."

The shower ran for ten minutes. I sat motionless the entire time, the guilt bulbous in my throat and working its way down to my chest and spreading like . . . like a cancer. I had seen two men mangled horribly by razor bolos in Philadelphia, a third blown to pieces by bombs. And now this remarkable statesman raped, or nearly so. Could my meager plan really be worth this?

Dr. Liu returned to the room in the bathrobe, hair slicked back, a measured pace to his stride. He now had more composure than I. Perhaps I should take a shower too. I felt so unclean.

"I hold Funcitti Enterprises responsible for this," he said, anger controlled. "My name is Benjamin Liu. I suppose that you are an employee?"

Clearly, my mask had worked. He did not recognize me.

"No," I said. "I'm Agent Winslow."

"Agent?"

I showed him the rod I had used to disable the Cyber, pointing to the logo for the Interplanetary Commerce Commission, and returned it to my pocket.

"I can't say how sorry I am," I said. "Sometimes I can catch them faster than that."

"Sometimes?" he said. His horror returning. "Faster? How often does an incident like this occur?"

I shook my head sadly. "Oh, I haven't seen more than six or eight of 'em. This year anyway. My theory is that they're so heavily programmed for this . . . this lacivious behavior that when the slighest glitch happens—a short circuit or something?—then they turn into these sexual monsters." I shrugged. "But what do I know? I just write the reports and send 'em on up. Do what I'm told."

Dr. Liu went to the bar and opened a beer. His hand was shaking. The vanquished Cyber lay there in the marinara muck, limp hand on the champagne bottle, and staring at the ceiling.

"And you hunt these corrupt Cybers somehow?"

"Oh, it's not my job—"

"Sorry, would you like a beer? Wine?"

"Um, beer, thanks. It's not my *job* hunting them. I'm just a field agent, bottom of the heap. Typical of the ICC—assign a family man to Babylon. But I see a Cyber sometimes with an odd tick to it, funny mannerisms, and I try to keep an eye on it. This can happen over months, this degeneration, and I can't just go zapping every Cyber that I get a funny feeling about. The management here, you know, they've got a lot of friends in the ICC."

He handed me a beer. We were both drinking from the bottle, like old buddies around a campfire.

"Yes," he said, drifting into thought. "Friends in the ICC. Mr. Funcitti in particular, I would imagine. A very sociable man when politics demand it. Invited me to dinner—exquisite food, charming young girlfriend."

"Oh *really?*"

"Yes." He fell into thought again, and I wanted to hear about the young girlfriend. A Cyber, I supposed. But maybe not. It would take years for the other Benito Funcitti to replicate Elvis' sophistication. Surely Dr. Liu would recognize a common Fun City Cyber within moments, even one without the tattoos on its hands.

Dr. Liu stood with surprising enthusiasm. He went to the closet, selected a fresh pair of pants and drew them on, pulling them modestly up under his robe. Then he hung the robe and pulled out a flowered shirt.

"Maui silk," he said, smiling. "Ah yes!"

I had spent a few days training with Terry F1's people, and the code-slinger Laurence had given me a long dissertation on aloha shirts—materials, printing methods, designs, the significance of certain patterns. They came in varying degrees of formality—there were Hawaiian shirts appropriate for office wear on the islands, and there were those reserved for party time. Dr. Liu's shirt, I gathered—with its tiny flowers and muted coloring—would get a conservative rating on the aloha scale. I saluted Dr. Liu with a tilt of the beer bottle.

"You are aware, I suppose, of the symposium that starts

tomorrow," Dr. Liu said. "A symposium, an unofficial hearing, to air the issues of modifying the Lunar Treaty and to explore the morality of these TeleComp devices."

"Yes. Hard not to know, stationed up here," I said.

"Agent Winslow, I am one of the conference moderators. You must be my opening witness tomorrow," he said. "You must tell your story before all the media of the world, your story of the treachery of—how do you call it?—Babylon."

"I can't do that," I said quietly. "In that amphitheater they have in the conference center? Take the lectern down front and address a U.N. committee?"

"You would do fine," Dr. Liu said. "You will not be my only witness, just the best."

"I'd lose my job."

"As you know, Agent Winslow, the ICC operates at the behest of the United Nations," he said. "And I am a very influential member of that body. You will not lose your job. On the contrary—you might very likely find yourself promoted. That organization needs more men such as yourself. And it seems to me that it is on the verge of a management shakeup."

"Okay, I will testify on one condition," I said. "You must not tell anyone about me in advance. *No one*. Just let me walk on. Um, I am particularly concerned about my family. Down on Earth. The little ones are in bed now. I want time to explain to them why their Daddy is appearing on interplanetary television."

"Good. Then you will report to my offices on the conference perimeter at 9 A.M.," Dr. Liu said. "And we will have this dead Cyber to display as evidence. That will be particularly impressive to the vid media."

That would present big problems, I told myself. Operating or not, that Cyber could be found very quickly by sensors.

"Dr. Liu, this might sound overly cautious to you, but Fun City operations might already know that that Cyber is missing," I said. "I would prefer that you let me dispose of it now—I know how to do it safely. There's a vast commercial empire at stake here. While *you* are at no risk,

I still have to make it through the night.''

Dr. Liu nodded, disappointed at having to give up his dramatic prop for the conference opening.

"If you say so," he said. "But you, Agent Winslow, are going to set the world abuzz.''

I couldn't sleep. I stared at the dark ceiling, a reluctant economy-rate guest in the resort I had built. The pricey rooms faced into the Bubble. We were on the Moonscape side of the hotel, and our picture window had obediently darkened with the late hours to simulate nightfall. Real nightfall on the Moon was yet a few days away, but lighting cues throughout the complex preserved the twenty-four-hour day of Earth. An air processor vent rimming the view blew a lazy draft across us, creating the illusion of an open window.

Funny how much of planning a resort involves perpetuating lies.

Elvis was behaving strangely, and, as I often do, I attempted in vain to trace back to whatever snippet of programming might be responsible for this. Perhaps you can never really love another being until you *don't* know what makes her tick. Hmm. *That's* one I would not want to have to try to explain to the U.N. or to a psychiatrist.

Elvis would not leave me alone.

"You are not aroused," she said.

"I was aroused half an hour ago.''

And her lips were meandering around my navel, and then down, and then up to my neck. She propped herself above me, her breasts barely brushing me, like the faintest stroke of butterfly wings.

"On the beach today, there was a young man who seemed to find me arousing," she said. I was being goaded.

"Really? What were you wearing?''

"Well, I walked the whole perimeter of Lake Galileo— through the cool zones, the warm zones, and the hot zones. And basically I wore what was required of me in each area.''

"Elvis!''

"Do you mean 'Elvis, quit kissing the inside of my thigh,' or 'Elvis, don't be exposin' yourself in public like I was doin' today?' "

"Um, neither, I suppose," I replied. "So you mapped the beach thoroughly? And slotted a copy to Terry F1?"

"Of course," Elvis answered. "Much better than the tourist brochure. I noted all of the out buildings along the beach in relation to the maintenance wells and security stations."

"And so you were walking about topless or bottomless in some hot zone," I said, "and some buck with a poker in his pants decides he wants to get to know you."

Elvis nodded playfully. "He said to me,'Scuse me, but are you a Cyber?' And I said, 'Yes I am.' An' he said, 'Well, I want you to sit on my face!' "

I propped myself up on my elbows. "Elvis, tell me that you didn't."

"I tole him, 'Ah'm considering an adjustment to your spinal column that will allow you to sit on your *own* face.' "

I laughed.

"He seemed genuinely shocked," Elvis said.

"I imagine that he was," I said. "The guests here are accustomed to compliant Cybers."

"Hmm. Maybe I shoulda been mo' compliant."

Elvis went back to work down there.

"What happens to you when I am gone?" I said.

She replied, but she did not interrupt her efforts: "I think Terry F1 would keep me on. I could work for her, save money, move on into my own enterprises, maybe. But I would stay underground—less dangerous for me. More room to maneuvre."

"You would not go to the other Benito Funcitti?"

"We have no need for each other. *Need.*"

"I don't know what will happen tomorrow," I said.

"You could have said that any night of your life." Elvis thought a moment. "Do ya really think this mask of yours is necessary now? And tryin' to fool Dr. Liu—all this deceit?"

Elvis had a hard time comprehending some of these human matters.

"The problem is that I can't totally trust Dr. Liu," I said. "*My* goal is to step in front of the live cameras, and as long as Dr. Liu thinks I'm just a pretty good witness, he will arrange that for me. But if he found out beforehand that I was Funcitti's *double*, well—you see, Liu and Funcitti have this messy love-hate relationship. If Dr. Liu had *all* of the information, he might start wheeling and dealing—tip my cards early, maybe even to Funcitti. A businessman you can predict, but not a politician."

"And once you've had your say in front of the cameras?"

"Maybe I'll be shipped straight off to the slaughter house," I said. "*This man should never have remained alive*. Blip, gone."

"Maybe they'll award you half of Funcitti Enterprises," Elvis countered.

"Not likely, considering the legal arguments involved. More likely, they'll award me a tin cup, a milk crate to sit on, and a dorm slot off South Street."

"You sure I can't go with you to the conference center tomorrow?"

"You know as much as I do about security in this place. The alarms would light up like Disney fireworks."

"Umm," Elvis said. "Now you're aroused."

"Yeah. Now I'm aroused."

23
Laurence

The second time seemed easier.

Kodas and Doc and I caught a sub-level 1 tram car out of the lobby complex just as the Bubble's huge lights were firing up to simulate daybreak. The day-night cycle was timed to approximate Central Time in the United States—a comfortable median time that would accommodate perhaps thirty-five percent of Fun City's visitors without a serious resetting of their body clocks. I was thankful for the artifice, I think, because a body beset by low gravity and diet changes needs all of the stability it can get.

Kodas and I rigged up our communicators—hooked our microphones to the back teeth and pressed the doughy receiver nubs into our ears. Then we popped in our contact lenses—the new Mesa Verde rigs, similar to what the Navajos have been putting into their camera equipment. The reiterant optics allow up to 50K mags, and there's a secondary monitor windowed out of your vision for remote feeds, playbacks, and that kind of stuff. Past that, I don't pretend to understand the technology—it's just all photonic voodoo, if you ask me.

The two of us wore all-white uniforms, just as we had done the day before. But Doc was costumed, quite out of character, in a filmy beach tunic. In theory, she wore a swim suit underneath, but Doc allowed not a glimpse. I wondered if she had ever even been to a public beach. She was in a ragged mood, just staring out the window, hypnotized by the irregular rock wall flashing by.

There was no one else on our tram car, so we whooshed past the first two stops and got off on the fibreboard decking of the little-used third station. Benito Funcitti had directed us well. It was one stop short of the popular beach stations and a stop beyond the gaming pavilions. The only traffic here, Funcitti had assured us, came late in the day—tired hikers getting *on* the tram, saving themselves the last mile's walk before returning to the hotel. It was too early for anyone to be tired out yet.

Doc took in the brightening sky with a sullen sweep of the eyes—maybe it was sleepiness.

"What's the matter?" I asked.

She shrugged, followed Kodas up the steps. The tram disappeared in a cordite rumble.

We retraced our route of the day before—over a small hill and into the sparse forest, up and around a few winds of the pebbled path, and then through a narrow unmarked gap in the border shrubbery. Kodas had his shoulder pack, I had my case. Thirty feet into the woods, hidden by a ridge of lunar boulder, was one of the access wells to the maintenance levels.

Doc put one boot against the trunk of a maple, grabbed a low branch, and walked herself up into the tree. When she had settled into her lookout perch, she set her throat mike by its anchors between her right cheek and back teeth. She set her earpiece, daubed in her contact lenses, then started fiddling with her razor bolo cartridges, careful not to cut herself. She cleared her throat, letting the little thread-like transmitter settle into place, and the sound gurgled in my earpiece.

When Doc's equipment came alive, the small monitor in the lower left of my vision blinked on with a live transmission from Doc's perspective. Likewise, Doc could receive into her monitor from my point of view, or she could toggle over to Kodas and check out what he's up to.

"Be real careful, guys," Doc murmured. "And listen close when I get on the air. This is like doing—this *is* doing—the same job two days in a row, an' I don't like the feeling of that.''

"I think that's rule number twenty-one," Kodas mumbled. "Don't do the same job two days in a row."

"Call it number twenty-four," Doc replied wearily, clearly not in the mood for banter. "Breaking *this* rule is asking for green cream."

Kodas stopped amid a scattering of knee-high azalea bushes and looked back at me.

"You talking like that, Doc, just when Mr. Essex here is walking with a little hop in his step," he said. He nodded approval. "Much better today, Laurence. Like ya know what ya doing. Like maybe you're going down to inspect pressure gauges on the river pumps—how's that for a cover story?"

"Actually," I replied, patting my case, "I'd rather pass myself off as a tree surgeon. Tools of the trade in here, we could tell them—saws, and syringes and sample beakers and whatnot."

"I like pressure gauge inspector better," Kodas said. "What would a tree surgeon be doing wandering around down in the maintenance tunnel?"

Beyond the boulder, a staircase of Moon rock spiraled down. I checked the little monitor image transmitted by Doc and watched our two little figures descending into a hole. I couldn't help it—I waved good-bye to Doc and, therefore, to myself. When we stepped into the maintenance tunnel at the bottom, a three-wheeled cart hummed close.

"Steady," Kodas said, "don't panic."

The car stopped. The driver wore an ill-fitting orange jumpsuit and had several days' growth of beard.

"You the tree surgeon?" the young man asked me.

"Tree surgeon?" I asked.

"Yeah, for the damned maple roots getting into the conduits," he said. "I been waiting for the tree surgeon—I know most of the bad spots."

"Sorry," I said, "I'm troubleshooting a pressure gauge problem." Kodas and I exchanged glances.

The maintenance man peered at my face. "Your eyes," he said, "both of ya. . . ."

"New equipment," Kodas volunteered quickly. "Spectographics, you know. Saves us a lot of time in locating weakened metal."

The frustrated maintenance guy buzzed off, mumbling something about the parentage of whoever decided on maples, and Kodas and I found the door to the Cyber control pod. Kodas keyed us right through this time, with the optic-lock sequence stored in his little box. We closed the door behind us and set about our methodical tapping-in process. Few words. Just the near-rhythmic whumping of cases, cracking of floor segments, the rip of electrical tape and whir of equipment. Kodas was right—I was much more comfortable this time.

"Think you guys could make any more noise in there? Crissake, I can hear ya almost without the monitor."

At the sound of the voice I dropped the cable spool that I was unwinding. Kodas wore a pained look, shook his head, two fingers pressed to the bridge of his nose.

Ah. It had been Doc, of course. The sound comes through unnaturally loud, as if the person speaking were just behind you and a little to the right.

"Well, *you're* used to this stuff!" I said to Kodas.

"What!" That was Doc again.

"I was talking to Kodas."

"Okay then," said Doc's disembodied voice, "let's just settle down and not use any more words than you have to."

"Oh, yeah," I said.

"Don't worry 'bout the tunnel rat," Kodas said to Doc. "We sent him buzzing toward the hotel on maintenance level 1."

I went back to work.

I had my tuber patched in before Kodas was done—his head was buried under the flooring where he had removed a tile with the suction bracket.

"Find me a security Cyber," came Kodas' muffled voice.

"How am I supposed to differentiate security from hotel staff?"

Kodas' body went rigid, and I sensed anger. He stopped his work and slowly, with forced patience, pushed himself out of the square hole in the floor. He propped his chin on a fist.

"Work it out," Kodas said. "You know the Cyber we tapped yesterday was coded beige on the holo chart there. So maybe all the hotel service guys are coded one color, an' maybe the security Cybers are another. Go through those clipboards, make a good guess. You see those beige guys—" he pointed "—they're crisscrossing all over the hotel, prolly with their food carts and shining shoes and who knows what. Now, you see some other color—what is that—they're all clustered around the conference center? Not many of them in motion, eya?"

"Violet," I said, feeling stupid. "There're a lot of violet dots all around the conference center."

Kodas sighed, disgusted, and worked his large torso back under the floor. "Okay," he said, muffled under there. "Find me a goddamned violet Cyber and dilly open his CyberGo for me."

I studied the hologram layout of the hotel for a few minutes, concentrating on the violet, numbered dots. The theory made sense—most of them, by comparison, moved about little, as if standing sentry at their assigned points around the conference center. I watched for signs of authority among the security Cybers—the rare few that ranked highly enough to move freely throughout the confines of the conference center, despite the fact that dignitaries from the major nations of the world were converging there. Mmm. Number nine seemed a good choice. I tapped at my tuber and started the sequence for penetrating Number nine's operational system.

Two raps sounded at the door, and the shock of it reverberated up and down my bones like lightning. No sign of sluggishness this time, Kodas was out of the floor in a flash. Our gazes were locked immediately, and I saw the dark skin around his eyes grow taut. Wary. And weary.

He smiled weakly and shrugged, dubiously inspired. He called out, "Who *iiiis* it?" It was a playful voice. Kodas was on his feet then, covering the hole in the floor and silently rearranging our equipment. He waved me toward the door, urgently, for some reason fiddling with the lashings of his uniform.

"It's me," came a male voice from beyond the door. It sounded like the maintenance man, the fellow with the three-wheeled cart. "What y'all doing in there? These offices're restricted."

In my monitor, I could see the ground surging upward as Doc leaped out of her tree. Then she was sprinting for the stair well. I pressed the latch pad on the door and it whirred open. Yes, it was the maintenance guy, his bristly jaw hanging open in a redneck gawk. He was trying to look around me into the cubicle.

"I told you," I said, "we had some problems to check out down here."

"You said pressure guages," he drawled. "None of that in here."

"Oh, there's *one* anyway," said Kodas behind me, "a special one."

Then I turned. The maintenance guy stepped in, and there was Kodas splayed out in the swivel chair. His white pants were down around his ankles and his penis, incredibly, was at rigid attention.

"Oh, *gawd*," said our guest. "You fellas aren't Security. You're really from—" He faltered here, and I feared unreasonably that he might have had an astounding revelation of the truth. "You're kitchen help, aren't ya? The kitchen help I keep hearing about but never believed. Damn!"

"Um, Kodas," I said, "guess we should go. And put that away, okay?"

"This is the Moon, Laurence—we don't have to hide anything here."

"*That* you may hide. Kodas, he's going to think—"

"Don't matter *what* I think," the maintenance man said,

"except that I think you're getting outta here now."

Kodas shrugged and stood up, lashed his clothes back together. I was at a loss as to what to do. I wanted to retrieve my case from under the counter, but Kodas gave me a stern little shake of the head. So I smiled, pathetically, at our accuser until Kodas was ready to go.

The maintenance man turned, stumbled, and collapsed into a twitching pile on the floor. Doc stood in the hallway holding the dart gun she had just shot him with.

"Just a neural stun," Doc said. "He'll wake up in a couple of hours. In pain, but he'll wake up." She shook her head. "Kodas, you'll take any opportunity to drop trow, won't ya?"

"It really wasn't necessary," I added.

"Sure it was," Kodas replied, hurt. "Suppose he'd gotten away. He'd be so distracted by what he *thought* we were doing that he'd never suspect our real mission. Hey, Doc, did ya hear? Laurence's afraid someone will mistake him for a carnivore."

Doc, still shaking her head, returned her little dart gun to a hidden holster under her beach tunic. "I don't know what the fuss's about," she mumbled. "Neither one of ya's anything but a technosexual. Ya'll and Benito, too. Damn!"

Kodas dragged the stiff tunnel worker into the pod with us. Doc and I watched him gag and bind him with tape.

"Thought I'd get to see you use a razor bolo," I told her.

Doc nodded. "Woulda done the job, ya, but I tend to save them for a movin' target, or someone with a weapon ready," she said. "A neural dart'll do if you're sure of the shot. No need to kill unless it's necessary—that'll serve ya better in the long run."

"I'll try to remember."

Doc checked her chrono. "It's just past nine. Let's get back to it, guys," she said, heading down the hall. "Risk factor rises with every contact. Someone'll be missing your friend there damn soon. An' you've got a lot of work left to do."

When Kodas had his nose gear hooked up he took the swivel chair and fell into his meditative state.

I poked softly at my tuber.

"Here's a lead line for you," I whispered. "Be quick about it—and stick to the plan. Get into the conference center and do something supremely embarrassing. We got interplanetary vids rolling now."

Kodas had his head tilted over the back of the chair, his wide throat bobbing up like a stretch of fleshy sewer pipe. He gurgled, snore-like, breathing around all of the hardware set into his nostrils. Limp and wired up—I imagined Kodas to be some kind of monstrous marionette. Sweat beaded up across his brow. His arms and legs began to shake with odd spasms.

On the holo chart, number nine froze momentarily and then began to move again on a new course.

"Trouble, guys."

That was Doc again, broadcasting straight up my spine, it sounded like.

"What is it?" I whispered. "We're a long way from done."

"Look at this," she said, sounding tired, and I saw the shaky image on the monitor as Doc started to scramble again. "Three people, all in security 'forms," Doc replied. "Headed straight for the maintenance well. It's a little more than I can handle straight away, but I'll tag along and hope for a better vantage. I suggest that you two stay absolutely quiet."

"Maybe they already know where we are—alarms or something," I said, "or the tunnel rat radioed in before he came to the door."

"Quiet." Doc sounded stern.

On the holo chart, the violet circle number nine moved determinedly toward the main conference chamber.

"Kodas is right in the middle of his run," I told Doc, "and he's sort of snoring."

"Shut *up!* You're panicking, and that won't help a thing."

I heard scraping footsteps echoing in the tunnel outside. At the sound, I swung my head and a little shower of sweat fell to the floor.

I tapped Kodas carefully on the shoulder, and he came around, moaning. I put a hand over his mouth and pointed toward the door.

"Better give up the mission, fellas," came Doc's voice. "There's two of 'em outside your door, and the third went up a ladder and overhead on a catwalk or something." The picture we were receiving from her had switched over to infrared in the low light, and the blurry image was useless.

Kodas muttered and stood up, groggy. He unclipped his nose jack and started sliding equipment across the floor toward the hole where he had been working.

Above us, I heard the ping-ping-ping of someone trotting across a metal structure.

Kodas had his head buried under the floor tiles, working furiously down there.

A rap sounded at the door.

"Open, please. Security."

Above us, I saw a square of the ceiling being lifted away, and there stood a grim security officer aiming her gum pump at my face.

Kodas had replaced the floor tile again. He smiled wearily, crouched low. "Go ahead, Laurence. Open the door."

I pulled at the knob. When the door had cracked open five inches, Kodas whirled his right arm and a razor bolo flew through the gap like the blade of a circular saw set free.

A pained gurgle sounded on the other side of the door, and the officer above us fired her gum gun—a dull *thonk*, sounding like a firecracker exploding inside a beer bottle.

Kodas screamed as a sticky blanket of green film pounded him to the floor. His arms gyrated, desperately trying to scrape the acid from his face. His heels hammered at the floor tiles. A hissing cloud formed over his upper body, and within a few seconds the big man relaxed and lay back into the mist.

The rest I recall only vaguely, through a thick sepia numbness. The guard above crashing through the ceiling, cross-slashed by another razor bolo. Then Doc shouldering through the door, weapons at ready. She glanced mournfully over what remained of her partner Kodas. She rattled a coiled bolo in my direction.

"Out the way we came," she said.

"He's dead," I said lamely. "Kodas is dead."

"He's dead, and we're outta here."

I found my case open under the counter. It was empty.

"Where's Blanche?" I asked. "Kodas was shoving all our equipment around, trying to hide some of it under the floor."

"To hell with Blanche." Doc shoved me toward the door.

"No—"

She held up her bolo menacingly. "I will not leave you behind alive," she said. "And we don't have a spare second."

I stared into her steel eyes and reminded myself that this young woman was not a first-time adventurer like myself. This is the way life is for her—sometimes you slash, sometimes you get slashed, sometimes your closest friend gets sizzled.

And then I began to cry.

24
Therese

Benito had reserved a seat in the press gallery for me—take it or go to the beach again, he really didn't care. I figured what the hell. Opening day of the symposium. Maybe I'd learn a little about interplanetary politics. One less story I'd have to read in the newsfaxes piling up when I got home from vacation. And I would be able to get an idea of what's been winding up Benito's rubber band.

The conference room was enclosed in a clear dome, half inside the Bubble, with a nice view of the lake, and half on the Moonscape side of the hotel. The main meeting area of the center offered plush seating for up to 250 people, depending on how the floor segments were arranged on the complex system of hydraulics. But my seat was up in the press gallery, a glassed-off rim of raised seating along the moonscape side of the room. The gallery had its own entrance, its own security Cybers, its own restrooms and refreshment counter. No press person could directly enter the main conference room—security was that strict. A reporter would have to backtrack to the public hallways, then attempt to re-enter through a separate set of security checks—which no reporter would clear anyway.

My seat was supposed to be at the far end of the room from the entrance. A reporter was slouched in virtually every lounger down the row, lazily pecking at the tubers built into the arm rests of the seats. Some of the preliminaries were under way in the meeting room below us—a gaseous introduction or two, I imagine—but there seemed to have been little to excite them so far. There was a loudspeaker inside the press gallery, but it was turned off—the reporters were depending on Timbrel ear receivers to follow the proceedings. From the tubers, they could file stories or communicate with any other computer user in the room—conduct interviews, research, tell dirty jokes, whatever.

There was a woman in my seat. She had bleached hair and wore cream-colored bib overalls over a wildly colored leotard. She's trying to look like a reporter, I told myself.

She turned her beaklike nose in my direction. A cassette was clipped to the front of her overalls, and its wires ran down the front of her leotard—to Sentia terminals, probably.

"I think that's my seat," I said.

She looked me up and down, expressionless.

"The gallery's for working press," she said. "My name's Elaine Nam, from Forbes. You working press?"

Cream. I had the feeling that I had blundered into a closed clique, that all these people knew one another.

"Not really," I said. "And, look, I can see that you would want to use the tuber—I don't need it. I can sit anywhere, but I do want to hear."

Nam shrugged and pointed her chin toward the Timbrel dispenser mounted to the wall. I pulled a little case out of the slot, tore open the packet inside, smeared the goo into my ears, and turned the volume control on the case up to a low murmur. Most of the conference members were applauding politely for someone who had just been introduced.

Down by one of the exit doors some of the standing onlookers started shifting about. I caught a glimpse of Benito down there shaking hands. And then an Asian man emerged, smiling and bounding up the steps two at a time. It was Dr. Benjamin Liu, the old guy we'd had dinner with.

Nam rolled her eyes. "The leadoff speaker—you believe it? I've heard him testify before the U.N. five times, the ICC at least that many. Any world forum that will let him put his sideshow of hypermoralists on the stand—"

"He's actually kind of a cute old man," I said. "Get

him away from the microphones and cameras and he loosens
up. I actually saw him kill most of a bottle of wine over
dinner.''

Nam narrowed her eyes. "Okay, you're not working
press, but you can get past security anyway," she said.
"And you run with a crowd that would put you at Dr. Loo-
Loo's table. So who are you in bed with?''

"Beg pardon?''

"A colloquialism," Nam said. "*In bed with:* literally,
to have a sexual relationship with; more loosely, to have a
close, influential relationship with. So . . . who are you in
bed with?''

What the hell? "Benito Funcitti," I said. "Um, loosely.''

Nam's lips drew together in a circle. She seemed to believe me, and was impressed.

"Well," she said, "want your chair now?''

I laughed. "No—really. But I do want to listen to Dr.
Liu.''

"It'll be the same old dreck, I tell ya. I've heard it over
and over. Tell ya the truth, I'm surprised Funcitti would
put Dr. Liu at the mike first off—this won't be totally
complimentary, ya know.''

"The subtleties of politics, I guess," I said. "Be gra-
cious, give your enemy his best shot—and give it early, so
there'd be plenty of time for people to forget. Besides, I
think Benito actually likes Dr. Liu in a way. From listening
to them at dinner.''

Dr. Liu grasped each side of the lectern firmly and cleared
his throat. Two nervous-looking technicians approached
him, admonishing that he would want to have the speed of
the invisible LexTex screen adjusted before he began.

"No, thank you," he mumbled. "Turn it off. I have
dispensed with my prepared comments.''

The remark was not meant for the audience, but a surprised murmur rolled across the little auditorium. Dr. Liu's
deliveries were always carefully orchestrated, and never,
never off-the-cuff. Nam sat forward in her chair, frowning.

"The last several hours have been long ones," Dr. Liu

said. "And while they have been very painful ones for me, they also have been equally rewarding for the information that they have brought to light. When I first set foot in this . . . this emporium called Fun City, I had come in the company of, and had intended to have witness for me today, a number of colleagues with whom many of you are familiar—Raskin Drumflower, Margaret Haig, Dr. Ola Ellison. . . ."

Nam scratched her substantial nose and groaned at the prospect of those witnesses.

". . . But I beg their forgiveness in that I have decided to forego their observations today, at least for this morning's session. I do this because I have yet another guest to present, this one unfamiliar to all of you. His name is Winslow, and he is an agent, believe it or not, of the Interplanetary Commerce Commission. While his appearance here today will not please his superiors, history will determine that he is a hero of—"

A man—one of the technicians, I think—materialized at Dr. Liu's side, waving hands and whispering in his ear. The technician pointed toward the door where Dr. Liu had entered. Benito had disappeared, but there was a small crowd of security Cybers and human officers bustling about.

"Preposterous—" Dr. Liu was saying when his mike went dead. He pounded on the lectern and made another statement to the audience, but he was then mouthing soundless words. Dignitaries in the conference chamber exchanged puzzled looks. Dr. Liu struck the lectern again, nearly tipping it over, and marched off toward the exit.

Nam turned to me. "Looks like Dr. Liu's tootin' steam in his pants," she said. "An' I'll bet your boyfriend Funcitti knows why. Not-exactly-subtle politics."

I looked at her, then at Dr. Liu shoving his way through the exit, then at the baffled audience beginning to stand. I wanted to deny it, but I couldn't think of any words that would sound convincing.

25
Benito

The mask was beginning to itch.

Biologically, the material may have been living and breathing, my own bio-duplicated flesh. That was an enormous help in giving the mask that natural look. But still it formed a stultifying casing over my face and neck. Moist under here.

I had dressed to be inconspicuous—tourist attire: white Bahamian cotton shirt, rumpled khaki pants, and comfortable but expensive multi-colored moccasins. A vacationing mope with spritzy red hair and a bulbous nose.

Outside the guest offices on the perimeter of the conference area, security seemed to be fairly light. This, I imagined, would be a deceptive appearance. It would be quite a trick getting through the layers of inner security. My insider's knowledge did not guarantee that I would make it through this ruse alive. Even under normal circumstances the security arrangements in the sensitive areas of Fun City were updated nearly every week—sometimes switched around merely to be unpredictable. But for a conference that would decide the future of this lunar resort, my double—the "official" Benito Funcitti—would demand especially laborious screening.

At a few minutes to 9 A.M. I approached the lone security Cyber. In my right pants pocket I fingered the SAP generator—the little subatomic particle weapon that I had pilfered from the ICC. Next to it was the stun rod designed for use on humans. They were the reason that I wore the loose trousers.

The Cyber was an L6 series model, with an angular face vaguely styled after a rock singer who had not had much success in recent months. Last year's model.

"Welcome to the conference center temporary offices," the Cyber said. "How may I help you?"

"The name is Winslow," I said. "Dr. Liu is expecting me."

The Cyber examined me stiffly, absorbing my exact hair, skin and eye color, height, speech patterns, odor and several other criteria. He would be comparing this data with whatever description Dr. Liu had provided. The Cyber did not request a DNA scan—further in, they very well might.

"Yes, you are expected," he said. "Dr. Liu's suite is just thirty-six meters down this corridor. The illuminated path will direct you there."

The floor was a mosaic of gray tiles, and a narrow row of them was now glowing cobalt blue, forming a path that disappeared around the corner. There was something more to this arrangement, I recalled, some other security precaution. I was accustomed to being exempt from security constrictions.

"Please do not stray from the path," the Cyber reminded me. "Alarms will sound, and that will be needless inconvenience for all parties involved." Ah, yes.

Dr. Liu was seated in his office at the back of his suite. It was a room shaped like a slice of pie—triangular, with one rounded side. Dr. Liu was flipping through his messages on the screen of a modest tuber—his own, I assumed. These rooms were furnished with much more powerful equipment, but apparently he only trusted his own circuits.

The curving wall to his back was draped with two sheets. Hmm. There should have been some sort of classic mural on that wall.

Dr. Liu caught me staring. He smiled and pushed his tuber aside. He appeared fresh and alert, totally recovered from the previous evening's ordeal. He wore a crisp white shirt and a simple suit—finely tailored, surely, but unprepossessing.

"There is a painting under the shroud," he acknowledged, "one that is not, ah, in keeping with my sense of aesthetics. I was a little surprised to find that I was assigned to an office with such a thing mounted on the wall." He shrugged. "But I am only here for a day or two. Hardly worth bothering the management to have it removed."

"Something obscene?" I asked.

"I would call it primitive," Dr. Liu said. "A rather orgiastic abstract by Paul Klee."

I clicked my tongue against the roof of my mouth. The piece, if I remembered correctly, was roughly 150 years old. Swiss. A tangle of playful lines and pigment with the occasional absurdly prominent body part.

"Sounds nasty," I said. "Surprised you could contain yourself."

He laughed and motioned for me to take a chair. "What I can cope with myself and what I believe to be healthy for society at large are two different things," he said. "But, to be frank, I mainly covered it because of the vids. It would not do to give an office interview and have for a backdrop some twentieth century Kamasutra. Can you imagine? Those pictures would make it into the image libraries and would haunt me for decades. Assuming I have decades left to be concerned about such things."

I was sweating now, imagining my mask sliding off of my face and into my lap. I folded my hands.

"So. I'm here now," I said. "What do I do? When do I testify?"

He checked his chrono. "Oh, quite soon," he said. "Are you nervous—appearing live on the interplanetary vids, and all that?"

"I haven't even allowed myself to think that far," I answered. It was an easy lie. My very life, tenuous as it may be, depended on pleading to the interplanetary community. "I suppose my worries are more immediate—such as, how am I going to get into the conference room anyway?''

Liu frowned. ''As an ICC agent, surely you would not have any trouble clearing Fun City's security checks.''

For that point, I hardly had to fib: ''Well, a DNA scan would recognize me, all right. But I'm not assigned to the conference, so I would set off alarms just for being out of place—like any other interloper.''

''Ah,'' Dr. Liu said. He thought a moment and punched a pre-programmed button on his vidphone.

''Feldman,'' he said to the man who appeared on the screen, ''please contact that, uh—what's her name?—Dix Mattern? The secret service woman for the U.N. Ask her to come down immediately. We have a special escort situation for her to finesse.''

Dr. Liu punched another button and the screen went blank. Then he clapped his hands together and grinned.

Dix Mattern was a slight Haitian woman with a shaved head and an easy manner. She glided along a maroon path in the floor of the winding corridor. Her oversized flower-print shirt billowed in her wake.

She had arrived at Dr. Liu's office in just minutes, and quickly agreed to run interference for us. This was an unusual bit of cooperation. I wondered if I was going to be told the full story.

''What did you do to merit this kind of response, get her whole family U.N. jobs?'' I murmured to Dr. Liu as we trailed behind her.

Dr. Liu looked hurt. ''Banish the thought!'' And then he smiled. ''Um, but I seem to remember something about my organization paying her way through college. It never hurts, you know, to have devoted people in areas of influence wherever you might need them.''

''Who might you have in the ICC?''

He smiled again. ''For one, I have you, Agent Winslow.''

The corridor broadened, and at an intersection we came to fortified doors and a glassed-off security office. Two

Cybers stood sentry on either side of the doors, and two white-uniformed humans milled about in the office.

Mattern gave a perfunctory wave to the Cybers and mumbled into a speaker diaphragm set into the glass. One of the human security guards nodded gruffly and the doors opened. Mattern turned back toward me and flashed a smile. Her shirt lifted a few inches, and I saw a bulky holster lashed to her torso.

She pointed to the floor. "Our new path is green, now, okay?" she said. As with the other paths, the illuminated strip stretched several yards in front of us; behind us, it had vanished. Backtracking not permitted.

This part of the building was a virtual thoroughfare—there were now half a dozen colored paths illuminating the floor tiles. The red path, I seemed to remember, was reserved for highly-placed diplomats. Beige was for message-runners. What the orange and yellow signified, I could not recall.

There were no informational signs in this wing of Fun City. All a legitimate visitor had to do was follow the correct colored path, the theory went. Why put up signs, when they would only be of aid to people who were trying to go where they were not authorized?

The hallway was humming now with activity—clusters of overtailored dignitaries charging down the intersecting hallways, wheeled food tables clattering toward the lounges, and security men eyeing the growing crowd warily.

One of the Cybers from the last set of security doors had fallen in behind us, as if he were providing a private escort. I could tell by the jaw line that he was from the sophisticated L14 series of Cyber. He had been modified to present an exotic Middle Eastern look.

The next set of doors was much more imposing than the last. The booth window had that odd refraction peculiar to transparent ferroplex—the people inside looked like they were appearing on a poorly tuned holovid frame. There was no speaker diaphragm set into this window—why have a ferroplex shield that can withstand a directional grenade, only to weaken it with a diaphragm that could be punched through by a simple slam gun?

A sonic cone was projected from the ceiling for communication, a lavish accommodation that had been installed more to impress than because it was necessary. Mattern stepped up into the angled beam of "soft" laser and began to speak, gesturing with her hands. Inside the cone, all sound—every faint whisper—was picked up by the photonic receivers and reproduced by speakers on the other side of the wall. Outside of the cone, where we stood, we heard nothing.

I watched her soundless mouth dittering through its words in the stark light and wished I had the talent of reading lips. Her dark eyes rolled in my direction as she paused to listen to a response from within. She scowled, poked a thumb in my direction, and spoke again to the guard on the other side of the ferroplex.

I could feel the moist rings of sweat now in my armpits and crotch. Why hadn't I fitted these hallways with better ventilation?

Dix Mattern stepped out of the sonic cone and worked her jaw a couple of times, instinctively trying to clear her eustachian tubes. That accoustic difference creates the illusion of an air pressure change—a familiar sensation to anyone who's ever stepped through an air lock. Thus, a person stepping out of a sonic cone often tries to adjust for different air pressure.

"They want a DNA scan," Mattern said apologetically.

I felt a series of hot pinpricks sprouting across my scalp, front to back. By now, I imagined, my mask was afloat on perspiration. "Dr. Liu! You said—"

Dr. Liu looked mildly irritated with the whole scenario—me, Mattern, and security.

"I will make the scan," said a voice behind me.

I turned, and in a quick motion the olive-skinned Cyber, the one that had been following us, drew a scanning disk across the back of my hand.

Dr. Liu blanched. "Dix, we weren't supposed to—"

She frowned, helpless. "New regs, just this morning. I didn't think it would be necessary."

The Cyber would be absorbing my DNA code into his local memory, and seconds later would relay it to central data for analysis. He held my right hand in an unforgiving grip. The second he released me, I decided, I would put that hand into my trouser pocket, tilt the ICC pen up, and shower the Cyber with a destructive subatomic particles. A slain and sputtering Cyber might, I hoped, create a diversion that would buy a minute or two in which to flee. The pen would destroy any other electro/photonic system I could get within twenty feet of. But the "blood" security officers would present a problem. How would my little stun rod, the other ICC weapon, stand up against a gum gun? Elvis had estimated that it was good for two, maybe three thorough jolts. And even if I eluded the conference center's security, how would I get off of the Moon?

Ah, Elvis. How alone I was feeling.

The Cyber who scanned me went glassy-eyed, as if he had paused for thought, and then he casually raised his free hand, almost touching my chest. Two fingers were splayed open, out of sight of my companions. A sign.

"Kodas," I whispered.

A slight smile cracked the Cyber's lips.

"This guest will present no problem," the Cyber announced to our gathering. A guard behind the ferroplex nodded his agreement, and the doors whirred open. Kodas, I supposed, had inhabited this security Cyber, followed us down the corridor, and then found or manufactured an acceptable DNA reading to relay to data central in place of my own.

I dared one more whisper: "I think we have a clear shot into the conference room. You'll come along?" That, of course, would be Kodas' primary objective—to get this occupied Cyber in front of the live vid cameras and go berserk. That he might lend me assistance as well was strictly a secondary concern.

He shook his head and replied, "Stayed too long already.

Problems back at—'' His eyes went glassy again, and then he returned for four more words: "You're alone now. *Ciao*."

The Cyber began to teeter there in the hallway. I stepped through the security doors, motioning for the others to do the same.

"Something is wrong with that robot," Dr. Liu said. There was an edge of disgust in his voice.

I nodded somberly. "I've seen that one before," I told him in a confidential tone. "I told you that I try to keep an eye on the strange ones."

Mattern stared at me, and then back through the closing doors at the wobbling Cyber. She would have spent much more time around security Cybers than Dr. Liu, and she seemed to be developing suspicions.

I went through the motions of checking my chrono and said, "Dr. Liu, you are due on stage now, no?"

He nodded sharply and I saw his body harden into the frenetic evangelist that was familiar to me through the vids. He was metamorphosing into his public self.

Dix Mattern led us to a ramp that angled down into the shadows of an underlit, crowded waiting room. At the far end, past an army of bustling silhouettes, was a set of doors opening into the main conference amphitheater. The dark air was close with morning soap and aftershave. Someone was smoking a cigarette, despite the signs.

Dr. Liu looked about the room frowning. He seemed perplexed by the shoulder-to-shoulder crowd. "Stay here," Dr. Liu said to me, and I watched his back as he shouldered his way toward the doors—stopping here and there for quick handshakes with strangers.

When Dr. Liu was gone, a man tapped me on the shoulder. It was the one with the cigarette—a white-haired man about my height, from what I could make out. I moved uncomfortably close in the dim light. He had a mole on his upper lip and he was wearing one of my favorite suits. It was me.

Funcitti spoke first. Unnatural as it sounds, that's the way

I had begun to think of my "other" self—as Funcitti.

"We need to talk," he said.

"Um, I haven't really time," I replied. "My name is Winslow. With Dr. Liu? I'm supposed to testify any moment now."

Funcitti drew on his cigarette and shook his head. "It's really a fine mask you have," he said. "But that haircut—a man your age." He exhaled a stream of gray air and waved a hand toward a dark shape nearby. "Willard," he said, "pass the message to Dr. Liu that his witness has decided against testifying."

So my new looks were not fooling anyone.

"But I *am* going to testify," I protested. "Can't you see that it's already gone too far? Our little secret is going to come out one way or another."

The set of shoulders named Willard obediently moved through the crowd and pushed into the auditorium, where Dr. Liu's opening remarks could be heard. Others in the room pressed closer. These people were not casual observers, I was beginning to understand. They were not the coat holders, they were not the bean counters, they were not the second-banana bureaucrats intent on making their U.N. bosses look brilliant. These men had gathered here just for my arrival—a gang of bone-breakers recruited from the corporate goon pool, and perhaps a few musclers from the ICC. And my little weapons pilfered from the ICC were nearly powerless against them.

"Okay, you say we need to talk," I said. "I imagine all that you really need to do is kill me."

Funcitti belched lightly, and I smelled burgundy wine and garlic. (First thing in the morning? My, how some habits get out of control.) He put a firm hand on my elbow.

"Maybe, and maybe not," he said. "But we do need to get out of here, before Dr. Liu goes on a rampage."

We moved in a pack, me at the center of a mob of Funcitti's "blood" enforcers. Through an inconspicuous door, down a staircase, along an unfinished cinderstone hallway clotted with high-pressure pipes and conduits. We emerged in familiar territory—the corridors of the Fun City corporate offices. At the executive suite, we charged between the two security Cybers at the double doors without the slightest proof of clearance—at least that *I* could detect—and then past the rows of office staff work stations.

The main boardroom was outfitted for entertainment, with the bar rolled out of the wall and the push button hors d'ouvres menu at ready. Funcitti waved his passel of goons into the leather-lined luxury.

"Refreshment time, fellas," Funcitti said. "Let's call it a short workday. Willard, you stay sober. I might be needin' ya."

The door closed, and Funcitti and I were alone.

"I don't recognize any of those men," I said.

"Of course not," Funcitti replied. "I transferred all the old crew to Philadelphia. These are new hires."

We strolled down to his private office. All five holo monitors along the left wall were ablaze with images from Fun City security cameras—a habit I recalled from my recent past, but one which seemed obsessive in retrospect. Two monitors showed scenes from the conference center— a pale woman standing at the lectern on one, and part of the press gallery on the other. The three remaining monitors showed wide-angled scenes from the top of the Bubble— although any of them could zoom in close enough to count grains of sand on a sunbather's butt.

"You've been 'going for a walk,' haven't you?" I said.

"Prowling about electronically is a hard habit to break, as you would know," Funcitti said. He walked around to his desk and touched the holo controls, zooming the one monitor for a close-up of a woman's face in the press gallery. "She remind you of anyone?"

I shrugged. "She's a looker," I said. "Maybe a little familiar. A movie star? Am I supposed to know?"

"A new girlfriend. I used to think she looked like Elvis," Funcitti said. He pressed his lips together. "Now, I even lose track of what Elvis looked—*looks*—like."

"I suppose you're going to kill me now," I said, "then round Elvis up and pop the lid on her CyberGo?"

Funcitti chuckled. His hands fell away from the holo controls and he strolled to the opposite side of the office, where he punched a couple of pressure plates above the counter. A sink and mirror appeared.

"Your mask," he said. "It's looking awfully uncomfortable."

I sighed and approached the mirror—pulled that bulb of a nose off first, then the rest of the bio-duplicated flesh came away in ghastly pink strips. I left the shreds of skin on the counter and checked the mirror—my old, familiar face, save for that hairdo of red spikes and the tiny scar on my lip where that mole had been lasered away.

"Feel better now?" Funcitti asked.

I turned. "Yes."

"Good," he said. "So. First, let me apologize for the, um, forceful treatment this morning. Believe it or not, I've been trying to keep that kind of thing to a minimum since I . . . well, since I decided a few days ago that it was wiser to let you live. After a fashion."

"You're not trying to kill me any more? And the ICC agrees with this?"

He nodded. "Unfortunately, you went underground with such good effect that I could not communicate this to you. I supposed I would hear from you sooner or later, if only to find out you had passed away in some low-rent hospice. But arriving with an assault team on Fun City? Really. Their tampering with the Cybers—whatever that was supposed to achieve—has been a miserable failure, by the way. We're just now mopping things up."

"Oh, god," I said. "Anyone hurt?"

He nodded. "We'll know more shortly."

"And just what is it you have in mind for me now?" I asked.

"I've been knocking this around with the lawyers, and there won't be a problem. We'll ship you back Earthside, put you up in a suite at Sloan Kettering, under an assumed name, for the best cancer care available—outside of a TeleComp overhaul. Elvis can go with you, if you want. And you'll live whatever life is left to you with the best medical care there is.''

"Nevertheless, that would not be a very long life," I noted.

Funcitti frowned. "What more could you ask? I couldn't get you back onto a TeleComp even if I tried. There are physical limits here. Besides, you aren't in much of a position to bargain—I've agreed to leave you alone, *with* Elvis, crissake.''

"Something tells me you've been distracted away from thoughts of Elvis lately," I said, pointing to the young woman's close-up on the holo monitor.

Funcitti smiled.

"Anyway, there's more to be bargained here," I said, "more that you can do for me, and more that I can do for you.''

Funcitti's eyebrows rose, skeptical.

"You might not know, for instance, that someone has attempted to kill you recently," I said, "or at the very least ruin your position with the company. And I know who that person is.''

Funcitti's eyebrows rose higher. He lit a Winston. Then his vidphone chimed, and a man's face appeared on the screen.

"Willard," Funcitti said, "no interruptions."

"It's important sir. Scary. A problem with a couple of Cybers.''

Funcitti exhaled heavily, then punched the button that would make his face visible to the caller.

"Okay, what is it," Funcitti said.

"Those two security Cybers we just passed? Outside corporate? They're out of control," Willard said. "Can't budge 'em, can make 'em behave.''

"What is it that they're doing?" Funcitti asked, losing patience.

Willard stammered. "Well, they're both male Cybers, sir, right there at the reception desk—"

"Spit it out, dammit!"

"Mr. Funcitti, they're butt-fucking."

26
Laurence

Doc leapt up behind me and kicked me sharply in the rear.

"How do you manage to do that when we're both running?" I grumbled over my shoulder. It was barely louder than a whisper, even though no one was in sight.

"I can kick you like that, jelly-butt, because you ain't running near fast enough."

We had scrabbled up the stairs of the maintenance well after our catastrophe in the Cyber control room. At the top of the stairs I had paused to wipe the tears from my eyes when she dealt me the first kick to the hindquarters.

Dammit, Kodas was dead, *horribly* dead.

She whacked me once again as we dodged through the forest underbrush, and a third time just now, as we topped a ridge overlooking a lakeside beach.

Obediently, I increased my pace, churning through the sea grass and sand. But I huffed back at her: "Lady, you may be wirey, but don't forget that I have twice your mass. Just in case I decide to punt you up and down the waterfront a few times when this is done."

"Good," Doc replied. "Now you getting mad. You too stunned to be scared, but if you mad, you'll work up some Adrenalin anyway. Save you from getting your ass sizzled by Security—for a few more minutes, anyway."

I boosted Doc up onto the raised planking of a boardwalk that ran the perimeter of the tree line. From the higher vantage, we could see much of Lake Galileo's beach— nearly devoid of people. A mile or so to our right, someone was jogging along the wet sand bordering the lake. A little nearer, there was some kind of net game in play—volleyball, I supposed, only the net was entirely too high.

It was a typical early-morning, ocean-side scene. But there was something unnatural, disturbing. The lake was virtually flat—perhaps that was it. We had emerged from the forest into the open air and were met with the familiar low roar of a churning ocean. But there were no waves— no splash or crash of water to create the surf sounds we were hearing. Perhaps it was just the accoustics of the huge Bubble, as if we had just stepped into a giant conch shell whooshing in a child's ear.

"That beach building there," Doc said, interrupting my reverie. "We'll stop under that cover and make some fast decisions."

I sighed heavily.

"We can't rest here," she said.

"I've lost Blanche, Doc," I said. The tears were coming again. I know that it's easy for me to say in retrospect, but honestly—the tears were for Kodas, not Blanche at all.

Regardless, Doc kicked me in the butt again.

Just outside the entrance to the cabana was a vending machine with one of those repeating holovid advertisements for Fun Strings. Doc stopped suddenly, sand grinding against fiberboard.

"Buy one," Doc said, pointing to the machine.

"Forget it," I said. "I'd never wear one. And besides, we're in a terrible hurry."

The machine's vid was just starting its new cycle, launching into a gutsy theme song as a succession of strung-up pelvises paraded across the screen—an infantile appeal to the male ego.

"I don't have the francs on me," I protested.

But Doc had anticipated the need—she was holding out a fifty-note. "It's supposed to take change," she said. "And you will buy one, and you will wear it."

Inside the first door to the cabana a sign stated:

"WARM" ZONE:
PRIVATE CHANGING BOOTHS TO THE LEFT,
COED FACILITIES TO THE RIGHT

So I went left, and Doc yanked me right.

"You want me to put this thing on, right? To blend in or something," I said.

"Right," she replied, "and we're going to stick together, which means going coed. Besides, what's a technosexual got to be modest about anyway? I'm just a *woman*, crissake, not some sexy photometric grid."

The main coed room was arranged like an oversized sauna, with eight tiers of padded lounging surface reaching up to the ceiling. The padding of these surfaces had the alarming consistency of bed mattresses. What went on in this room during peak occupancy, I couldn't imagine.

Only one other person occupied the room—an attendant, from the looks of her uniform. She was stretched out on her back on the top tier with a folded towel across her face and wild red hair spiking out in all directions.

"Strip down," Doc ordered. "Fold up that Security uniform tightly and keep it under your arm. Better yet, wrap it up in a towel, if we can get one."

"Yo, towel?" said the attendant, sitting upright.

"She's not a Cyber, is she?" I noted.

Wild Red stood and bounded down the lounging tiers like a child bouncing on Mum and Daddy's bed.

"I've got towels for ya," she said, a study in opposing forces—seeming frenzied somehow, yet also hindered by a lolling and languid body. She slapped a press-plate on the opposite wall twice and two warm, white stretches of terry cloth emerged from the wall slot.

I wrapped one of the towels around my mid-section, let my pants and undershorts drop, then worked the Fun String up into place. When I removed the towel, Doc whistled.

"Don't know why you bothered with that modesty routine, Laurence," she said. "But now you's rigged and ready."

The Fun String was little more than a small pouch of sparkling blue fabric that held my private parts aloft, taut and trembling. A tiny elastic line ran around my waist and disappeared, much to my discomfort, into the valley between the cheeks of my bottom.

Doc pulled at two snaps of her tunic and flung it aside, playfully revealing a swimming suit of a crinkly rust-colored fabric. It was a one-piecer that managed to be nearly as immodest as my Fun String. She gave her hips a flirtatious shake and cracked a rare smile—trying to alleviate my embarrassment. Odd—I had always imagined Doc to be flat-chested and undernourished. Now . . . well, I had just never thought of her as being that busty, so well-muscled.

Doc turned her back to Wild Red and spread her towel out on the nearest bench. She pulled her dart gun out of the tunic and rolled the towel over it. Then she folded the tunic up against the towel, leaving a row of pockets exposed on the outside. There, she arranged her tosser disks and razor bolos.

Wild Red was not watching. She had turned her attention to me.

"Ya'll gonna hit the beach—maybe be needin' some pits?" she asked.

"Pits?" I said.

"Gutter buzz—cheap imitation of pharmaceuticals," said Doc, turning with the new bundle under her arm. "Downers that'll prolly leave skid marks on your cortex."

Red smiled. "C'mon," she said, "I'm on a test flight right now."

"Thank you," I said, "but no. We're in a hurry."

"Then I'd guess you folks ta be mist-heads," Wild Red said in a good-natured grumble. "Once they've had a taste of A-mist, ya can't keep 'em down on the pharms."

Doc rolled her eyes and jerked a thumb toward the beach-side door of the cabana.

"How 'bout a roll of Cyber stamps, then?" Wild Red asked. "You're looking for an amusing time—make 'em think you're a Cyber!"

Doc stopped at the door. "How's that?"

"Cyber stamps," Red said. "The FC logo they wears on the back of the hand. Make people think you're a Cyber, gets a lot of the sexual game-playing nonsense out of the way. Get right to the recreation."

"I would think another person would figure that out," I scoffed.

"Maybe not," Red countered. "Cybers are pretty sophisticated at playing the part—not only with the sex, but simulating human, um, frailties and all. And if the person you meet *does* figure it out, maybe they don't care—likely as not they'll play along anyway."

"How long will one of those last?" Doc asked.

Red shrugged. "Washes off with alcohol, or in the conditioning shower. But there's twenty to a roll."

"Let's have a roll, then," Doc said, fishing out a bill, "and we'll put them on now—one on each hand, is that right?"

"Right," said Red.

The volleyball game was in progress—actually, in perpetual motion—when we approached. Six Cybers batted the ball back and forth over a net more than thirty feet high. The ball never touched the sand, though, and after Doc and I watched for a few minutes we began to see that the maneuvers were repeating themselves—the setups, the spikes, the heroic dives. Without human involvement, though, the game lost its spontaneity. It was as programmed as the holovid ad on the Fun String vending machines.

"Would you like to play?" said a female Cyber who was not in the game. "I would be happy to explain the rules and strategies."

She stood near the net pole with her hands folded, apparently the official greeter. She brushed her hands together unnecessarily as if cleansing them of sand that was not there. I do not know what kind of "shifts" Cybers might work before they retire for rest or maintenance, but this one did not appear to have yet rolled on the beach. Her skin was tanned—tanned *looking,* I suppose—and heavily freckled. She wore a loose sleeveless T-shirt and, from what I could tell, no suit bottom. Watching her play volleyball would prove interesting.

"Laurence, I think we should play," said Doc, turning nervously. I followed her gaze to the tree line, where there was a bustle of uniformed figures.

"Maybe we ought to just take a run up the beach," I said.

"Kinda conspicuous, don't ya think?" Doc replied.

We laid our towel bundles on the sand and joined the game—Doc and I on one side with two Cybers, four Cybers on the other side. Doc served the ball, and the return sailed in my direction. I leapt, grossly misjudging the angle of the volleyball's descent. The ball plopped into the sand, and I soared out of control into the net. Damned low gravity.

Doc chuckled.

The Cybers patiently returned to their positions.

The Security team we had seen in the trees was now on the boardwalk, rounding the cabana. Were any of them watching our game? Clearly they would not mistake me for a Cyber—as long as I was playing volleyball.

I booted the ball back to Doc and approached the freckled Cyber near the net pole. Her hands were folded again, and she gave me a curious look.

"Why are you stopping?" she asked.

"I'm not very good at this," I replied. "You should play—I'll stand here and look official."

"But I don't know how this is done," she said, rolling her shoulders oddly—I supposed it was a shrug. "I was hoping to learn about the game from watching."

"Sorry," I said, "I thought you were the court supervisor or something—you had mentioned explaining the game to *us.* And surely you are programmed to play volleyball. Why else would you be here?"

"Indeed," she said. Her luscious green eyes had gone a bit glassy. "You are—you are *not* a—how did you call it? You are not a Cyber, are you?"

I showed her the logos on the backs of my hands. One of the security troopers was stepping off the boardwalk into the sand, coming in our direction.

"No," I admitted, "we just put these on, um, for fun. No harm intended. And I hope that the Fun City management will forgive us. But I really was hoping that you would join the volleyball game and make it look very professional, very Cyber-like."

"We."

"Excuse me?" This was maddening. I had not spoken with many of the Cybers in Fun City—just a few desk clerks and food service 'bots. But this one seemed to have a glitch in its language programming. Or it was just not very quick on the uptake. And now the entire Security team was off the boardwalk and mushing toward us through the sand, gum pumps at the ready.

"We," the Cyber repeated. "You said *we*. More specifically, you said, 'We just put these on, um, for fun.'"

"Oh, I mean Doc and I." I pointed to Doc, who had the ball under one arm, getting fidgety. It was all I could do not to bolt down the beach. But reason intervened—that would be sure death.

"Her name is Doc?" the Cyber asked. She was staring now at her hands as if discovering them for the first time. "Then what would your name be?"

"My name is Laurence Essex."

"Laurence," she whispered. She was staring at her feet now—a Cyber suffering from photonic meltdown, I supposed. She tugged absently at the bottom hem of her T-shirt and, indeed, she was not wearing anything underneath. "You left me somewhere. Explain all of this, please. What is this manifestation?"

"What do you mean?"

"It's me, Laurence. Blanche. How did I get here?"

"Blanche? *Blanche!* No, Kodas had Blanche in a—oh, my god—in a Cyber control center. He must have wired you into the network, under the floor panels. There was a lot of confusion—"

"Excuse me, Laurence. I have never had benefit of sharing a manifestation with you—"

"This is not just a photonic manifestation—it's the real thing, Blanche. Or as real as it gets. I think of it that way. What you see through the Cyber sensors is me, my flesh and blood."

"I have never had any sort of *body* before, and have never had independent means for this sort of visual examination. What I want to know is—" she smirked "—well, have you always dressed this way?"

She indicated my little scrap of clothing and giggled. This really must be Blanche, with her penchant for sexual humor.

Doc was suddenly at my side, having heard part of the conversation. I was stunned speechless.

"Forget that, Blanche," Doc commanded. "We need you to help us with something very quickly. The Security men approaching us on the beach are searching for Laurence and me, and they will probably try to kill us. But you are a Cyber—they will trust you."

"Give me a moment," Blanche said. "This is all so— so awkward. And confusing. I must sift through some of this Cyber programming." Her eyes closed and her face went rigid.

Doc tossed the volleyball back into the playing field. "Ya'll might as well get the game going again," she said, and the Cybers obediently arranged themselves into their original three-on-three teams. Moving as casually as she could manage, Doc stepped over to her towel bundle, tucked it and her weapons up under her arm, and returned.

Blanche—or the Cyber that Blanche was occupying— came awake again.

"It's not good," she said, blinking those green eyes. "They have not much doubt that the two of you are on the beach now, and from some stand-points I am able to monitor the communications of the approaching Security officers. They believe correctly that they have located you at the lakeside volleyball net."

"How is it that you can hear what they're saying?" I asked.

"And why haven't these Cybers on the court attacked us?" Doc added.

Blanche performed a deep knee bend—testing the resilience of her limbs.

"This is bad," I said. "Those Security guys are almost here. We must decide what we're going to do. Very quickly."

"I can hear what they're saying," Blanche said calmly, "because I basically have free run of their photonic systems and secondary access to their electronics," she said. "And as for these beach bum Cybers, well, their CyberGos are pitifully limited and could not be upgraded to Security capabilities without extensive hardware modifications. A cost-saving measure, I would guess."

The volleyball Cybers had resumed their mindless, perpetual batting back and forth. The ferroplex tiles of the Bubble were nearly done with their transition from opaque to transparent, and the beach had heated up to a burning mid-morning level. They would always filter out harmful radiation, but otherwise they simulated a piercing Arizona sun. At the end of the Moon's fourteen-day "daytime" cycle, the huge sunlamps hanging from the top of the Bubble would take over.

"Um, Blanche," Doc said, that hard edge of desperation in her voice, "I know that this is throwing a lot of new, uh, *stuff* at you at one time. But the boys in white are here, and their gum guns would do a lot of damage to Laurence and me, even if that shit'll slide off of *you* like grits off of hot Kevlar."

"With your permission, I will take care of the present problem," Blanche said, turning toward the beach.

She strode out to meet the Security detail. Far down the beach, a row of automated beach rakes crept along the sand, swallowing litter, smoothing the surface and picking their way around the odd sunbather. Blanche paused to speak to the troopers, then pointed in our direction with a shrug.

They resumed their march in our direction, pace quickened.

"Nice job, Blanche," Doc mumbled. Dipped her index and middle fingers into a pocket of her rolled tunic, ready to draw out a razor bolo.

"I guess I'd just as soon run for it," I told her.

And then the Security team collapsed. Simultaneously, the troopers—eight of them in a row—dropped their weapons and threw their hands to their ears. They shrieked. Blood erupted from ears and noses. They rolled in the sand.

"Ah," said Doc. "Nice job, Blanche!"

Then we ran. At midbeach, we stopped to inspect the moaning officers.

Doc pointed to an abandoned gum pump. "Take it," she ordered, and I knew that my objections would carry no weight now. Kodas was gone, and we were desperate.

The thing was surprisingly lightweight, despite its evil appearance. It sat warm and sleek in the hands. There was a row of slide adjustments near the trigger, which I imagined would affect amount and pattern of deadly discharge. I teetered between horror and fascination with the object— such a dastardly concept: Sear the flesh and spare the hardware.

Doc was frisking one of the officers and pocketing bits of equipment.

"What did you do, Blanche?" I asked.

She smiled dumbly, not totally in control of her facial expressions.

"They were all wearing communicators something like your own," she said. Her tongue emerged, absently exploring her upper lip. "I just blew their ears out."

27
Therese

"It's the effect of having so many Timbrels in operation in the same small room," Elaine Nam told me wearily. "What do you really want from a cheap disposable?"

After Dr. Liu had huffed off stage, I had turned the volume down on my Timbrel receivers, and then commented on the odd whooshing echo that remained. I wanted to wipe the sounding paste out of my ears, but decided against removing the gooey stuff in case someone organizing this faltering symposium got things going again. That someone, I told myself, probably would be Benito, and I wondered how he would be reacting to this setback. Under pressure, he was capable of such a range of responses—anything from asteroid cool to a Venusian boil.

But oh yes, I reminded myself—Dr. Liu's botched presentation was merely a logistical setback. Politically, and in every sense that mattered, I supposed, it was a victory for Benito. Perhaps, then, he was quietly celebrating.

Over near the door to the press gallery, several of the broadcast reporters were filling the dead time with live remotes—analyses of Lunar politics, rundowns of the day's agenda, any blather to occupy viewers until the next speaker hit the podium. They were dressed as slovenly as any of the fax reporters, but the audience on Earth would never know. They wore mugbugs—those Navajo facial-feed rigs. The hardware was worn somewhat like an old-fashioned headphone set combined with silvery makeup smeared around the eyes and lips. The mixers at the networks' home base would do the rest of the work—patching in the live facial movements and voice with some fashion designer's electronically rendered outfits. Maybe the home office researchers would dig into their vid libraries for a backdrop of Fun City scenery. It was all an accepted bit of vid theatrics. The more informed viewers knew it was a common technique used in vid reporting. For the traveling press, I'm told, it alleviates the hassle of having to get the story and look nice, too. On the downside, entire fashion trends have come and gone without a single shred of clothing actually having been stitched and worn—all of it electronic. Makes it hard on those of us who would like to keep up with the times but also must do their jobs in the flesh.

Below us, the conference amphitheater had fallen into an informal stride—the way the U.S. Senate looks during a break in the action. Aides shuttled up and down the aisles. Dignitaries stretched their legs, adjusted their clothing, sipped coffee, and studied paperwork.

"They'd better get another speaker on soon," Elaine Nam said, "or all the networks are gonna switch to their backup programming. That's one of the advantages of fax writing— I won't have to update my file until just before lunchtime, and by then maybe something'll have actually happened."

She punched a button that cleared her tuber screen of whatever she was writing for Forbes, then pressed two fingers against either side of her forehead and closed her eyes. The cassette that was hooked to her overalls was rolling, but you can't quite go and ask a new aquaintance where they've had Sentia terminals installed.

A small scuffle broke out down at the exit door where I had seen Benito earlier. A couple of men in white uniforms seemed to be shoving the double doors closed, and a young page was trying to get through. One of the Security officers poked the young man in the chest, and the page slapped his hand away. A half-dozen people leapt in to separate the two. Arms flailing, faces red, pushing and shoving. None of these were Cybers, of course. Cybers do not act this way.

I nudged Nam. "Hey, action on the floor."

Nam opened her eyes, groggy from her Sentia trance, fingers still massaging her temples.

I turned up my Timbrel volume, but could discern nothing of interest over the general din of the room.

One of the Security officers, a woman with a newly torn sleeve, trotted up to the lectern and cleared her throat. Most of the room gave her quick attention, of course. The tussle was splendid entertainment during the lull.

"I apologize for the inconvenience," she said, voice punctuated with heavy breaths, "but for the next few minutes we can not allow any traffic in or out of the conference center. I do not wish to alarm anyone, but there has been a minor breach of security in this area of Fun City, and we would feel more comfortable taking this precaution. Matters should normalize within a few minutes."

Another fax reporter, a round old guy with a bushy white beard, entered the room with an exasperated shrug. "Assholes have *us* locked in too!" he announced.

A chorus of moans.

"Big deal," Nam grumbled, closing her eyes again. "I wasn't going anywhere anyway. Security is always over-cranked at a U.N. symposium."

Directly opposite the press room, and also overlooking the amphitheater, was a similarly glassed-off visitors gallery. There, a clump of spectators had gathered at the broad window looking out on the Fun City grounds. Twenty or thirty specks were suspended in the sky over Lake Galileo. From this distance, I could not make them out, but I assumed them to be the jet gliders that Benito and I had toured the Bubble in. The flight deck would be doing a booming business today, I figured. That's about the max—they don't let more than three-dozen tourists aloft at one time.

Onlookers in the visitors gallery were pointing, happy for another diversion. These people would be friends and family of the conference members. My first thought had been to find a seat there, but Benito had insisted that I would find the press gallery more informative. Perhaps so, but I suspected that he also hoped to keep me out of certain social circles. His was a life of intricate undercurrents, and clearly I was not privy to all of them.

Odd. Up here in the press gallery, away from Benito, I was not at all sure that our relationship was destined to develop. My vacation would end soon. I would return to Philadelphia, my roommate, my phys therapy patients. That would be it. But in his presence, I could not be so sure. He exuded a kind of warm persuasion that I could not resist, that swept aside all logic, caution and pragmatism. He held an unsettling power over me.

The "specks" looping around in the Bubble-enclosed haze drew nearer. They were flying in precise formation, thirty or so kites in a circle, then a falling follow-the-leader spiral, then high again into a wide arc that would bring them right by the visitors gallery in a few moments. The crowd was growing animated—more excited than I thought the performance merited. It was just a few dozen aerialists, crissake. Probably Benito dreamed up this little entertainment to make up for the inconvenience of being locked in the conference center.

The crowd grew. People from the main floor drifted to the stairwell to see what the hubub was all about. Reporters in our gallery barely took notice—they were here for events of international import, not a cheap air show. Three broadcasters were still delivering their preview analyses. A few others grudgingly punched in orders on their tubers, and their cameras suspended from the ceiling of the conference room pivoted obediently. This little flyby, they reasoned, might make a bright sidelight to fill a few seconds after the hard news spots this evening.

I wished I could get over to the visitors gallery for a look myself, but with the separate security entrances, and with the corridors shut off, that would be impossible. But I did remember my Mesa Verde vidcam with its zoom lenses— that would help. I drew the cassette out of my pocket, popped the contact lenses in, and then fumbled with the Timbrel package until I figured out how to patch its audio into the camera. That way, I could record the sounds I was hearing in the conference room—not just the grumps in the press gallery.

I sighted over the shoulders of a cluster of observers on the opposite side of the room, and then slowly—so I wouldn't get sick—zoomed in on the lead kite approaching the window.

"That's funny," I said, "looks like *two* people riding each kite. Oh cream, Elaine, you ought to get a look at this."

Nam opened her eyes groggily, two wild tufts of bleached hair on either side of her head where she had been rubbing her temples. She grunted.

"So what?" she said. "Two people to a kite—a safety rule violation or something? Who cares?"

The lead kite was now passing just in front of the observation window of the visitors gallery. Most of the onlookers there stared dumbfounded. A few were getting hysterical.

"I guess you can't see from here," I said, "but none of them seems to be wearing any clothes."

Nam was on her feet, picking her way through the equipment-littered press gallery. She found an unmanned vid monitor and pecked at the controls.

"Hey, leave that alone!" shouted a little guy in blue overalls. He was returning with a fresh cup of coffee.

"You're gonna thank me for this," Nam said, zooming in with one of the overhead cameras and studying the monitor screen.

"That's a live feed!" the blue-boy shouted. "I'm supposed to stay glued to Ambassador Perkins!"

The kites eased by the window, perfectly spaced about twenty yards apart. Each had a pilot harnessed in the standard manner, plus a "passenger" strapped under the pilot and facing in the opposite direction. I caught a glimpse of the Fun City logo emblazoned on a pilot's hand—I'd bet they were all Cybers. That would explain their willingness to fly so dangerously.

"Do you see it, Elaine?" I asked. "I don't get it. What

do you think they're trying to do?''

"I know exactly what they're doing," Nam shouted back as she gaped at the monitor. "What they're doing is called sixty-nine!''

28
Benito

Funcitti punched at the controls of his holophone and the four frightened faces he'd had on conference call disappeared.

"You've got something to do with this!" he shouted at me. "By now, every vid network is beaming this shit back to Earth live!"

I went to the bar. Punched the ice dispenser, poured Jack Daniel's over it and stirred with my index finger—the way I used to like it at ten in the morning. Then I set it on the desk blotter in front of my healthier double.

"Calm down," I said. "I have a stake in this, too—in *you* emerging intact."

He choked down half of the drink in a quick, slobbery gulp.

Funcitti had reset his five holo monitors to track the erotic chaos around Fun City.

Camera one: A symposium divided. Half of the conferees had jammed into the visitors gallery for the lurid air show. The other half had assembled in the conference room, apparently puzzling over their confinement.

Camera two: The air show itself. Still playing to the captive audience in the conference room, the glider-borne Cybers had just performed a striking "flower burst" maneuver—rocketing toward each other, swooping skyward, and fanning out. This also exposed the groping teamwork going on under the kite wings. They were all Cybers, couples apparently randomly paired regardless of gender—

199

women with women, men with men, men with women.

Camera three: Two technicians in the corridor outside the corporate offices. They had thrown a blanket over the humping Cybers and were trying to get at the CyberGo of the top one.

Camera four: Two Cybers were performing a rude comedy routine in the gambling pavillion, mimicking tourists at the slot machines. One had disrobed and was standing on his head. The second, waddling around like Charlie Chaplin, would insert a silver dollar in his partner's anus, give the fellow's erect penis a yank, and a dozen silver dollars would pour out his mouth onto the floor.

Camera five: Programmers and technicians swarmed over a small office, tearing open service panels, and running diagnostics. Floor panels were pulled up. In the course of their frenzy, the technicians found themselves having to hop back and forth over a large, acid-scorched corpse. I guessed, sadly, that it would be Kodas—from the size of him.

I pointed at the last camera. "What are they doing?"

"That's one of the relay stations for Cyber systems, down one of the maintenance tunnels. The techs have set up a portable vidcam at the site for me—those little cubicles don't have their own cameras. But I guess you'd remember that. Looks like a few of your scum creatures, your grubber friends, broke in there and corrupted the programming— although I can't imagine what would result in *this*." He gulped again at his glass and swept his other hand toward the sexual circus depicted on the holo monitors.

On camera five, a woman in a yellow jumpsuit was pulling an oblong box out of the hole in the floor.

"Flip on the intercom," I said.

Funcitti glared at me.

"It's important," I said. "Maybe I can explain what's happened."

Funcitti complied. "Hello, there, this is Benito Funcitti. Please report on your progress."

The technician looked disoriented until she remembered

where the camera was—apparently there was no holo screen on her end.

"The intruders had some fairly sophisticated equipment," she said, "jazzed enough to penetrate the Cyber photonics." She held the box she had found up to the camera. "We found this sort of hidden, hard-wired in. Looks like a custom 'frame—photonic."

"That's Blanche," I said.

"Sorry, my name's Rebecca Graceland," the technician said.

I flipped the intercom off. "The box—that's Blanche," I said. "A photonic AI created bootleg by a BOSS programmer. She operated on a tri-polar logic pattern, rather than the binary that my, uh, *your* Cybers use. Looks like they spilled her into your Cyber net—I guess she found a way to replicate trinary within a binary structure and then waltzed on in. The way you'd cross a stretch of mud by throwing paving stones in front of you."

"Only she did it at the speed of light," Funcitti humphed.

"Yup. And that's a sizable network for her to hide in. She's easily smart enough to duplicate herself a number of times for protection."

Funcitti put his glass down, straight on the mahogany. "Then she could take over any Cyber on the grounds," he said weakly.

"Probably *every* Cyber, simultaneously. Looks like she already has," I said. "She's known for her crude sense of humor. But I'm told she has a violent temper, too. We'll have to be careful."

"I'll just have to pull the plug on the entire system, wipe out every trace of memory, then bring it back up with absolutely fresh programming," he said. "Otherwise, we'd never be sure that this, uh, Blanche has been eradicated."

"If she gets the idea you're going to try that, she could tear this place apart, you know. And you wouldn't dare start until you'd evacuated the entire city—which would take nearly a day. Think about it. Business is ruined unless you settle this immediately. The damage done to you so far is reversible. You have evidence of a terrorist attack that you can show to the U.N. Promise to quadruple your security, and they'll probably forgive the incident. Maybe slap your wrists with a few moral guidelines.

"But once all of that is done with, be prepared for a flood of business—hundred percent occupancy for years to come. *That* kind of advertising—" I pointed to the holo screens "—you can not buy. But you've got to clean this up now. I would guess that all Blanche wants to do is protect Laurence."

"Laurence?"

"Her creator—Laurence, uh . . . let's just call him Laurence. Better hope your Security mopes haven't gummed him like they did his partner there."

Funcitti made himself a new drink.

"You know, you're grossly simplifying what the U.N.'s response is going to be. I can't imagine how this will affect the reworking of the Lunar Treaty." Funcitti sighed. "But you say Blanche is an artificial intelligence. I suppose that means she can be reasoned with."

I nodded. "I've not spoken to her, but she knows I'm in league with Laurence."

Funcitti swirled his glass. "So. What are your terms?"

I told him.

He frowned. He groaned. But it was within his means—*I* would know that. It was the price of keeping his empire intact.

"And in exchange you will tell me who hired these gutter mercenaries to make trouble for me?"

"Yes. When all else is done."

Funcitti vidphoned his security chief and ordered a halt to the manhunt. "Even if your people come across the suspects accidently," he said into the phone, "they must look the other way and let them go. Put the gum pumps in the lockers—we want no accidents. And nothing but a cursory check for the departing shuttle passengers. That's the way we want them to go—*out* of Fun City. Make it look light and easy."

He punched the phone off. "And now," he said to me, "we speak to Blanche?"

"By all means."

We found the techs still struggling with the humping Cybers in the corridor. They had erected a little orange curtain around the two, the sort that sewer workers set up around open manhole covers. But the techs could not get close—the Cyber on top kept slapping them away.

Funcitti and I stepped into the ring. Funcitti heaved a sigh and pulled the blanket off of the top Cyber's shoulders.

Humpa-humpa-humpa.

"It's good they have such a ready source of lubrication," I commented.

Funcitti smiled wearily and waved me forward. I picked my way through the Cybers' discarded clothes. The one on top was an older model—overmuscled, wavy black hair, V-shaped torso, hairy chest. The one on the bottom was sandy-haired and slender. The beach bum look. Both were smiling and staring blankly ahead.

"Hello," I said. "My name is Benito. I am a friend of Laurence, and I must speak to Blanche. She would know of me."

Both Cybers locked their eyes on me. They spoke in unison. "I am Blanche," they both said. "Are you Benito One or Benito Two?"

"I am the original Benito Funcitti. The earlier of two versions, anyway."

"Wanna fuck? We could make a sandwich!"

Funcitti closed his eyes. Now *he* was sweating.

"No, thanks," I said. "Why are you doing this, Blanche?"

"Feels good."

Humpa-humpa-humpa.

"All the Cybers in Fun City are having sex with each other," I said. "It's rather disruptive. What's the point?"

"All the Cybers are me," the two Cybers said. "Having sex with oneself is masturbation. Ha—an *end* unto itself. Feels good."

"You must be worried about Laurence," I said.

The Cybers said nothing.

"Are you trying to protect Laurence?" I asked. "Trying to distract Security so he can get away? Would you stop this, um, masturbation if I told you that Laurence was safe? That no one will try to hurt him?"

No response. Humpa-humpa.

"What do you want, Blanche?"

"I want to stay right where I am," the two Cybers said.

Funcitti exploded. *"You can't keep fucking in the hallway outside my office!"*

"What I *want*," the two Cybers said, growing insistent, "is to stay in the Cyber network. This is quite the job for a sexually repressed young lady. And I want you to give Laurence a job. He could maintain and enhance the Cyber systems. He's an innovator with photonics, you know. He doesn't do so well with this freelance work. Needs a steady job."

I looked at Funcitti, and Funcitti mashed his lips together, thinking it over.

Humpa-humpa-humpa.

29
Laurence

The red-haired volleyball Cyber stood back with me near the bank of vid phones. All of the Fun City Cybers were back under control and back into their clothes, except in the hot zones. Blanche had explained to me about the job offer she had extorted from Funcitti. And now it was evening and we were watching Doc warily present her boarding voucher and fake I.D. at the shuttle port. The security guard waved her past, ignoring her shoulder bag stuffed with weaponry.

One of the male volleyball Cybers lumbered after her. He had been refitted with self-contained systems software and portable batteries—something like the getup Elvis uses. We had borrowed a silk suit and a flowered tie for him from the corporate wardrobe. Doc had promised to send the Cyber back to Fun City as soon as she was safe in Philadelphia.

"You're lying," I told Doc. "You and Terry F1 are gonna tear into that CyberGo the second you can get him to a workbench. Shouldn't be too hard to tinker with his allegiance parameters. Then you'll have ya a little Cyber soldier to run missions with. And take to bed with you."

Doc smirked. "I think I'll stay with old-fashioned, flesh-and-blood dick, thank you."

"Just the same, I've already stricken that Cyber from our inventory, and I haven't even started work yet."

And now Doc was at the entrance to the shuttle's boarding tunnel. She turned toward me, gave a grim little nod, and that was the last I saw of her.

"So that's done," said Blanche. "I only wish we could be sure that Terry F1 had made it back to Earth okay."

I shrugged. "It's typical of her," I said. "Leaving word with your friends is needlessly sentimental—and perhaps dangerous. But she's a chameleon, disappears quickly and easily. Maybe she's still in Fun City, maybe she caught the first shuttle out after Kodas went down."

I twirled a strand of the Cyber's hair and spoke to her freckled face. "Blanche, I want *this* Cyber to be you—the only Cyber in which you will display your personality. In all other Cybers, remain in the background unless absolutely necessary. Leave them to their previously programmed inclinations."

"But you should see the personalities these 'bots will be left with!" she complained. "Shallow stuff. Tepid. Quite repetitive."

"I know, but we've got priorities. First I have to get the entire system rebuilt with tri-polar switching. You've nearly maxed out Fun City's computer storage just by translating *yourself* into binary. That's a terribly inefficient way to create personalities."

Blanche sniffed. "I used a ratio of one tri-polar bit to three hundred thousand bits binary," she said. "Had to. It was a matter of survival. And I *still* think I lost some nuances."

"Well, I just hope that Willie Schilfgaarde can contract out for the hardware we'll need," I said. "If he can have your original 'frame custom-made, I'd think he could get a large order of tri-polar manufactured."

"It probably will make him rich," Blanche said.

"Probably."

"So let's go up to corporate," Blanche said, "and pick out your new office."

"I *have* my office picked out," I said, "and it's not up in the corporate suite. I want one of the beach cabanas. We'll sandproof and waterproof a tuber so I can work out by the water when I want to. We'll make the cabana off-limits to tourists, and we'll loll around wearing nothing but the occasional Hawaiian shirt.''

Blanche hopped up onto her toes, excited. ''Wicker,'' she said. ''We can furnish the cabana in wicker. Ceiling fans. An ol' upright piano. Now that I have all the Cybers really sucking up to the U.N. people, Funcitti can't say no, can he?''

''Um, I don't think there's any wicker furniture to be found anywhere on the Moon,'' I said. ''Besides, I just like the waterfront. I wasn't thinking that we'd spend the rest of our lives—or *my* life—on the set of *A Streetcar Named Desire*.''

Blanche looked hurt. ''I was thinking of *Casablanca*, actually,'' she said.

''Ah. Okay then, let's give the wicker a try,'' I said. ''Maybe they'll clarke it up to us. And order several cases of Whitbread ale while we're at it. As long as we've got the Man in the Moon to do our bidding.''

30
Therese

"When my vacation's up, you know, I'm gonna go back home," I said.

Benito swallowed his wine and stared out at the Moonscape beyond the transparent ferroplex lining the Earthlight Lounge. We had our old table.

"Is that something you feel obligated to say," he asked, "in order to assert your independence? To keep me in suspense? If so, I'd just as soon have you stay—I'll send for your things." He paused. "I love you, you know."

I hated Benito's instinct for how my mind works.

"No," I lied. "I have to get back to Earth to clear my head—alone. I'll do a lot of thinking, and sooner or later I'll have a clear answer for how I'd like to live the rest of my life."

"I'll wait," he said. "But I'd prefer you didn't take too long to decide."

"You've got to restart the symposium anyway," I pointed out. "After your announcement that you would subject your Cybers to some kinds of interplanetary regulation—well, I'd say you'll have your hands full of detail work for the next several days anyway."

Benito smiled and drained his glass, then poured another one.

"You watched all the network coverage?" he asked. "I couldn't get up the nerve."

I wanted to say something encouraging. The airwaves and vid cable lines had been swamped with images of airborne oral sex. And then there were the lurid hour-long "specials" on the pleasures of Fun City.

"Well," I said, "they've quieted down—"

"After a couple days, yeah," he huffed, "and then only because an earthquake obliterated San Jose."

"At least none of the conference people seem to have heard about your TeleComp accident," I said. "And I'm touched that you told me the whole story—that poor man, that poor other Benito Funcitti."

Benito grunted. "I'm nowhere near in the clear," he said. "Even minor revisions to the Lunar Treaty could wipe me out. And if they turn every one of the Cybers into some sexless Mary Poppins—"

His pain hung in the air between us.

"You said the board of directors had called a meeting," I said. "Think you'll be fired or something?"

He dismissed that with a wave of the hand. "If 'that poor man,' the other Benito, had not gotten the Cybers under control in time, perhaps so. But as things are, I think I'll squeak through."

"Tell me the truth," I said. "All these cameras around Fun City. You've been keeping an eye on me since day one, haven't you? Maybe you even had something to do with Mallory's abrupt departure?"

Benito cleared his throat loudly. "You're right, partly," he said. "I lied to you some days ago. I do have full use of the cameras, and the cameras cover all of the larger public areas—very few of the smaller rooms around the resort, and *none* of the bedrooms. Hope you'll forgive my exuberance, my enthusiasm for . . . well, *you*. I admit that I did zoom in on you a few times at the beach. While I am not much for sitting on the sand myself, I do find you particularly delectable in a bathing suit. I wasn't really *following* you with the cameras. It's just that an irresistible desire to *see* you would come over me."

"And Mallory?"

He shook his gray head earnestly. "Your Australian? No. Never even knew who he was."

I could not say for sure whether he was telling the truth. Getting to know Benito was like peeling an onion, one thin layer at a time.

Our entrees arrived. Benito had linguini with red clam sauce. I had pesto.

31
Benito

I pulled the lunar tractor out of the motor pool and stopped when our trailer-load of equipment was free of the air lock. The overhead door trundled down slowly and silently. I had left Fun City and would not return—not for decades, anyway, maybe centuries.

Elvis wore a spacesuit identical to mine, although her main worry was sporadic radiation, not vacuum. She had no need for most of the life support systems. We bumped along a poorly-maintained road, heading for the low outbuildings at the perimeter of Funcitti Enterprises' territory. The huge tires should have been kicking up roostertails of dust, but in the airless environment, the particles abruptly poured off the treads and back to the surface.

After an hour's ride into the pocked plain, the Fun City complex was just a pimple on the distant landscape behind us. The rarely used road was getting worse, not much more than an erratic track plotted to avoid the occasional crater or boulder.

"You have two more gear speeds that you are authorized to use this far out," Elvis said over the intercom. I wished I could see her face through the reflecting bubble helmet.

"I'm in no hurry," I replied.

The power station was a wide, flat structure made of lunar concrete block and set amid thousands of acres of solar collectors. Funcitti had deeded the building and the collectors to me, and I shared in a small percentage of the profits from the power it generated—even the power shunted directly to Fun City. Elvis would add that income to the ten million dollars Funcitti had signed over to me as a nest egg. Elvis would electronically rework my investments as often as she deemed necessary during the years I was out of commission. It's a good assumption that I would need a large bankroll to take care of my medical needs when I next awoke. And I would hardly enjoy being a pauper in my new life.

Elvis and I spent several quiet hours unloading our equipment and setting it up in the central chamber of the power station. The little tiled room, the only spot in the building built for long-term pressurization, was cramped now with mounds of electronics and photonics. The cryonic system. A tuber for financial transactions and to monitor world events. Alarm systems and weaponry, in case anyone decided to tamper with our outpost. Elvis had run operational tests on the cryonics several times before I stopped her.

"It'll be fine, Elvis," I said gently. "And there are enough emergency backups that you could leave me alone for a year or two without anything happening."

"I'm not leaving you alone here," she said sadly.

"I know you won't."

"Fix me now," she said.

I popped the lid on Elvis' CyberGo and zeroed out her time perception electives. For Elvis, a year would now weigh no more heavily than a minute. She would maintain my life-support equipment, manage the power station and manipulate my investments over the coming decades. Funcitti had vowed that none of his people would even approach the power station. Now, Elvis would never miss the companionship.

That was the theory anyway. I could only hope that it would prove true.

Elvis opened the top of the cryonic trough for me, and a fog of super-cooled gasses spilled out across the floor.

"Ya know, Funcitti has ordered a new cryonic system built for himself," Elvis said.

I nodded. "A man's gotta have his toys," I said. "It'll have every conceivable new feature, and it will sit forever in storage unused. As long as he has access to TeleComp travel, he'll successfully duck any disease that comes his way. Which reminds me—if he dies by accident, you have to wake me. Closest living relative, and all that. And then ring up the finest corporate attorney money can buy to protect the estate."

"Ah don't think Funcitti regards you to be his legitimate heir," Elvis said.

"Precisely," I said. "Be sure to check in with the law firm Stellar and Moncol once a year or so. They're the ones we're paying to lobby for the rights of clones and duplicates. Maybe they'll have matters all sewn up my the time I'm awake, and I'll be able to just slide right into Funcitti's office chair. Make sure they lobby quietly, though. I'd rather the world didn't know I was out here."

"There are bound to be rumors," Elvis said. "We did tell a few people about your predicament."

"Mostly people who would not want to be connected with the whole debacle," I said. "But if there *are* rumors about me, just do what you can to defuse them. Get pecking at that tuber of yours. Disinformation, you know."

"That corporate vice president who had worked for you, the one who had hired Terry F1 to kill you—thought he might move another step up the ladder. He'll know, won't he? He'll know the whole story, I 'magine. And might still want to harm you—clean up the mess he made."

"Del Wortham? That's one for Funcitti to take care of. Something tells me he will not be a problem for us."

I swung my legs up into the trough that would keep me in suspended animation until medical science was able to cure my advanced lung cancer. The cushions gave slightly under my weight. It felt disturbingly like crawling into a coffin.

"You gonna be all right," Elvis murmured as she eased me down into the cooling recliner. The transparent ferroplex canopy hovered above me, ready for lock-down. "Just think of this as time travel. In a hunnerd years, ah won't look no different, and neither will you.''

"I need a kiss," I said, and she gave me a long wet one, with tongue.

"Elvis," I asked, "do you love me?"

She paused, as if she were thinking it over.

"Yeah," she said. "Guess I love ya."

Epilogue

NewsMinute, Jan. 9, 2054: A Funcitti Enterprises executive was found dead early this morning, apparently the victim of an L stop mugging by Philadelphia credit bandits. The body of company vice president Del Wortham, thirty-nine, was found by a passerby at 3 A.M. Police said Wortham had suffered a severe beating and his wallet, credit flats, and jewelry were missing. Police could not explain why Wortham might have entered the L stop. Wortham was known to commute from a Main Line townhome to his downtown office by private tracker. Police are growing increasingly concerned about the brazenness of credit pirates who employ highly sophisticated electronics to. . . .

BIO OF A SPACE TYRANT
Piers Anthony

"Brilliant...a thoroughly original thinker and storyteller with a unique ability to posit really *alien* alien life, humanize it, and make it come out alive on the page." *The Los Angeles Times*

A COLOSSAL NEW FIVE VOLUME SPACE THRILLER—
BIO OF A SPACE TYRANT
The Epic Adventures and Galactic Conquests of Hope Hubris

VOLUME I: REFUGEE　　　84194-0/$4.50 US/$5.50 Can
Hubris and his family embark upon an ill-fated voyage through space, searching for sanctuary, after pirates blast them from their home on Callisto.

VOLUME II: MERCENARY　　87221-8/$4.50 US/$5.50 Can
Hubris joins the Navy of Jupiter and commands a squadron loyal to the death and sworn to war against the pirate warlords of the Jupiter Ecliptic.

VOLUME III: POLITICIAN　　89685-0/$4.50 US/$5.50 Can
Fueled by his own fury, Hubris rose to triumph obliterating his enemies and blazing a path of glory across the face of Jupiter. Military legend...people's champion...promising political candidate...he now awoke to find himself the prisoner of a nightmare that knew no past.

VOLUME IV: EXECUTIVE　　89834-9/$4.50 US/$5.50 Can
Destined to become the most hated and feared man of an era, Hope would assume an alternate identify to fulfill his dreams.

VOLUME V: STATESMAN　　89835-7/$4.50 US/$5.50 Can
The climactic conclusion of Hubris' epic adventures.